Willo

Willo

Karen Snow

Street Fiction Press, Inc.
Ann Arbor

Fragments of this fiction have appeared in: *Anon, The Beloit Poetry Journal, The Ladder, The Lake Superior Review, Michigan Quarterly Review, Parade Magazine, The Periodical Lunch,* and *We Are All Lesbians,* the editors of which I greatly acknowledge.

*** THIS BOOK was photocomposed in English Times at H&Z Typesetting Company, Ann Arbor, Michigan. Colors separated by Lemar Graphics, Brighton, Michigan. Printing and binding were accomplished at Thomson-Shore, Inc., Dexter, Michigan. Book design assistance by Patrick Mullaly, Inc., Ann Arbor, Michigan.

Library of Congress Cataloging in Publication Data

Snow, Karen,   1923-
    Willo.

    I. Title.
PZ4.S6733Wi [PS3569.N62]   813'.5'4   76-15987
ISBN 0-914908-29-4

STREET FICTION PRESS, INC.
201 East Liberty Street
Ann Arbor, Michigan 48108

Manufactured in the United States of America

for Warren Jay Hecht

Willo

"Don't cry!"

The towheaded tyke picks up the fragments of white china from the kitchen floor. Her mouth turns down at the corners, but she blinks back the tears.

"Don't cry!" Her mother lays the sock she is mending in her lap and wags her scolding finger. "If there's one thing I can't stand, it's a *baby!*"

The child, who cannot speak for fear of sobbing, holds out the pieces of doll's cup towards her mother.

"That's nothin." The worm-lips squirm to make a wry mouth. The large red hand picks up the sock, and the other hand, clumsy as a mitten, resumes the prodding with the needle. "When I was a little girl, I didn't have a set o dishes ta break. I didn't have *no* toys. Think of *that!*" She pumps her head like a work horse. The gruff voice matches the hawk-nose. It matches the mannish hands. It does not match the thin body. She looks up from her mending to study the effect of her statement on the child. Nor does the voice match the large blue eyes. She points to the chair. "Look at that: two dolls!" The lemur-eyes return the dolls' innocent stare. She points to another chair on the other side of the table: "A teddy bear!"

The child stands downcast before her.

"Well, I did have one toy. Didn't I tell you before about my little blue dishes? No? I told Cora....It was right after my mother died. I musta been about five. My big sister Agnes give em to me. Got em with some soap coupons, I guess. Little teeny blue dishes. Oh, yours is jumbos compared with those! Why, the cups—" She thrusts up the tip of her pinky. "The cups was no bigger'n that—like a thimble. I was just

15

crazy about em. Carried em everwhere with me. Took em to bed with me. Carried em to the table. Then I got it in my head that somebody'd steal em, so you know what I did? Over by the house where I lived there was a vacant lot—you know the one, it's all growed over with weeds n brush now an' it's fulla snakes n bad bugs, but when I was a kid it was all sorta sandy. Well, I went over there an' dug a hole an' buried them little blue dishes. Wasn't that *dumb?* After a coupla days I couldn't stand it without those dishes, so I went back an' dug. Well, I dug n I dug n I dug." The big blue eyes wander, confused, all around the kitchen. "They was gone." The voice bleats, "I couldn't bleeve it. I dug n I dug until my fingers was bleedin' but they was gone." The gaze still searching the room. Dazed. "I went back an' told Agnes, an' she helped me dig. Then when my pa came home from work, we told him, an' he helped us dig. I told my brother Milo an' he helped. Agnes had give him a little celluloid train that she got with the coupons same time she got my dishes an' boy! did Milo hang onto that train! We dug n we dug. My pa asked my big brothers because they was always up ta mean tricks. Oh, they could be catshit mean! But they swore they didn't take those dishes. Sikes n Casey, they even went out an' helped dig." She shakes her head. "They was gone. We never found em."

She studies the child's face.

"When I was a big girl—fifteen, sixteen—I still went back there an' dug. No luck."

The child ponders the pieces of cup in her hand. "Daddy will fix it."

"Naw! Didn't you even listen to what I told you? Why, when I told Cora, she throwed her arms around me an' she said: 'Oh, Mamma! When I get big I'll buy you some little blue dishes just like the ones you lost.' Would you do that?"

Large lavender eyes gaze out of the baby-face. The snowy head nods, dreamily.

"Tell me, Mina, *would you?"*

The little girl pumps her head like a horse.

16

The woman places her bent arm across her flat chest and hooks the hand over the shoulder. She rests that way a while. "Wouldn't you feel bad if you lost yer only toy?"

"You had teeny scissors."

"I didn't have no scissors!"

"The ones you n Milo made with two straight pins on the railroad track."

"Haw! You remember that?" The boney fingers squeeze the shoulder, then climb up to squeeze and squeeze the back of the neck, where it always aches. "Milo n me used to take two straight pins an' cross em a little bit an' lay em on the railroad track. Then the train would come along an' mash em an' we'd run out, an' golly, they'd be just like a little teeny pair o scissors."

"Can I do that?"

"Don't you dare! Don't you *ever* go on that railroad track."

"I'd watch for the train."

"Naw!"

"I'd listen for the train."

"Naw! Don't you dare."

"I wanna make those little teeny scissors."

"You got real scissors. I told you that just ta show you how poor we was."

Mina's gaze returns to the white fragments in her hands.

"You gotta learn ta think of someone worse off n yerself!" She hooks the other hand over the other shoulder and resumes the massage.

—If Cora were here, she'd be rubbing the sore places for Mamma.

"My mother died when I was five. Just think of that. What would you do if I died, huh?"

"Cora would tie my shoes an' then she would read me the funny papers."

"Haw! I can't put an old head on yer shoulders, can I? Just think, if Cora was in school, who would cook a meal for you?"

17

"Aunt Agnes?"

The thin lips stretch in a smile. "Yer the limit."

—I'd sit on Daddy's lap and he'd show me his book with Adam and Eve wearing aprons made of leaves and God chasing them out of the Garden of Eden and then they'll go and find a farm and Adam will grow corn and beans and Eve will make warm clothes for them.

"When I asked Cora that, you know what she did? She throwed her arms around me an' hugged me so tight an' she said: 'Oh, Mamma! Don't die!' Sure! That's what my pickaninny said!"

Mina looks solemnly at the pieces of cup in her hand.

Mamma stamps her foot. "You just *gotta* learn ta think o someone worse'n off 'n yerself. *Look* at me."

The child looks up into her mother's face.

"Are my eyes black?"

Mina looks carefully. She sees nothing but those two bruise-colored eyes in that buttermilk-colored face.

"Tell me! Are my eyes black?"

The child sees the black dot in the middle of the blue. Her mother has told her before that she does not mean *that.*

The woman places her fingertip beneath her eye. "Do I have black *circles* under my eyes?"

Mina sees nothing but little wrinkles in the yellowish skin. If she says "no," her mother will keep asking. *—Black eyes? Black circles? Cora sees them. Aunt Agnes always sees them: "Oh, Kate! Such black circles under yer eyes today!"*

The woman places the fingertip on the other cheek beneath the other eye. "Do I have black *rings,* huh?"

Mina nods.

"Huh?" Thrust out like a beggar's cup.

Mina pumps her head like a horse. *—Later I'll see them. Later I'll understand it all. Cora says when you go to school you learn to read and then you know. Daddy says, "Pray. God will make it all plain."* His voice laves her. *"When you get to Heaven, God will explain everything."*

Mamma keeps the pointing finger on the cheek. She presses

it in deep. "Wisht somebody'd give me a big kiss."

Mina stands on tiptoe and kisses the cheek.

Mamma presses the fingertip into the other cheek. The little girl kisses that spot, too.

A thin smile wavers on the woman's face. "I can't kiss you. My breath is bad." The smile broadens. "How much do you like me?"

"Ten bushels."

"Show me with yer arms."

Mina lays the pieces of cup on the table. Then she reaches up over her head.

"Oh, more'n that! Show me a *hundred* bushels!"

Mina reaches her arms out around her as far as she can, then stands on tiptoe and reaches way way up above her head.

Mamma claps her hands. "That's my sunbeam! Wisht I could hug you but my hands is so chapped." She claps the hands again. "Is that a smile I see on yer face: Sure! See! You forgot all about that broken cup. You thought of someone *else!*" Proudly, she pushes the hairpins into the big tan bun at the back of her neck.

Mina goes to the table and moves the white fragments on the oilcloth to the place where her father will sit for supper. "Daddy will fix it."

"Gee! You got it in yer head yer Daddy can fix *ever*thing." She studies the small face. "Just think. Next year at this time you'll be in school. I won't have no little girl to kiss my cheek. Boy, will I be lonesome!"

"I'll kiss you when I come home."

The big blue eyes blur with tears. "Bless yer little heart. Yer my candy kid with the gumdrop ear, that's what you are." The gaze drops to the large rough hands in her lap. "I won't take ya ta school that first day. I got such raw hands. So round-shouldered. Can't tawk good. I won't shame you."

"Daddy will take me to kinnygarden."

"Naw. He has ta work on the railroad. Why do you think yer daddy can do *ever*thing?"

19

"Cora will take me."

"Maybe."

Mina climbs into her father's chair. Painstakingly, she arranges the white shards. She cannot make the cup. What she makes looks something like the corolla of a flower.

On the swayed stoop of an abandoned shanty, Mina is blowing dandelion seeds with a boy named Nicky.

"When will you be five?" she asks.

"I don't know."

"I'll be five next May."

"Then you'll have to go to school."

"Not in May."

"But you'll have to go after you're five."

"I know it." She blows a seed out over the fields towards the railroad tracks.

"I think I'll be five when it snows," he says.

In the September sunlight, they are a pretty sight: she with an aura of pearl-colored hair; he with his thatch of rich brown.

He blows a seed out into the field. "My brother says school is dumb."

"My sister says it's not bad."

"I don't want to go." His tone is grave.

"I do. I want to learn to read." Her tone is snippy.

He puffs a seed to her arm. "You have to print your name."

She puffs a seed to his arm. "I can print M I N A. My father showed me how."

"You have to print your whole name."

"I can't print 'Von Musson.' " She puffs a seed to his cheek.

"You'll have to print it. Else you won't pass." He puffs a seed to her cheek.

"Then my father will show me how."

He puffs a seed to her knee. She puffs one to his knee. She

lifts her dress. He puffs one to her stomach. — *Yes.*

He lifts his shirt. She puffs one to his stomach.

She glances towards the door...which he squeaks open. Indoors, they stand, displaying bellies, fair and smooth as two loaves of bread. His is fatter. Her button is round. It gazes. His is a wink.

She blows his a seed. He blows hers a seed...which spills to the edge of her pants. She eases the pants down a bit. He blows her a fluff. Her pelvis tastes it, stinging sweet as a lemon drop.

He eases his pants down. His pelvis likes fluff, too.

A wriggle urges her pants to her knees. A ditto-wriggle; his pants obey. She feels herself pucker at the sight of him.

"Yours is like a thumb," she says.

"Yours is a crack."

She blows his a fluff. "Look. It's thumbing a ride."

"Sure." He blows a fluff to hers.

A black pounce. Her mother is yanking, snatching, spanking—like a spider that jabs and stabs and bundles its prey into two paralyzed packages.

"Does Daddy know?"

Her mother looks away.

"Did you tell Daddy I'm bad?"

"Maybe I did. Maybe I didn't."

"I'll never do it again."

"You'd better not."

"I know I won't."

"Buh!"

In and out...up and down...'round and 'round...like a yoyo in her mother's hand.

*   *

"You've been thinking nasty thoughts," hisses Mamma when Mina gets up from her nap. "It shows in your eyes."

"No!"

"Sure! Come here. Let me smell your hands."

"Shame! Shame!" sneers Cora when she bathes Mina in the tin washtub in the kitchen.

"Pew!" says Mamma when she washes Mina's face. "Nasty breath."

Mina hides in her father's lap, behind the big Bible in his hands. Mamma and Cora stick their arms through the doorway and begin to wipe their right scolding fingers down their left scolding fingers: *Shame! Shame!*
Daddy says, "Oh, leave her be!"
But they keep stropping those fingers. Daddy sighs.
Mina slips off his lap. He doesn't say, *"Come back here, Mina."* He just sighs and goes on reading the Bible...and the fingers go on stropping.

"Does Daddy know?"
Her mother shrugs.
"Please! Does my Daddy know?"
Her mother leaves the room.
Mina, who has always slept upstairs with her father, while Mamma and Cora sleep in the bed downstairs, hitches herself like a cocoon to the edge of the bed. He doesn't tell her stories anymore. He coughs. He snores. He stinks.
She whispers, "Daddy? I can't sleep, Daddy."
He says, "Pray. 'Pray without ceasing.' "
—*He knows.*

*   *

One morning in April, right after Daddy has gone to work and Cora has gone to school, Uncle Milo comes to the door. He's all shaky.
"Oh, God! He's had the D.T.'s again!" Mamma whispers. "Mina, go upstairs."
Down in the kitchen, Mamma cries. Uncle Milo cries, too. The house fills up with his sour stench. Then the washing machine chugs.

23

Staggering around in her father's clothes, he opens her door. He grins, grabs her long hair, jiggles it in his shaky hands. He lifts her skirt, pulls at the elastic edge of her pants. "Whatcha got in there, huh?"

With hands suddenly stronger than his, she pushes him away.

After he has left the house, with a big bag of lunch under his coat, Mina says, "Mamma, Uncle Milo tried to look in my pants."

"When?"

"While you were washing his clothes."

"Are you making that up?"

"No. He came to my room and grabbed my hair and lifted my dress and—"

"Milo is my twin brother. He's got no home but this."

"Will you tell Daddy?"

Silence.

"Shall I tell Daddy?"

"Don't you dare." She shakes her head. "I can't put an old head on yer shoulders. Before the booze got Milo, you wouldn't bleeve it but it's true, he was such a gentleman—so smart n strong n good-lookin. Yer father couldn't hold a candle to him."

All spring, all summer, the worry lashes back upon itself, again and again, like pulled taffy.

"Will Cora tell my teacher I'm bad?"

Silence.

"Please! Cora won't tell my teacher, will she?"

"I don't know."

"I'll be good."

"Let's hope so."

"Then will you tell Cora not to tell?"

"I'll think about it."

"Is it still in my eyes?"

"At times."

24

"Is it still on my breath?"

"Just a trace."

"I don't want to go to school."

"You have to. Else they'd put me in jail."

On Labor Day Mamma and Cora decide that Mina should wear the white dress with blue trim the first day of school.

"Such a pretty dress, an' bran new shoes n socks," says Mamma. "You don't know what a lucky little girl you are."

At the dining room table, Dad works on the note.

"Don't write it in pencil," Mamma says. "Use pen n ink."

The pen scratches and splatters the ink.

"Don't write it," Cora says. "Print it."

Wads of paper lie on the table around Dad. He sits very erect over the lined tablet, like a pole that must hold up a thrashing tent. At last Cora chooses the best note.

Slowly and solemnly, Dad reads it aloud to the three of them: "Name—Wilhelmina Von Musson. Address—1618 North Kramer Street—Bronson, Michigan. Born—May 31, 1923. Health—good. Father's name—Otto Karl Von Musson. Place of employment—New York Central Railroad. Mother's maiden name—Cornelia Nella Koeneig. One sister—Cora June Von Musson—age nine years—student—grade four—Parklawn school."

Mamma's hands fumble in her apron. "There, Mina." She grins wryly. "Yer jest as good as the next one."

Slowly and ceremoniously, Dad folds the note and fits it into the envelope. "Now, Mina, you join your sister in the privilege of going to that fine school. My, how the dear Saviour has blessed us!" He looks very solemnly into Mina's face. "Only one thing to remember: *Obey your teacher.*"

Mina looks solemnly into his face, too. "I will."

"That's what I told her," Mamma says. "Obey. Do zackly what the teacher says."

"I will."

"Another thing—" Mamma ducks her face into her hands.

25

"If you can't learn, don't feel bad. I know what a heart-ache it is to be at the foot o the class."

The tent pole pulls against her groveling: "Why, Katie, this girl is a regular little scholar!"

"Well, if you learn easy," Mamma says through her fingers, "don't make fun of them that are backward."

Dad arranges his lean, handsome face into a mask of utter dignity. "Now I told you: This girl is an A-number-one *scholar.*"

Mamma sighs. "Naw! I don't ask fer that. You know I don't. All I ask is a good C-student, like Cora. No more."

"Cora is a little scholar, too," Dad says. "She reads and she writes just perfectly. When I was nine, I hadn't set foot in a schoolhouse. I was eleven years old before that privilege came to me. Eleven years old: my first day at school: I felt like a prince!"

"Well, one thing I'll say fer my girls: They *mind.* They don't talk back. No one has ever complained about their behavior."

"The Saviour has blessed us with two fine little ladies," Dad says.

*   *

On Tuesday, they wait until Nicky and his mother have passed the window. Then Cora takes the note in one hand and Mina's hand in her other hand.

"Remember," Mamma says to Mina, "it's not nice manners to breathe in anyone's face." She opens the screen door. "Where's that smile, Whitey? Yer jest as good as the next one. You, too, Cora."

Cora walks very fast. She is dark and swarthy, like an Italian, but she has none of the Italian animation. Mina is so fair that the excitement has turned her cheeks a bright pink. They look nothing like sisters. All they have in common is a very sedate posture, as if they share with their father that mission to counteract the frenzied, demeaning motions of

26

their mother.

"Look at all those babies that have to have their mothers along," Cora whispers out of the side of her mouth.

At the door of the kindergarten, she hands Mina the note. Then she hurries on to the fourth grade room.

The kindergarten teacher, glancing across the thirty little bobbing heads, and all the mothers' heads, sees the white one enter alone   and move swiftly to a chair in the far corner where she will sit, with that note in her lap, scarcely moving, scarcely breathing one hour one hour and a half nearly two hours until all the other children have left with their mothers smiling and still, less like a girl than a trillium.

Down the railroad tracks, just beyond the papermill, stands the house. It's something like a crooked caboose; a yellow-tan, with windowsills repainted so much that they're like green gum. Soot webs this house. The yard is mostly cinders. Mamma was born and raised here. Now her brother Casey lives here alone. He's a nightwatchman at the papermill.

Mamma opens the back door. She and Mina tiptoe inside. It's dark. All the shades are down. It smells of blindrobins and coffee and pee.

"Don't turn on da light!" Case crouches in a chair in the corner like something caught in a trap.

Mamma and Mina come here every Tuesday and Friday afternoon. Mamma brings Case half a pie or a cake or a pot of soup. Then she cleans the house, fixes his sores, and takes his laundry home.

Mina stands in the kitchen beside the bubbled oilcloth, the vinegar cruet, the coffee pot. She stands there waiting to get used to the dark.

"Feelin better?" Mamma says to Case.

"Naw!" He crouches foreward as if he's sitting on the toilet. He spits on the floor. He's very dark. "Nig" they call him sometimes. His beak-nose and his jutting chin snap together over his slit of a mouth like a monkey wrench. The narrow head jerks, and one of the eyes is looking at the small blonde child. She tries to remember which eye is blind. "Dat's my Whitey," he says.

Mamma starts snatching wads of his sour clothes up off the floor.

That one eye keeps watching the child. He grins. "Gee, I

wisht I could go ta dat kinnygarden wit you, Whitey.''

Mina looks away.

"Tink dey could teach ole Case ta read in dat swell kinnygarden, huh?'' he asks in a singsong voice.

"We don't read in kinnygarden. That comes in first grade.''

"Haw!'' He throws his face towards his knees like a hatchet. He jerks his face up, grins at Mina, then sticks out his finger. "Comear.''

Mina looks quickly to her mother. The woman's face says *git to the porch*. The child exits. She's crammed with her mother's coaching: answers, exits, entrances: *When Case sticks out that finger and tells you to pull on it, don't.* Twice Mina pulled, and twice he broke wind: Haw! Other instructions: *If he fiddles with his pants and asks you to look at his thing, just laugh n say: "No thanks. I got one o my own ta look at." Or do I say: "I can't hold a candle to you?" I get it mixed up with what I say to the people at the store. I hate to go to that store. That's where I'm supposed to keep Mamma from making blunders. Cora did it fine. Now I have to do it. I never know what a blunder is. It's saying "rice kripsies," I think. I'm supposed to say it for her when she points to the box: "Rice Krispies." If she makes too many blunders, I'm supposed to take hold of her hand and say: "My mother's nerves are bad today." Cora always did it just right. Last week when Mamma croaked "Hot do! Nice day!" I thought she said it wrong and I grabbed for her hand and she was mad at me. . . . Then the clerk said to me: "Where'd you get that pretty white hair?" and before I could think of the right answer, Mamma snatched at my lip and said: "Yellow teeth. White hair. Ever see such a freak?" The clerk said, "Aw, Mrs. Von Musson, she's got such a sweet smile." Mamma said: "Naw! That's jest a nervous smile."*

Mamma pokes her head out the door: That means *come inside now.*

Case is picking his nose. Mamma starts smearing clover salve on a sore on the back of his neck.

29

He looks at Mina. "Gee, I wisht my daddy worked on da railroad. Wisht I had a pass ta ride on da train."

Mina knows this answer: "We're not rich. He's just a section foreman."

"Don't mess wif my tattoo!" he yells.

He and Mamma tussle and squawk. "Punch n Judy!" Mamma yells.

She looks like Case, except her eyes and her skin and her hair are light. People are always thinking Case, not Milo, is her twin.

"Niggers n the Irish!" he yells.

Their shoulders lurch. They start swaying together: warming up for their song: "Oh, the niggers n the Irish...They don't amount to much!...But still they are better'n the gollildarrrrrned *Dutch!*"

Case spits on the floor.

She grabs a piece of underwear from the heap and wipes up the blob.

"Yer dumb, Kate," he says.

"Yup, I'm dumb."

"Dummern me."

"Yup."

"That's goin some."

Case grins at the little girl. Carefully, he crooks his fingers, one over the other, then sticks out the pretzeled pile to her. "Hey! My fingers is all stuck tgether. Wisht a Little Sunbeam'd kiss em apart."

Mina looks to Mamma. She's still wiping the floor.

Case squeezes his eyes shut. He's been playing this game as long as Mina can remember. "Wisht a Little Sunbeam'd kiss my eyes open." Singsong. He fiddles with his pocket. Mina starts for the door. Mamma says to her, "Hey! It's O.K."

Case takes a paper out of his pocket, unfolds it, and thrusts it to Mina. "Found it in a magazine in da mill. 'Golly,' I said when I seed it, 'dat's my *Whitey!*' " He flaps the paper at her.

"It's O.K." Mamma says again. "Take it, Whitey."

30

It's a picture of a blonde girl in a white dress, with a bunch of lilies in her arms. She's looking up to heaven.

"Know what she is?" asks Case.

"A sort of angel?" Mina says.

He throws a wheeze to his knees. When he straightens up, he says, "She's a *healer.*"

"What'dya say ta yer uncle?" Mamma says.

"Thank you."

"*'Thank you!'*" he tweets. "*'Thank you!'* Ain't you the limit?"

"She's *refined,*" Mamma says, in an apologetic way. She means *persnickety.*

Mamma grabs a bottle of Lysol and a scrub brush from under the kitchen sink and jerks her chin in a motion that signals Mina to go outside with her. It's time to clean the outhouse.

Mina waits on the cinder path. Mamma yanks open the squeaky door. "Don't look!" she calls over her shoulder.

Mina has already seen. Her gaze flees to the vacant lot matted with the tangle of weeds and shrubs. *—Snakes in there; bad bugs. Please, God, let me find those little blue dishes for Mamma before she dies.*

Mamma leaves the kitchen door open while she goes back into the house to put away the Lysol and the brush and to stuff the stinking underwear and shirts and pants and clotted hankies into a blood-spotted pillowcase. From the steps, Mina hears Case spit on the floor again. She hears her mother scurry to wipe it up.

"Yer a damned fool, Kate."

In the doorway, Mamma jabs her finger towards the sky: *I'll have my reward.* This has been their parting act for as long as Mina can remember.

They start out up the railroad tracks. A spotted hound trots behind them in a lopsided gait. He keeps sniffing that bundle. The woman stamps her foot. "Git!"

"Why did Uncle Case do that to that picture?" Mina asks.

31

"I *told* you not to look!"

"I saw it before you said that."

"Git!" she yells to the dog.

—*Her nerves are bad today. Please, God, don't let us go to the store.*

"That was a picture of Gladys. She used to be Case's wife. When you was a baby. She run off with another guy. Broke Case's heart. Poo!" She makes a swatting motion with her hand. "She was a pretty thing, but she had fits. Fell down in a faint. Foamed at the mouth. It's a big word. I can't say it, but the doctor, he give her some new pills n just like that she never had another fit. Got stuck on herself then. Flirted with the guys. Run off with another man. Case ain't much, but he give her his paycheck ever week...n she jest made a fool o him. Poor Cuss."

Mina lets her picture flutter to the cinders. —*Maybe the dog will grab it.*

"Pick that up!"

Mina obeys.

Mamma puts her bundle down, snatches the picture, and looks at it warily. "It's clean. I thought maybe he'd stuck a coupla boogers on it fer tits. He's a corker sometimes." She tucks the picture into Mina's pocket. Then she starts grabbing threads from the hem of Mina's dress...starts grabbing threads from her own hem and from her sleeve, pokes at the hairpins in her bun.

—*Please, God, not the store today.*

Mamma takes off her shoe, rearranges the folded newspaper in the sole to cushion her bunions; then she grabs up the bundle and sets off in a fast, teetering stride, like a starling. Mina hurries along behind her. The hound turns around and ambles back to where he came from.

—*Another time in the store, Ilene's mother said: "Ilene told me Mina draws the best pictures in her grade." Mamma twisted her face up sour and screwed her fists into her eyes: "Boo hoo!" I cried first day of school. Not in school. Just a little when I got home. Then I threw up. Mamma tells every-*

32

one. When Ilene's mother told her again about the nice pictures I draw, Mamma said: "Naw! Yer girl's got that pretty round face. Look at Mina's skinny little face. She can't hold a candle t'Ilene!"
She's striding past the store. *—We're going home. Home to our gray bungalow. Thank you, God!*

In the kitchen, the woman stares down into the girl's face. "Whassa matter with you today?"
Mina shrugs.
Mamma starts unbuttoning Mina's sweater. She shakes her by the shoulder. "Whassa matter, huh? Yer so *stiff.*"
Mina shakes her head. *—I keep trying to find the answer.*
"Those refined kids in that school ain't everthing. Snub yer uncle n you'll give birth someday to the most deformed kid you ever saw!"
Mamma takes the picture out of Mina's pocket, unfolds it, lays it on the table. "Boy, wouldn't that be somethin—ta *heal?* Jest with a touch a the hand—hunchbacks, cripples, crazies.... You used ta look like that. Sure! A regular *sunbeam.* Now you've got so *stiff.*"
—I want to go to the other room to cry.
"Sit down!"
Mina folds herself into the chair and looks away from the food her mother is setting on the table. She's still trying to answer that question. *—Lately I always feel sick. That's the answer I gave last week, and it made her mad.* "The doctor at the clinic said you was O.K. fer school. Underweight, but that's nothin. Yer bones are small. That's nothin ta be stiff about. If there's anything I hate, it's a BABY!"
"Yer always blinkin yer eyes. What's got inta ya? Boy! You got it too good, that's what: Three meals a day, like clockwork. Anthing you ask for: milk, jam, jelly, peanut butter, graham cracks. I even got you *Ovaltine!* Yer clothes washed n ironed n mended. Yer bed made. When I was five, I didn't have no mother ta do any of that fer me. Had to shift fer myself. Just over from the Netherlands. Couldn't speak

33

nothin but a little broken English. My poor pa nearly went crazy. . . . Yer a *princess,* that's what you are! You got a *servant!''*

Mina looks away from her, out the window. —*Maybe my nerves are going bad. That's another answer that made her mad, too. That's also being a baby.*

"Whassa matter? The teacher snub ya? That's it."

Mina shakes her head.

"I'm sorry, but you gotta go ta school. The law. Else I go to jail." She scrutinizes the child's worried face. "Maybe that teacher is snubbin you in some way you don't catch on to. If you don't know what a blunder is, maybe you don't know when yer being snubbed."

—*The teacher is nice to me. The kids don't pick on me. She won't believe it.* —*I get sick in the store, mostly, I want to tell her. But that would make her mad: BABY!*

The woman pretzels her fingers, thrusts them to Mina. "Wisht my Sunbeam'd kiss my poor fingers straight."

The child does not move.

The woman squeezes her eyes shut, points to them with the clumped fingers.

—*Kiss her. Get it over with.*

"What's *wrong!* What happened to my Little Sunbeam? Huh?"

—*Kiss her. Don't cry. Just kiss.*

"What happened? Where'd my Little Sunbeam go?"

"Maybe you used her all up."

"Haw!" She swats the table. "Yer the limit!" She shoves her false teeth out, like the drawer of a dresser; sucks them back in. Clatter. Click.

Mina looks down into her lap.

"My Little Sunbeam used ta smile at that. Wisht she'd come back." Singsong. "So I used her all up, huh? Wait'll I tell Case. What'll he say, huh? He'll say, 'Wish in one hand, shit in th' other. See which one gits full the quickest.' Haw!"

34

"Look! Look!" the children call from the teeter-totters.

Loitering in the doorway over the balky buttons of her coat, Mina hears the teacher call, "Don't frighten it!"

Mina hurries out to the cold gray playground.

"It's lost! It's lost!" the children call; and through the snowflurries, she sees them all running after something.

Then, like a bit of blown tumbleweed, it is suddenly at Mina's shoes—a tiny kitten, more lavender than gray. It lifts a pansy-face to her and mews.

"Mina has it!" the children shout, and the stampeding feet rush towards her. Mina stoops to stroke the kitten, and she feels through the fluff a body like toothpicks.

"It's cold, Mina," the teacher says.

And Mina lifts the shivering kitten and tucks it inside her coat.

"It trusts you," the teacher says.

"It's Mina's kitten!" the children call. "It's Mina's!"

The pussy-willow toes tread out a *thank you, thank you* on Mina's collar bone...and the faint purr says *please please please* against her neck.

With the kitten peering like a corsage from her coat collar, Mina opens the kitchen door.

"No!" Mamma says.

"But it's starting to snow."

The kitten sniffs the warm kitchen air and utters a small pink mew.

Mina lifts it out of her collar. "Feel it, Mamma. It's so thin."

"No cats, Mina. They're nothin but trouble."

35

"Look. It's toes are like red raspberries. And look! The snow is coming down harder."

The kitten buttons large lavender eyes to the grumpy face. Mamma looks away. "Only fer tonight," she sighs.

By evening, cozied with warm milk and a pillow-bed, the kitten watches Daddy turning the pages of the newspaper. The big round eyes move up and down, up and down, wonderingly, like the eyes of someone watching the city park fountain sink and soar, sink and soar, in changing colors.

Daddy says, "Mina, what do you figger you'll name that kitty?"

Drying dishes in the doorway, Cora says, "Sure, Mina, think of a name."

All through the cold winter, while Mamma and Daddy spatter the rooms with stormy bickering, and while Cora and Mamma tangle the air with scoldings and gossip, Mina sits on the stairsteps with Wisp, who purrs a silky umbrella over their two heads.

Wisp follows Mina everywhere. Out-of-doors, she chases leaves and cuffs bushes and flowers with her paws. "A real show-off," Cora calls her, but Cora has to smile.

Often she scoots up and down the trees, like eighth notes in a scalloping song; pauses, with head cocked, on a high limb, then spills down, and with a trilling motion, scoots up the next tree.

Sometimes, when she scampers out in front of a dog or a car, prayers stick like pellets in Mina's throat...and for the moment, she turns brittle against this charmer, who bounces in her Love, like a clown in a trampoline.

One morning in late May, Mamma says, "Mina, I bleeve Wisp has got a birthday present for you."

Nested in Daddy's old coat, Mina sees four palsied moles, one with a head like a marshmallow, three with heads like wet Shinola applicators.

"They were in her belly," Mina says.

"Naw!" Mamma says.

Mina looks at the wetness on the inside of Wisp's leg. "Yes, they were in her belly. I kept telling you something lumpy was inside her belly."

"Naw!"

"And they came out through her rear end."

"Say! Don't talk like that."

Mina looks at the stems on the four little bellies. "Then where did they come from?"

"None o yer business," Mamma says.

Wisp lifts a paw and rolls back to reveal a double row of pink nipples.

"She's nervous," Mamma whispers. "She don't want us to touch her babies fer a few days."

"I can wait," Mina whispers, gazing into the proud tea-colored eyes. "I can wait as long as you want me to wait, Wisp."

Within a week, the kittens have wriggled off the boweled look of birth, and by late June, they are four balls of fluff lit with eight jewel-eyes.

"We can't keep five cats," Mamma says. "Better be bring-in chums in ta pick their pets."

"Not yet," Mina says.

"Any day now. It's best. Before ya get too attached ta them."

Mina, who knows there is nothing so wilting as being looked at with devouring eyes unless it's being patted with pestering hands, stations herself in front of the box of kittens, like a cannon.

"Here, Kitty! Kitty! Here, Wisp! Here, Kitty! Kitty! Kitty!" Mina calls and calls into the hot Saturday night.

"I declare," Daddy says. "She was here all afternoon while you three were shopping. Such a proud little mother, washing those kitties. Then just half an hour before you came home, she went out."

He has said that same thing over and over, four or five times.

"Here, Kitty! Kitty!" Cora calls, too.

"Here, Kitty! Kitty!" Even Mamma tries.

The babies in the box are a quartet of pink-tongued pleading.

In the saucer, the milk shrivels to a sour sore.

Early Sunday morning, Mamma tells Mina, "She's under the back steps—all bloated."

Mina squats and sees: Wisp does not even raise her head.

"Poison! Some goddamn neighbor!" Mamma cusses.

"I declare," Daddy says, and he shakes his head.

Mina lies in the grass on her stomach, looking into the big tea-colored eyes. —*Dear God, let it be Milo, instead, or Casey, or Agnes, or Sikes—*

The eyes go milky with the seeping poison.

—*or my teacher. . . or the black kitten. . . or the white one . . . Thy will be done.*

"Come away, Mina," Mamma keeps saying. "We'll get an eyedropper n some Pet Milk n some warm water. She'd want you to take care of her babies."

—*This second is a snapshot of all Life: The chirp of the sparrow. . . the clang of the streetcar. . . the silence of the clouds. . . and Mamma's call to breakfast. . . all ALL are sounds of The Great Conveyor Belt.*

"Cora, get a doll's blanket. . . and that doll's little nursing bottle."

Mamma's voice is alien as a voice heard in a high fever.

"Come on, Mina, get a little blanket."

Daddy just shakes his head.

A week later, at the corner of the back yard, there are four rectangles of fresh turf: one as big as a shoe box, and lined up beside it, as if they're still nursing, three tiny ones, like match boxes.

Every cell of Mina's flesh votes against this plaid dress, these brown sandals, the ripe cherries, the bragging robin, the clanging streetcar...the whole row of bland-faced petunias...the whole row of fat-faced zinnias...against Mamma, who brings her the one survivor:

"Here, Mina, 'Every cloud has a silver lining.' "

Drooped and dulled from his loss, this orphan does not even mew.

—*Worse...worse, Mamma...so much worse than your little blue dishes.*

The model-T Ford has been rattling along the highway for a long time. The backs of Mina's legs are chafed from sitting on a pile of papermill felts, which Mamma's washing machine and Agnes' washing machine have been chewing all summer, like a couple of Eskimos, into the semblance of woolen blankets. All this for Milo.

"Watch fer the Lowden county line!" Agnes keeps calling from the front seat.

Strangers always think Agnes is Cora's mother. Both have full faces and small black eyes and gushes of black hair. Both hold their heads to one side when they smile, which Mamma thinks is cute. Agnes is chunky. She's Mamma's older sister, an old maid. Sikes is driving the car. He's Mamma's older brother, even older than Agnes; a dwarfish old batch with a gargoyle face; a janitor in the Bronson insane asylum. All the way from Bronson, over the clatter of the flivver, they've talked about how Milo *must* stay over the county line for two years. The judge has sentenced him to that. *If he crosses the line, he will be put in jail again.*

Mamma says, "Member how he drawed them pictures so good?"

Agnes remembers. Cora remembers. Mina doesn't remember. She's glum.

"Them cats!" Mamma explains to Agnes. "A whole year, n Whitey still mourns." Then Mamma says to Mina. "Think of the nice things about Milo. Why, he drawed Major Hoople n Neb n all them people in *Out Our Way* just like in the funny papers!"

"Sure!" says Agnes, "n he'd write them comical sayins ta go with the pictures."

"Sure!" says Cora.

Sikes says, "Christ! Drawin silly pictures. What's that? That don't earn a livin." He speaks out of the side of his mouth.

Mamma has warned them: *"Sikes has his bellyfull of Milo. Be thankful he'd drive us out ta Lowden."* Mamma also explained: *"The judge hates to keep lockin Milo up fer drunkness. It don't do no good. The judge says Milo is such a nice bright guy; he shouldn't be in jail."*

Agnes is saying, "Hey! Youse girls didn't even tell me we crossed the Lowden county line!"

Mamma points to Mina. "Wake up!" She points to Cora. "You, too!"

The sisters wince at their negligence. Together they worry about their lapse until they are bumping down a dirt road into a woods. Then, dark and ragged as a gypsy, Milo is strolling out through the trees, waving his arms and grinning.

Mamma throws open her door and yells, "Happy Birthday!"

And they are all carrying gifts to his tarpaper shack. All but Sikes. He's gone to sit on a stump with his back to them. Back and forth they scurry with their loads: sacks of canned goods—peaches, beans, salmon, sardines, Pet Milk—two can openers; brown bags of cigar clippings...medicines...coats, underwear, mittens, galoshes. Mamma and Agnes have been assembling this heap all summer.

Then Cora and Mina are sitting on the running board next to Sikes, and Agnes is leaning on the fender; all four have carefully turned their backs to the tarpaper shack. Behind the trees, Kate and Milo, arm in arm, walk back and forth, round and round, like a couple on a merry-go-round. Sikes keeps jerking his mouth towards his ear, muttering to Agnes. Agnes keeps glancing over her shoulder with those little raisin-eyes. Phrases from Kate and Milo flutter back to them, singsong, blurred:

"Rats! Oh, Milo, that's what I worry about: *rats!*"

"Aw, Kate, they can't do me no harm!"

Sikes mutters, "Little pitchers—"

Agnes says, "Look, girls! Was that a bluebird?"

"Fire! I worry so about that kerosene stove!"

"Aw, Kate, it's a good little stove."

"Hey, girls, was that a jackrabbit?"

"Oh, ain't that a pretty flower?"

"That's called 'Indianhead,' Kate. Here, let's pick some."

Sikes mutters, "He's gettin her all worked up."

Mina is thinking of what Milo said to her and Cora last time he was at their house: *"Next time you see yer Uncle Sikes, ask him how many bodies that old face o his has wore out."*

Agnes whispers, "Come, Cora. Come, Mina. Let's look fer pretty stones."

"Don't ever tell me the name o them rich ladies!"

"You'd burn their house down, wouldn't ya, Kate?"

"Worse'n that!"

"Aw, Kate, it's all water under the bridge now."

Mamma told Cora and Mina last night: *"Milo wasn't drunk. Just a little lit up. He was takin a leak in the gutter when two rich ladies come along n reported him to the police. 'Indecent exposure' they call it. But all Milo was doin was takin a leak. He didn't know them ladies was watchin. Honest."*

"You was smart in school, Milo. You coulda learned a trade."

"You wasn't dumb, Kate—just bashful. You wasn't *dumb!*"

Sikes sputters, "He's got her all worked *up!*"

Sikes and Agnes confer. Then Agnes waves her arm and yells very loud, "Yoo hoo! Time ta go, Kate!"

"That dominie!" she bleats. "He preached Ma in Hell, didn't he?"

"That still preyin on yer mind? Why, that dominie was crazy!"

"That's what Otto said. He told me that church was

narrow-minded."

"*Katie!* Time ta go!"

Agnes takes a little box camera out of the car. Kate and Milo stand by the car, smiling, and Agnes snaps their birthday picture. Then Sikes climbs into their car, and Kate tells her daughters they may shake hands with Uncle Milo.

His hand is trembling. "Thanks for coming, girls," he says. "Thanks a lot."

In the car, the four of them turn their faces away from the farewell. The girls have never seen a kiss or an embrace between adults. When parting time comes, they usually make little swatting motions at one another, like poor swimmers trying not to drown. Sometimes a slap or a shove. Sometimes one will pick a booger from his nose and pretend to flick it to the other. Whatever, the girls know they must not look now.

"Much obliged!" Milo is calling.

"It was nothin!" Kate calls back. Hugging the flowers, she climbs into the back seat of the flivver with her daughters. The motor sputters, and they go wobbling down the dirt road.

"Don't Milo look good!" says Mamma. Her slack cheeks are bloused like Priscilla curtains: she's smiling. "Oh, don't he look *good!*"

"He does look healthy," says Agnes.

Sikes gnaws his lips.

The scent of the flowers seeps through the car: Queen Anne's Lace, Brown-eyed Susans, Daisies, Indianhead, ferns. Mamma keeps dipping her face into them. "In the mill," she says, "people used ta say Milo looked like—who was it, Agnes?"

"Rudolph Valentino."

"And who'd they say I looked like?"

"I fergit."

"It was some actress."

"Oh. Greta Garbo, I guess."

Mamma's eyes bloom like two orchids. "Yeah! Rudolph Valentino n Greta Garbo!"

Agnes purses her lips. "It was just a joke, Kate."

"But more'n one said it." Those eyes blooming, hugely.

"Kate! I told you: It was just a *joke!*"

Mamma throws her face towards her lap, and with that fast series of jabs to her nose, mouth, neck, shoulders, she mimes that familiar refrain: —*I know I'm homely: false teeth, hook nose, yellow skin, chicken neck, round shoulders, cat eyes.*

The sharp spice of Indianhead swells through the car like a sunset.

"I can't get over how good Milo looks," Mamma beams. "I don't care what anybody says, even if he is my twin, there's no man in the whole family that can hold a candle to Milo when he's sober."

Agnes leans back from the front seat to inhale the bouquet. She sighs: " 'Daisies won't tell.' "

Mina looks out the window.

Then Cora says exactly what Mina was about to say: "Was Uncle Milo ever married?"

Agnes hoots.

Sikes yanks his lips back to his ear, and out of that dingy slot he snarls, "Sure, he's married. You know his wife's name, Pickaninny?"

Cora looks to her mother for a hint.

Mamma looks up, befuddled, from the bouquet.

"Whitey," Sikes snarls. "Now it's yer turn to guess."

Mina looks to Agnes for help. Agnes shakes her head. Mina says, "I don't know her name, either."

Sikes yanks his lips way back, like a slingshot. "His wife's name is BOOZE."

Mamma ducks her face down into the flowers. Cora looks out of her window. Mina looks out of her window. They let fields of corn...fields of wheat...fields of clover...wipe the scribbles of knowledge from their faces.

"Milo told me I could be put in jail fer this," Mamma whispers, "but with you two girls along, we're just out fer a walk."

It's past bedtime, but they can't sleep. It's so hot. The streetcar keeps clanging past the house. A switch engine keeps chuffing back and forth beside the papermill. Dogs are barking; cats, fighting. Their dad is snoring. So they've left the little gray bungalow and climbed the steep hill to "the rich section." The Parklawn Elementary School is up here. Most of Cora's and Mina's schoolmates live up here, too.

"Yeah, Milo says it's window-peeping," titters Mamma, "but that's if ya stand still n look. Keep clippin right along."

There's a cool breeze up here. The leaves of the big trees rustle. Here and there, sprinklers are spinning great glittery webs of water out over the lawns. The sidewalks are wet. Wet and cool.

"Wasteful," Mamma whispers. "Money ta throw away."

"This is where Lenore lives," Cora whispers.

"Lenore? Her father owns that big shoe store?" says Mamma.

It's a large sandstone house, nearly hidden behind a tall hedge. It looks closed up, dark.

"Bet they're away on a trip," says Mamma.

"I think that one is Betty Holmes' place," Cora offers.

There are lights on here; a radio playing.

"Stinks o the mustard," Mamma giggles. "That's what I wisht we could have: a radio. Yer old fogey dad don't want none of them nice things."

A dog barks from a back yard, and the three figures scurry along. A scent of roses causes them to sigh in unison. It wafts from the park beside the school. The three sit on a bench under the streetlight. Cora points out to her mother the avenues and the houses where her classmates live. She finished Parklawn School two years ago, but she remembers clearly the names and the houses. So far, Mina has not spoken one word. She has hardly entered their conversations all summer. Mamma and Cora seem like chums. Mina has no one. She doesn't sleep in her father's bed anymore.—*"Shame on you, you big girl! Nine years old: Shame!"* Mamma and Cora have teased her. Stoically, she has accepted the teasing; has accepted the blame for crying to sleep in his bed when she was a baby. Gratefully, she has accepted the little cot in the hall, where she can hear Mamma and Cora whispering and giggling in their bed downstairs. Mina looks beyond the houses towards the end of the street, where the school looms big and lonesome. It seems years since she sat at her desk drawing with her crayons...will be years before she can sit there and draw pictures once more.

"...Marie Stacey," Cora is telling Mamma... "and down that way, Barbara Killwater, and over there, Margaret Tasswell."

"Tasswell?" Mamma gulps the name. "Her father's a dentiss. I gotta see their place."

The three rise in unison and move briskly past more darkened houses...past some lighted ones.

—*Oh, those sprinklers,* thinks Mina, *spinning plates of water and humming like phonograph records.*

"It's so quiet," Mamma says. "Bet most of the people are away on trips."

"It's the corner one," Cora whispers. She has pointed it out to them on previous summer nights, but somehow it's more adventuresome to pretend this is all a fresh discovery.

The Tasswells are on the screen porch, talking and laughing. Ice clinks in tumblers. The three walk very fast....At the other end of the house, a chandelier sparkles. A double garage. Two cars.

"Wow!" Mamma whispers after they have passed. "Is she

46

stuck up?"

"Sorta," says Cora.

They cross the street, gaze into another window, where a woman is playing the piano. Her hair is gathered at the back of her head in a shiny bunch of curls, like grapes. A man stands behind her, looking down at the curls, smiling. Love. Wealth.

They head back to the bench and seat themselves again. "Wow!" Mamma giggles. "Wasn't she a looker? Refined. I knew a girl at the mill, nice-lookin, somethin like that woman. Sadie was her name. Good teeth, took care o her hair n her complexion n her fingernails. Used good creams n good shampoos. Her mother washed her hair for her every week, taught her such good grammar. She was too good fer the mill gang. Smelled so fresh n clean. Not a high-stepper, mind you. She didn't use a speck o *paint* on her face, just the good creams—lemon n cucumber n I don't know what all was in them. Some said she used cocoa butter on her bust. Well, those was the smutty-talkers. Anyway, this Sadie she was too good fer the mill. She quit after a while n her mother got her a job housekeepin fer a doctor. Well, this doctor's wife was ailing: consumption or TB. I don't know what it was, but after a while, she died. The doctor kept Sadie on, and the next thing we heard, why he had married her. Sure, he did! They say he was awful good to her; gave her a charge account of her very own at Gilmore's. Took her to the Grand Canyon. That's really *true.* Sadie showed someone some snapshots to prove it."

The three sit in silence, relishing Sadie's good fortune tangibly as if they're licking lollipops.

"Will power," Mamma says. "You gotta have will power. Backbone. Tell yerself every day: I'm goin ta rise in the world. I'm goin ta get control over my nerves. I'm just as good as the next one. If my feelings get hurt, nobody will know it. Sure, teach yerself ta hold it inside. Put a smile on yer face. It works. Wisht I'd had a mother ta tell me these things when I was a girl."

She sits in silence, savoring her sermon. "Another thing: Don't steal. Don't you ever take one penny or one thimble that don't b'long ta you. That's what Agnes was accused of once, when she was housekeepin fer them Jews. Poor Agnes cried n cried. Lucky they didn't send her to jail. Her nerves got bad n they took pity on her. Jews ain't mean; they're just stuck-up. They went to a lotta trouble ta get Agnes' job back for her in the mill, but she ain't happy there. It's not her kinda work."

Heat lightning flashes. Mina sees the school in all its splendor. —*In September, when the teacher says, "Class, draw a picture of your summer vacation"... while the others are fumbling around in their desks and the sweaty boys are shoving one another and snorting and the nervous teacher is ringing her little bell, the Beauty will be flowing through my hand onto the paper, like colored icing out of a tube, and one by one, those nearest me will grow silent and draw near and will watch, as people gather at a bakery shop window to feast their eyes on the fancy cakes.... Oh, I have lain on that cot all summer, planning and planning what I will draw: three pink roses, their petals curved and folded elegantly... a single red rose so waxy everyone will want to touch it... a tiger lily dark orange at the tips, it's pale throat speckled like the throat of a brown thrasher... and in the center, WISP, silvery and fluffy, with eyes like Jesus' eyes when he said: "Lo, I am with you always." Flowing and flowing and flowing out of my hand... and after a while, I will look up and see them all standing around me in silence. The teacher will say, softly, reverently: "Class, take your seats." And they will part, like the Red Sea, to let my talent pass through to her astonished eyes.... I will look around me then and see on other desk tops: a crayoned beach umbrella clumsy as a lopsided bicycle wheel... a swimmer that looks like a rag doll stuck in a fish bowl. The pity! The shame! Are their fingers crippled? Can't they SEE?... And there, on Nicky's desk: a car? It looks like a tin can that has met up with a pair of eyeglasses.... And one by one, we will walk to the front of the room and*

hold up our pictures...and the class will vote—UNANI-
MOUSLY, as they have every September for five years—to
hang MINA'S PICTURE in the front hall....And I will bow
my head and whisper: "Thank you, Dear God."

The heat lightning is flashing again. Mamma is saying:
"Boy! That's what I'd like: to work in a rich house...learn
sumpin about good manners. Well, we'd better git home
before it rains."

The three rise and start down the hill. Mamma swaggers
with exhilaration. "I bleeve this is my favrite game!" she
giggles. "I can't help it if Milo says I'll be put in jail. I can't
help it if Sikes says I'll end up in the sylum fer cranin my neck
at the richbuggers. Shit! Ain't it FUN!" The rain patters
them gently. "When we was kids, Milo n me used ta do this
at Christmas time—look in the windows at the other people's
Christmas trees. Agnes used ta come along, too. She'll deny
it if you ask her, but she's the one that taught us. Sure. Talk
about *poor.* You kids don't know what *poor* is."

It has started to rain harder. They run.

"Boy, oh boy!" Mamma pants, "Won't we have sweet
dreams?"

Lying on her cot, listening to the rain on the roof, Mina
sees it clearly: *—a brand new picture on a sheet of black*
paper, maybe dark gray—drawn with sky blue crayon—the
water twirling out of the sprinkler...like a hoop...like a
plate...like a web....Yes. Ripening in my hand...waiting
in my hand...like a blessing.

Swooshing out of the cherry tree like Tarzan's Jane: That's cousin Maybelle in an old tire.

Standing in the back yard under another cherry tree is a handsome man: That's Lester, Maybelle's father. Mina's father is standing next to Lester. Otto and Lester, brothers, both straight and slim; Lester, very black-haired; Otto, sandy-gray. Their quiet talk about corn and wheat and hogs is strumming the summer air.

Swaying on the porch swing, behind a dollop of blue morning glories, is a plump blonde woman in a coral-colored dress all fancied with rickrack. Her big bubs blob. She laughs like a piano. She has a gold tooth. That's Maybelle's mother, Ida. Beside Ida on the swing is a scrawny woman, Kate. Her skinny arms are clutched around her ribs. It's summer, yet she acts cold. Her beak juts out of her yellow face. Those angleworm lips are trying to smile, but they make a snarl. Her hair is crimped under a hairnet. Ida's hair is bouncing as she swings. Kate keeps turning her face this way and that. She's very nervous. She didn't want to come here.

Billowy Ida is scooping Kate into the house. Good: Now the show can go on: That Maybelle! She's fourteen. Cora, sixteen, and Mina, twelve, haven't seen her for three years. Swoosh! goes that tire. It fans the sisters. Maybelle is all pink. She has huge blue eyes with great lashes that swoop down like wings and swoop up again. She pouts: a pink ladyslipper. She laughs: a string of bells. Her heavy tan-blonde hair wags like a sheaf of ripe wheat.

Otto and Lester are pumping water, washing their hands, snorting their faces into the water, drinking from scooped hands. When they walk around the corner of the barn and out into the corn field, Maybelle will tell her cousins the rest of her story.

Now! She plunges towards them again...her thin dress like water against her round breasts: two scoops of ice cream ...that thin dress flapping back like a wave to show her rosey thighs. "You wanna be born again?"

Zoom! She's gone again, her words wafting up like bubbles. In city dresses and white shoes, the sisters wait for this knowledge. Before Maybelle can tell them, someone strolls around the corner of the barn. His bare chest is like brown grass; he has a matching mustache. He hooks his thumb into the top of his pants.

"This is your shirttail cousin, Clayton!" Maybelle warbles.

Even his bellybutton grins. He says, "Hi."

The sisters look down at their chalky shoes.

Maybelle swishes again, like a pendulum, that hair flying like a plume. "Wanna know something?" She opens her pink legs.

"Yes!" the sisters gasp.

Maybelle swishes back, flashes her crotch: *an auburn kitten*. "Clayton can fuck you so's your toenails hum!"

The sisters look back at their shoes.

"She's Vicky Valentine," says Clayton, his words wavering like the sound of the pump.

Something pops out of the window like a cuckoo out of a clock. "Cora! Mina!" It's Mamma's face. "Come in here!"

Cora and Mina wrench themselves out of the web of enchantment.

"To be continued!" Maybelle wheedles.

The kitchen is as the sisters remember it, but more so: the windows wreathed in foliage: begonias big as poppies, geraniums on fire, African violets beckoning, baby's tears jiggling; from the ceiling, pots of fuschia dripping...Swedish ivy shining...blowsy petunias cascading...Ida's giggles cascading...her flesh cascading...steam from the kettle cascading.

"Youse girls have had a tiring trainride," Mamma says.

Her voice creaks through the lushness. "Set down n rest awhile."

Fourteen miles on the train, and they're supposed to be tired. They sit down. The sunshine through the pink glass bowl stains the tablecloth. The walls glow pink. Even Mamma looks pinkish. She dabs at Mina's sleeve with her hanky. There's no spot, but she dabs and dabs.

Ida says in a trilling voice, "You two beauties going to Hollywood with Vicky Valentine?"

Kate looks dazed. "They've never been to a movie." She points to her older daughter. "Look at that oily skin, blackheads, puffs under the eyes." She points to her younger daughter. "White hair, yellow teeth. Did you ever see the likes?"

Ida makes big round eyes. She puts her hands on her hips. "I declare, Katie! I never heard a woman carry on that way about her own daughters!"

Kate looks this way and that as if she's watching a fly zigzagging around the room. She's fidgeting for a statement to please this baffling sister-in-law. "Yer Maybelle's a knockout."

"Your girls are pretty, too."

Kate thrusts her hand up like a policeman's stop sign. "Naw! That Maybelle she's a knockout."

"I'm tickled pink with that girl."

That fly-watching look again. "Don't you worry?"

"*Worry?*" Ida's eyes big and round. Even the mouth round.

"That sumpin will happen to her?"

"Ho!" The plump hands fly up like quail. The coral bosom jiggles. "I figger the Lord wants us to be pretty. Else why did he make the gorgeous flowers and the birds and all the glorious things?"

Mamma spurts a glance out the window at that swinging tire. Again she thrusts up her stop sign. "*I'd* worry."

"Well, I guess you'n me's two diffrunt people, Katie." Ida waltzes over to Cora and plants a big kiss on top of her head.

"This is Clara Bow." Then a kiss on top of Mina's head. "This is Jean Harlow."

The sisters dare not look at one another, they're so embarrassed. They both curl their toes down inside their shoes.

Ida is chuckling, the gold tooth flashing, the face dimpling, the coral dress brimming. "And Katie, I'm going ta hug the worry right outa you!" She oozes down over the skinny woman...and the next thing the girls see is their mother's arm struggling like a grasshopper to get out from under a huge pink peony.

"I'd worry!" Katie shrieks. "A pretty girl is an awful worry!" Then, sensing her blunder, she jabs her pointing finger towards the doorway to the next room. "Look, girls! Ida made all them pretty things from remnants!"

Behold! All over the couch, all over the chairs, even on the floor: peach-colored, powder blue, lavender, white, but most of them that sumptuous *peach*-color: satin pillows...all tucked and puckered like petals, with tiny beads glistening in their centers...like great dahlias...asters...roses. Oh, lavish! Oh, bountiful! In the corner of the room, ferns cascading, ramshorn ramming, more fuschia dripping...goldfish flashing in their sunny bowl.

"Nothin to it." Ida shrugs. "I worked in the casket factory over to Vicksburg all winter; got oodles n oodles of remnants. Maybelle'll show you in her room pretty soon: slips, pants, brassieres, nighties, even the drapes. Did we ever have fun sewin that slippery satin!"

Bowls of apples, peaches, plums, grapes: everything round, everything brimming, everything beckoning...all lips...all tits...ah!

"Shoo now!" Ida calls to the girls. She winks. "We two hens wanna chew the fat."

The sisters try not to bolt out the door. —*Maybelle! Clayton! Here we are!*

"No bull," Clayton tells them. "She's going to Hollywood."

Swoosh! "My screen name will be Vicky Valentine."

53

A blazing day! Near the end of the visit Otto and Lester are standing together straight and tall against the sunset. Otto glows as if he's absorbed some health from Lester. —*Cowboys,* Willo is thinking.

Then Ida is handing her nieces slips of begonias and baby's tears wrapped in waxed paper, and Mamma is scolding: "Don't, Ida! Nothin grows in our house: that gas stove!"

Ida winks. "These'll grow. Give em a kiss an' a prayer." That voice like piano trills; the dimpled hands clapping. "Come, Nelson Eddy! Come, Jeannette MacDonald!" The gold tooth flashing. "Ooooops! I mean Vicky Valentine. Give your cousins a classy send-off!"

Clayton leaps like a tiger onto one side of the tire. Maybelle leaps like a tigress onto the other side.

Kate covers her eyes. "The limb!" she croaks. "They'll break the limb!"

"When it's springtime in the rockkkkkkkkies I'll be coming backkkkk to youuuuuuuu!"

Everyone laughing. Everyone waving. The tire spinning. The limb galloping.

"...Little Sweetheart of the mounnnnnnntains with your bonny eyes so bluuuuuuuuue!" Maybelle and Clayton gleaming in the sunset.

On the train going home, Kate pecks like a crow at the three of them. "I saw you drinkin that wine," she says to her husband.

He holds his finger and thumb apart exactly one inch. "Just a sample: blueberry."

Mina leans back in the plush seat. The pecking cannot touch her. She's languid; her breasts pushing like mushrooms against her starched dress; her feet swelling out of her city shoes. *Fuck.* Her brain doesn't know the word. Her body does.

Kate keeps glancing at Otto, then out the window, then back to Otto. He has arranged his face very carefully for her scrutiny.

"What did you think of Ida?" she asks.

He gropes around in his attic for something very small to hand down through a trap door to her. He takes his time.

"I *asked* you: What did you think of Ida?"

He feels around for something very small and very smooth that can be slipped through a narrow slot. "Why—," he says, "she's —*jovial.*"

Kate looks out the window, at Cora, at Mina, at the other passengers. Then she hooks her eyes into Otto again. "What you think of Maybelle?"

He looks out the window...at trees...fields of wheat... uddered cows...fields of corn.

Kate purses her lips. If they were at home, she'd be yelling at him. "Did you hear me?" she manages to say in a civil tone.

He keeps looking out the window. His Adam's apple bobs. "She's— *developed.*"

"She looks like a Fast One to me."

Mina speaks up: "She's very nice."

Now the crow beak pointing at the slight girl. "The Devil always comes in good looks. That Clayton: Did he sweettalk you?"

"No."

"Huh?" She looks at Cora. "Did he, Cora?"

Cora shakes her head.

Dad sighs. The tan is draining out of his face.

Kate is swatting Cora. "I told Ida! I told her!"

Cora has pinched the juice out of the begonias.

Mina is watching apple orchards, peach orchards, vine-yards, fields of clover, fields of corn, fields of grass...—*blue chicory looking up Maybelle's legs...tall clover touching her THING...ripe wheat kissing her THING...All flesh is grass....*

"Shiftless!" Mamma is sputtering to Dad. "My girls don't go back there again!"

—*When it's springtime in the rockkkkkies, I'M COMING BACKKKK TO YOUUUUU.*

55

Dad sighs. His grin has vanished. He's gray again.

Cherry orchards, peach orchards, pear trees, plum trees.

—Little Sweetheart of the mountains with your bonny eyes so bluuuuuuue—

Mamma takes another swipe at Dad. "I spose you approve of the way they're raisin that girl."

He keeps looking out the window. "That's not for us to judge."

Cherry orchards, peach orchards, grapevines, chicory, wheat, clover.

—My crotch has become an ear. My crotch has become an eye. My crotch has caught more knowledge in this one day than my face has caught in a whole year at school. My crotch is a sort of GENIUS.

"Never have I spent a worse Labor Day," Mamma sputters. "What a family I married into!"

Dad does not move. He does not speak. He sits there upright as that tent pole.

Fields...fields...fruits...flowers....

—Vicky Valentine: Born on Valentine's Day. That must be her magic. Flowers...fruits...flowers...My toenails are humming.

On a hot July afternoon, Mamma, Cora, and Mina ride a series of streetcars across town to a neighborhood of big elm trees and green lawns and twirling sprinklers. They knock on the door of a tall brick house.

Agnes comes to the door, wearing a green smock. This is her new job: The judge who sent Milo to Lowden has taken pity on Agnes; he has hired her to be his housekeeper for the summer, while his wife and children are at their lakeside home.

"Sit down! Sit down!" Agnes sings out. She looks proud.

The three seat themselves carefully on the silky green sofa, then look around at the swish curtains, the lush ferns, the silvery-striped wallpaper, and the soft mole-gray carpet. From the walls large portraits of a beautiful woman, a dapper man, and three lovely children gaze down upon these visitors. They see the red dent in the skinny woman's forehead. Her hat, which is now clutched in her huge-knuckled hands, is too tight, and she has a terrible headache. They see the larger dark girl wearing the squint-eyed smile of a girl who has been ordered all summer (with fingernails in her shoulder) not to cry, not to pick her nose, not to pick her pimples. Next to the dark girl, they see a slight one, almost abnormally blonde, wearing the wrung look of one who has witnessed atrocities.

THIS HAS BEEN A TERRIBLE SUMMER.

"I'll get youse some lemonade," says Agnes, very importantly.

"Don't use any good tumblers for us," says Mamma. "I'd be *sick* if we broke somethin."

57

"Come to the kitchen," Agnes orders her spindly sister. "Pick out the tumblers yerself."

The women leave the girls on the sofa. Their mother has instructed them all week that they are to leave her alone with Agnes to talk over her troubles.

The girls sit there, side by side, silent, looking at the floor lamp with its sugary cloth shade dripping a butterscotch-colored fringe. They're glad to be rid of their mother, if only for a few minutes. Mamma wants to leave Dad. She's talked of little else all summer; in fact, since the end of last summer. It all started with that hen-talk she had with Ida. Now she has come to Agnes to see about getting a job as a housekeeper in a place where her daughters can live with her and help out with the light work. Both girls are sick with dread.

The women's agitation pings through the hallway like popcorn in a hot skillet:

"That Maybelle! Goes with a married bandleader forty years old!"

"She'll end up with a disease," says Agnes.

"And he'll end up in jail—marijuana charge. Wait n see."

"Ida must be blind."

"Ida brags about it! Says she's 'tickled pink' with Maybelle."

"I brought you up better'n that."

"You bet! I never brag about my kids."

"You used to brag about Milo."

"I know. I learned my lesson."

Cora and Mina are gazing at a marvel: an amber bead curtain between this room and the next...shimmering, twinkling. Mina looks at her older sister: *Dare we?* Cora's face says NO.

"Maybelle was a big girl, nine 'r ten, still sittin in Lester's lap."

"It makes me *sick!*"

"Sure! Sittin in her father's lap, huggin n kissin."

"I thought our family was riffraff, but we're not as low as them *Germans.*"

58

"Ida swears it's true, Agnes: LESTER'S N OTTO'S FATHER NEVER MARRIED THEIR MOTHER."

"There's no worse sin. You must leave Otto, Kate."

"Ida just laughed about it."

"She's an igrunt woman. It's the First Sin. That's what Adam n Eve did."

"I know it. If it wasn't for my daughters, I'd throw myself in fronta a train."

"Now get control o yourself, Kate. You know what Sikes says."

"I know: I'll end up in the sylum."

"Otto, too. Sikes warned you. Pa warned you. I warned you."

"I know it. Sikes told me n all of youse told me the sylum is fulla people that lost their minds over religion."

"Your girls. That's the ones I feel sorry for: those poor girls."

The girls gaze at the bead curtain, hanging like icicles... discern the wavering pinks and greens in what must be the parlour...glimpse an organ, maybe, or a piano.

"I mean it: I could throw myself in fronta a train!"

"Don't talk that way, Kate."

Her daughters have heard her raging about suicide all summer. The suspense is awful. Their dad just says, *"The change of life is awful hard on your mother. Try to cheer her up."* Cora tries sometimes. Mina doesn't. Mina is sickened by the medallions of blood on the seat of Mamma's dresses ...blood on the chairs...pails of bloody rags in the cellar. The whole house seems painted red with change-of-life.

"I couldn't take no job where I'd have ta cook 'r serve at table. I can do a man's work, though: take care o the furnace, wash windows."

Mina keeps her eyes on the bead curtain: —*God, let me stay with my daddy. I'll pack his dinner pail every morning. I'll wash his clothes and sew on the buttons. I'll keep quiet so's he can rest and read the Bible.*

"Son of a bitch! That's what he is!" flails Mamma.

"Don't use that kinda language, Kate."

All summer she's been hacking at him. At the supper table, she always attacks: *"Son of a bitch!"* He says nothing. She pours vinegar all over her food, sticks out her tongue at him, thumbs her nose. He looks down into his plate and very slowly, he mashes his potatoes. She stamps her foot, slaps the table, screams, like a dog barking at a scarecrow. *"Sin! Sin!"* she yells. He goes on mashing his potatoes. *"Dear Little Sisters,"* he says to Cora and Mina. *"Satan is working awful hard because he knows he has but a short time."* His voice is melancholy, slightly lilting, like an old chair rocking by itself on a porch. Mamma mops up her plate with a crust of bread, pours herself a cup of black coffee. *"Sin!"* she screams. *"You was born in Sin!"* Slowly, he picks up an apple, takes a jackknife out of his pocket, unfolds the blade. *"We were all born in sin,"* he explains. *"The Dear Saviour came to save us from that sin."* The girls watch the red peeling curl down off the apple. Mamma mops at the vinegar with that crust of bread: *"Yer mother n yer father brought sin upon my daughters!"* Dad takes his time slicing the apple into quarters. *"My mother was a wonderful woman. Whatever mistakes she may have made, she'll answer for them."* *"Her sin is on your girls!"* cries vinegar-mouth. He slices the apple into eighths, wipes the jackknife on his big blue hanky, then folds the knife and puts it back into his pocket. *"No, Katie, the Lord is merciful. The Lord does not punish The Innocent."* She gulps at the coffee. *"Agnes says the sin is on my daughters!"* He chews one piece of apple, then another. *"Poor Agnes, Katie, please tell poor Agnes that The Lord holds each person accountable only for their own sins. He tells us so in the Bible."* She thumbs her nose. *"You ain't so smart. Sikes could stump you on the Bible."*

—Cool lemon beads. Mina looks at Cora. Her face says YES. They stand up, walk towards the curtain. Cora walks through it first. For a moment, Mina is alone. Then Cora walks back through the curtain, her face blissful as if she's just been baptized. Then Mina is walking through the beads.

—Cool beads blessing my forehead, my cheeks . . . the parlour: pink, rose . . . marble table, glossy pillows, brocade drapes, organ . . . then back to Cora.

"Cross my heart, hope ta die! I could throw myself in fronta a train!" Mamma is insisting.

"Get holda yerself, Kate!" Agnes is scolding.

Cool yellow beads, erasing the summer . . . back and forth they walk, like parched fishes flopping from gravel into water . . . tinkling beads, shimmering beads . . . *—Now we are angels ascending—*

"The *nerve* o you girls!" Mamma is yanking Mina's arm, swatting Cora. "Oh, the *nerve!*"

The sisters swallow their cries.

"Come, drink yer lemonade! Eat yer ice cream!" their mother yells.

The lemonade and the ice cream wait on the dining room table—rainbow ice cream in green glass bowls.

"Sit down!" Mamma orders.

Mina has turned sick. *—The portraits are watching me. The elegant man, the rich lady. Their well-mannered children. —I beg your pardon. Oh, I do beg your pardon!*

"Eat!" Mamma snaps. "Agnes went to all this trouble for us!"

Sickness engulfs Mina.

"Eat! Where's yer manners?"

Mina picks up the spoon.

"Eat!"

Mina touches the spoon to her lips, but they will not open.

"Bullheaded. Just like her German father!" Mamma says.

—The ferns are watching me. There's a knuckle in my throat.

"Don't get yourself all worked up, Kate," says Agnes.

—Even the lamp is watching me. My lips are paralyzed.

On the streetcar going home, Mamma pushes the hat up off the red dent in her forehead, like a drunk. "I'm so dizzy," she rasps. "If I faint and never come to, good!"

61

People across the aisle turn startled faces to them. Mina sits up tall, looking straight ahead.

"I'm sorry I slapped youse, both of youse," Mamma huffs. "I know I make youse girls nervous."

"It's O.K." Cora whispers. She looks away from Mamma, out the window.

"Naw, it ain't O.K. Agnes she means well but she always makes me act bad."

"It's O.K." Cora whispers again.

—the red welt showing on her cheek. . . my arm feeling like a chicken wing in the meat market. . . people staring at that Looney between us. . . Daddy, oh my daddy, I'm watching out the window for you walking along the street carrying your black dinnerpail under your arm.

Mamma has started to cry. Her skinny fingers clutch Cora's arm like a rope of poison ivy.

Mina leans further from her, out into the aisle. *—Everyone says I look like you, Daddy: we're both dignified.*

"You know I'd cut off my right arm fer you!" Mamma is sputtering.

—"The Spirit is willing, but The Flesh is weak."

"I married into a rotten family!" she tells the world.

—trying to rip open the faces of strangers, trying to mash her misery into any crack. . . . "What was your mother's name?" I asked Dad when we were alone on the porch. "Alice," he said. "I mean—her maiden name." "Alice Porter." It was like a canary flying through me. "It's a beautiful name," I said. "She was a beautiful lady," he answered. . . . "Alice Porter," I whispered to Cora. The canary flew through her, too. "Why, Mina, our last name is not Von Musson. It's PORTER!" For days, we tried it out: CORA PORTER. MINA PORTER. Yes! "What you two grinnin about?" Mamma asked. Cora told her. Swat! Swat! "Sin! Sin!" to Cora. Then to me: "You! Always takin yer Dad's side! Why? Huh? Why? He didn't want you. He didn't want a girl. He cried when you was born." "He likes me now." "Haw! You got him wrapped round yer little

finger. That won't last."

"Oh, what a family I married into!" she hisses.

People twist around in their seats to get a look at her.

—*"Sure, he cried when you was born. The Mother Superior—They had ta take me to the Cathlic hospital cuz I was so bad off.... Why, I come near throwin myself in the mill pond a coupla times when I was carryin you—and the Mother Superior said: 'Why, Mrs. Von Musson, cheer up. Your little girl was born with a'—well, I don't know the word, but Agnes told me it means a kinda veil over yer face—'God has somethin special planned for this little girl.' That's what the Mother Superior said. She come ta talk ta me in the middle o the night. She had the sweetest voice, n she brought me a dish o ice cream. Gee, right away I took such a likin ta her."* A sneaky grin crossed her face. *"I didn't say a word to yer Dad bout it, though, cuz he had no use fer Cathlics. But I told Agnes. Agnes was mad at me fer believing that junk. She told me it's just superstition. So don't let it go ta yer head. Sikes said n Agnes said, too, them nuns'r sly. Maybe she saw how nervous n dumb me n Otto acted n she thought she'd better say somethin like that ta keep us from harmin the baby. Some people do, ya know.... Maybe she was jest makin a fool o me. Anyway, don't let it go ta yer head."*

"I'd cut off my right arm fer you," she hisses at Mina.

Mina turns her face away from her. —*No thanks, Mamma, I've got one of my own, although you nearly ripped that off.* She looks past all the curious faces of their audience, past the trees and houses, and watches the clouds. All the way home, she sits very tall.

September:

Tall and tawny, he strolls into the classroom and announces: "This is section one of grade eight." His voice sounds like a cello talking. "This is American history, and I am Frederick Sinclair."

This utterance, captured in blue ink in Mina's notebook, spirals into spires she scarcely recognizes as her own.

He calls the roll: "Richard Dykstra...Johanna Nyboer...Nicholas Tilburtson...Wilhelmina Von Musson..."

It's like finding under old leaves the pearls of fungus.

October:

Before class the girls jingle their bracelets.

"Yikes! He's a *Brain.*"

Someone holds up a movie magazine: "Wouldn't you swear it's Mr. Sinclair? It's Gary Cooper."

The dark-eyed curvy girl named Virginia presses her finger into a dimple in her cheek. "Jeez, he's conceited. I hate him."

"Here, too!" squeals Johanna, and she draws a heart on her notebook.

That pimply Nicky keeps shoving his arm close to Mina to display what he has penned on his grimey wrist: NRA WE DO OUR PART. She leans away from him, away from the smell of his sneakers, and sits stately as a lily which holds in its throat, like a sweet, sweet scent—in case anyone should ask—her rehearsed opinion: *I have a lot of respect for him.*

November:

She cannot sleep. Cupped in her hands, her hot new breasts

are throbbing like baby birds. She keeps seeing His large hand on the back of the book, that large hand, tawny, green-veined, long-fingered, with hairs golden as pollen in the shaft of sunlight. The soft pink beaks in her hands keep chirping, mutely, *Frederick Frederick.*

At nine o'clock the next morning, He asks: "Wilhelmina, can you tell us about Elias Howe?"

She turns mute under that Midas-voice.

He walks down the aisle toward her, those golden-haired hands sparkling in the sunlight. "Would you write a report for us on Carl Sandburg—sometime before Christmas?"

She turns brittle under that Midas-smile.

Now, she tells her pillow that night, *I know what Lovesick means.*

December:

After gym class, in front of the long steamy mirror, the girls comb their hair.

"Did you see Mr. Sinclair's new roadster? Wow."

Some of the girls put on lipstick. Some powder their blackheads. One dabs calamine lotion on her acne.

"Guess what? Saturday night I saw him cruising down Parchment Street with a dame."

"Bet they were going to a night club."

The row of preening girls bloom like a windowbox full of flowers at the mention of this Sun.

"My mother says he gives us too much homework."

Mina fluffs her hair into a halo, like Jean Harlow's.

Fresh from the shower, wearing a gleaming white slip, Virginia pushes into the little crowd. "Gee, Mina, you're tiny," she says. "How old are you?"

"Thirteen." Mina pouts her lips like Maybelle. "I'll be fourteen in May."

Virginia raises her full white arms to comb her dark hair, and her wet armpits glow like black suction cups. "You're getting pimples on your forehead, Mina. Why don't you cover them with bangs?'' Her strap snaps, and she shrugs out of the crackling slip and stands in the white satin puddle. "I'm fourteen," she smirks. "I'll be fifteen in April.''

March:
"Write a report on one aspect—just one—of The Industrial Revolution," says The Sun.

They bow their heads over their desks. Nicky squeezes his thatch of brown hair into a crest, and with the other hand he writes across the top of his paper, in letters like black ants: *The Cotton Gin*. His pen drools a blob of ink, which he doodles into a wagon wheel.

Virginia gazes out of the window and screws her finger into her dimple.

Johanna gets up importantly and consults the big dictionary on the shelf.

Mina leans away from the stink of Nicky's sneakers, gazes out from under her skirt of bangs at Him. She looks out the window at the wind-wavering treetops, steals another look at Him, and her heart, like a kite caught in the crazy March gale, flutters out the title: *"Song of the Papermill."* All but panting, she lets her hand write: *"Down the railroad track my father laid on gravel and cinders long before I was born. I hurry to school. I hurry past the sooty dandelions. I hurry past the big dark red boxcars where the hobos snooze. I enter a big cloud of sooty, sour smoke. I hear a rumbling out of the cloud, but I do not look up. I know it's the papermill. I do not even glance at the loading platform where the gloomy roustabout stands in lumpy shoes powdered with lime. I hurry. I do not look up at the dirty windows of the sorting room, where the sad woman is looking out, where other sad ones are reading scraps of love stories on ripped yellow pages, and a man who cannot read is looking at smutty pictures."* Her nipples warble the words. *"I do not look up at the opened door, where the fan belts roar, where the kettle big as a kitchen rumbles with the boiling of gray glop made of rags and old catalogues and old books. I hurry. I do not look up at the dirty windows of the coating mill, where more sad people are putting the gloss on the paper. I hurry so fast on those creosote-soaked ties that my heart hurts. I do not even glance at the other end of that loading platform at that other roustabout in lumpy lime-powdered shoes. Maybe he is the bad wolf who floured his feet to trick the seven kids.''* Her breasts sing out the words. *"I never look up at that papermill, but I know that from every window, its gloomy eyes are watching me. I hurry hurry hurry to school. Past the sooty dandelions I hurry down the railroad track my father laid on gravel and cinders long before I was born, and my feet turn the ties into piano keys.''* From between her hot legs from somewhere in her new little nest, something moist whispers another two words, which she places, in loopy letters, like an AMEN at the end of her anthem: *WILLO von musson.*

June:

All but dancing down those creosote-scented piano keys, she knows that this blue rayon-covered autograph book in her hand will keep her from being parched during the three-month drought that stretches ahead.

Not because of what Richard Dykstra wrote in his knotty penmanship: *When you are in the kitchen/Frying meat/Think of me/Washing my feet.*

Not because of Johanna's message in lacy script: *As you pause on the crossroad of life/Reflecting on the past,/Remember you have a friend/As long as friends do last.*

Surely not because of what Nicky wrote with that splatty pen: *Dear Whitey, Your all right in your place but it hasn't been dug yet.*

But near the back of this blue book, which Virginia, with all the virtuosity of her fifteen years, handed Him at the end of the hour. . . .Now, past the papermill, behind the last boxcar, Willo stands still and flips through those silly pages to this One. Oh. In tall letters, rapturous, like trees: A grove that fills the whole page:

You are a poet, WILLO!
Best wishes from Frederick Sinclair
June, 1937

That girl in the coffin looks small and dry in that shiny turquoise formal, like a doll in a box at a carnival.

Ida says, "There's my little Valentine. Born on Valentine's Day. Now on her sixteenth birthday, we lay her to rest." She chants it like a nursery rhyme.

"Dear Little Sister," says Dad. He shakes his head.

—*Think of something else. Look out the window at the deep snow. See that huge icicle hanging from the sign: SYNDER'S FUNERAL HOME.*

Behind the Otto Von Mussons, people are coming into the door, stomping snow off their boots. Voices are muffled, words dipping like oars into a pond thick with lilies. . . voices feeling their way as if there's a heavy fog over the narrow pond.

"Her suffering's all over." A croaking voice, louder than the others. It's Mamma, looking around for an audience. She glances back into the coffin. "Wisht I could be in your place, Maybelle."

Cora has started to cry.

—*Don't look at her.* For three days, she's been giving herself these commands. She's holding something like epilepsy inside her.

Ida is moving vaguely towards the door. Lester is taking her arm. He steers her like a large clutch of balloons.

"Stunned," Mamma says in that gruff whisper. "She don't really *know* it's happened yet."

Dad takes out his railroad watch. "We may as well be seated."

They shuffle to the chairs and sit down. A few others are seated, murmuring a little, blowing their noses. . . taking off their coats. Still like people stranded in a narrow channel in a heavy fog. Services will begin in ten minutes. Willo looks at the flowers in front of the casket. —*Roses, larkspur, chrysanthemums. Tall. They hide her. Smell sweeter than flowers, like Easter eggs. Big ribbons on the baskets: gauzy, lavender, blue. —My first funeral, and it has to be you, Maybelle. I always thought it would be someone old: my mother, Milo, my dad.*

Mamma is looking all around at the crowd.

—*Exactly what she tells us not to do: "Don't stare." Her big eyes snatching clues from the other faces.*

A very tall man enters, alone. —*Mamma is elbowing Dad: That's HIM: EMMON, the bandleader. As handsome as Frederick Sinclair. Married. Three children. "Ought to be in jail," Mamma has been saying. "Ought to be hung," Agnes said. Lord, but he's handsome. He's sitting at the end of our row. Maybelle was a singer with his band: Chicago night club. Peritonitis, a disease. HIS fault, my mother says.*

More people are shuffling in. Snow from galoshes melting all over the floor. Voices dipping, warily dipping. "Some blizzard." "Worse at Three Rivers." "Road blocked." "Car stalled." There's Clayton in a big canvas coat. He's with a short girl who is hugely pregnant. —*His wife? Next to Emmon, you're a shrimp, Clayton.*

—*"Maybelle has appendicitis," my dad told us one night at supper. I thought I'd draw you a comical picture and write a poem to go with it. "Complications," my dad reported a few nights later: "They moved Maybelle here to the Bronson hospital." I thought: Good, now I can buy you a movie magazine at the drug store and take a bus to the hospital some afternoon... "Peritonitis," Mamma was telling us next: "No drug can kill the pain. Ida says she's bent all the rounds of her iron bed." My father cried. "Pray for her," he would say each night when we went to bed. Maybelle, I didn't pray. I thought they were just trying to scare us about screwing. I smiled and planned to bring you that movie magazine Friday after school....*

The room is filling. Lester and Ida are there in the front corner. Others sitting next to Emmon. —*He looks rich. The rest of us must look like Eskimos to him.* A chubby girl has settled herself at the organ. NEARER MY GOD TO THEEEEE.—*Take a detour. Make your own hymn.* People are coughing. —*Squeeze your fists inside your pockets. Look down at your galoshes.* The preacher is opening his Bible, looking out over the congregation. —*Don't look at him. Look at your galoshes. You have huge feet. Make your own sermon: Vicky Valentine: Hollywood's loss. When will that Beauty come to earth again? Is a beautiful daughter waiting somewhere in my chromosomes? I doubt it. I'm getting pimples. But I'm smart in school. I'll marry Frederick Sinclair, have two sons. From the corner of my eye, I can see Emmon looking our way. You looking for a stand-in, Mister? Not me. I lack padding. I can't sing. Nor Cora. She's puffy. She's having her period. She can't sing, either. I have to dig my nails into my palms. For a second, I felt like laughing. What's funny?. . . Then one day, my mother said, "It's touch-and-go with Maybelle. No cure for that disease. That damned man. He oughta have her suffering." You know my mother, Maybelle. Are you laughing? I still thought she was just trying to scare us. I even bought that movie magazine. It's still in the bottom drawer of my dresser. Cora has read it from cover to cover.*

Willo looks up. Dad and Lester are aligned in her view, tears sliding down both their long faces like wax dripping down a pair of beige candles. —*Leaping like epilepsy. I've got to keep it inside. Focus on the icicle. Harvest. The preacher said "harvest." Think of harvest. Everything in its season. Apples, berries, corn, pumpkins, squash, potatoes, walnuts, cherries, snowstorm. Cora is crying; tears splashing on her hands. Soaked hanky wadded in her hand. Don't you start! Harvest: everything in its season. God's way is not our way. See, Maybelle, I'm saving it up. I'm smart. Someday I'll write you a poem. . . .I can feel you looking at me, Emmon. Do you like my platinum hair? Is my profile inter-*

esting? A family resemblance? Where is your wife? What did you tell her? Did you tell your children? WHEN IT'S SPRINGTIME IN THE ROCKKKIES —A team of horses leaps inside Willo's ribs. WITH YOUR BONNY EYES SO BLUUUUUE She gouges her palms. *—I was counting on hymns. . . . Apples, peaches, pumpkin pie, how many years before I die? When I step out of this door, that icicle could drop on me. A car could strike me. The train could crash going home. God's way is not our way. We could all freeze in this blizzard.* Snow is pelting the window. Wind is shaking the window. *—Is that you, Maybelle, trying to get inside?* LITTLE SWEEEETHEART OF THE MOUNTAINS WITH YOUR BONNY EYES SO BLUE!

The people are standing, shuffling, fumbling with coats and mittens, coughing. *—Won't be long now. Don't cry. Nothing more to see. You saw her already. Anyway, that isn't really HER.* WHEN IT'S SPRINGTIME IN THE ROCKKKIES *All over again. Dig your palms. Save it up. —All those voices dipping like oars, lost lost.* Willo barely glances into the coffin. *—Peach-colored lining. Turquoise dress. Big ring on her finger. From Emmon? Didn't notice that first time. Great big blue gem. Look at that, not her face. Blue. Chicory. Morning glory. . . . My father is laying his hand on her hand. I wouldn't do that. Cora didn't. My mother didn't. Just my dad.* "Dear Little Sister," he says again.

ROCK-A-BYE, BAAAAABY *—Wild horses again. My palms must be bleeding.*

"The cars will never make it to the cemetery," Mamma says. Her voice is the only loud one. Not really loud, but not soft.

They're shuffling out the door. WHEN I GROW TOO OOOOOOLD TO DREEEEEEAMMM *—Oh, let me out of here fast* I'LL HAVE YOUUUUU TO REMEMMMMM-BER *—That must be for Emmon.* Willo clenches her face. Her nose wings flare as if they'll jump off.

"The cars will never make it," Mamma is saying again.

—That scrapy voice. SO KISSSSS ME, MY SWEEEET
—Emmon, are you kissing your Sleeping Beauty?
Now they are in the cars, engines sputtering, most of them
starting. Jerking and sliding through the snow. *—Clayton
out there cranking a truck. Dumb canvas coat. Crank, crank.
My toenails are frozen. Cora's face is all splotched. It will be
chapped tomorrow. Tomorrow at this time we'll be sitting at
our desks in school. My face isn't at all wet. I'm saving it up:
icicle.*
It's snowing very hard. *—Good: We won't be able to see
much. Maybe we won't see the grave at all. Dad said there
will be a canopy over it.* YOUR BONNY EYES SO BLUE
I'LL BE COMING BACK TO YOU *Just one tear. Hot on
my eyelid. No more.* ROCK-A-BYE, BABY *I never
dreamed they'd play that at a funeral. Maybe because of
Emmon. Maybe she sang that in the night club, or for Em-
mon's children. Rock-a-bye, Baby, your cradle has dropped.
Maybelle, Maybelle, I love you I love you I love you. Maybe
I love you more than anyone else has ever loved you. If it is
Thy will, God, let Maybelle be born again as my daughter.
Thy Will Be Done.*
The car is stopping. All the cars are stopping. They have
arrived at the cemetery. They are all getting out of the cars.
*—It's the way I wanted it: all blurred. People blurred.
Flowers blurred. Casket blurred. Voices blurred. Grave in-
visible. I will not look, will not listen. Apples, peaches,
pumpkin pie....*
"Oh, my little girl!" Like a shriek of a dog that's been hit
by a car.
—Ida: Now she KNOWS.
Squeak squeak squeak go the feet past the tombstones.
*—I love you   I'll always love you   Rest in peace   All of
you All of you   REST   Soon the rest of us will be here with
you   One by one   Who first?   My father?   He's oldest   One
by one   all ALLLLLLL*

On the train, Mamma keeps glaring at Dad. Tears keep

sliding down his flat cheeks. Finally, she pecks: "If you was a true Christian, you wouldn't be cryin. You'd be laughin."

The three look down into their laps.   snow   snow fields of snow.

Cora turns a soggy face to her sister and whispers, "Did that Emmon remind you of someone?"

—*Yes: Mr. Sinclair. But that's my secret.* "Some movie star?"

"George Saunders."

"Yes." —*I must look again in that movie magazine.*

Mamma says, "My! Didn't she have *long eyelashes!*"

snow   snow   snow   fields of snow

—*Rock-a-bye, Baby   Your bonny eyes so blue   I'll be coming back to you   Drip drip drip inside me   A little every day   It will drip until I'm eighty*

"I can't put an old head on yer shoulders," Mamma sighs. She's standing at the ironing board, that beaked face bobbing out of those hunched shoulders. "You sittin there over them books, day n night, bad as yer dad over that Bible n them WATCHTOWERS. All A's? What good are they? I'd rather see you have a chum; get out n have a good time, that's what I'd like." That flatiron wrangles the ruffles of Willo's blouse like a hawk trouncing a chick. "Cora, she's got the right idea. Be a tiz— stiz— stiznog—oh!"

"Stenographer," Willo says without looking up from her book.

"Yeah, *that.* Boy, that's what I'm proud of! She's got in with a nice bunch there. Why, did she tell you how Hannah can just look at a picture in a magazine—drapes, pillows, tablecloths, salad, hat— n she can make it herself? Sure! LADIES' HOME JOURNAL. She give one to Cora. Did you read that?"

"Mmmm." *—recipes, beauty tips, silly little poems. The gears of my mind kept slipping over those gears: no meshing at all.*

"Sikes sees plenty of them people with book-learnin locked up in that sylum: doctors, lawyers, perfessors; burned out their brains. You don't bleeve that."

Willo visualizes college: a sequence of titans, like Mr. Sinclair.

"Yer dad: guess you can see how his mind is gettin funny."

—Yes, I can see. In my private journal, I'm composing a poem: "My Dad's dinnerpail is a little coffin. Every day my mother packs it with slabs of something that is shrinking him

to its size.".. . LADIES' HOME JOURNAL, I don't need rhymes. . . . "My sister is wooden: my mother pecks at her like a woodpecker."

"The thing about yer dad, he don't keep his word." She hisses her wet finger on the tip of the iron. "Oh, the promises that man made! He come walkin down that railroad track past the papermill, looked real spiffy; blue serge suit, his shoulders throwed back, hair combed so neat, perfect set o teeth—" the words drifting singsong through the heatwaves, drifting past the girl who has heard this a hundred times. "He was carryin a suitcase that was fulla religious books. Not them Judge Rutherford things. He got them later. These had nice pictures. Well, he started talkin—not like a preacher, you know but very quiet. . . .Well, I fell fer it. Said he could make Milo stop drinkin. Oh, *boy!* I thought. I wanted that more'n *anything!* Said he could make Casey stop cussin. Said he could get me over my nerves. Gee!" those eyes shining like two candles " *'Pray!'* he said. 'All you hafta do is *pray.* Then read the Bible n keep thinkin about Jesus. *Bleeve!* You hafta *bleeve!'* Well, I did—that prayin, I mean. Not the readin the Bible cuz I couldn't begin to make out them big words n it made me nervous. He promised. Oh, how he sweet-talked me! Said he'd git my teeth fixed. They was all growed ever-which-ways n I was so shamed o the way I looked. 'Come on,' he says, 'I can make you look real pretty.' " looking up out of those huge Garbo eyes "He took me to a dentiss. That guy pulled all my teeth. Give me chloroform. Nearly put me in my grave." She slams the iron down. Garbo is gone. "Cheap dentiss! Shoulda sued him, my pa said. I talked worse'n before n people made fun o me. *'Pray!'* Otto kept sayin. *'Pray!'* Then he got me a set o false teeth. Boy! Talk about a conundrum! They slipped n pinched n made sores n I talked funny n my breath got terrible. Buh! Cheap teeth. Cheap dentiss. Ooh, I shoulda sued that man! But I was too bashful. Otto he just kept prayin n readin the Bible. I prayed until I was *dizzy!*"

She slams the iron onto Otto's shirt like a branding iron.

"Then Casey—" She jabs a huge-knuckled red finger at her crotch. "Casey, he started gettin after me. Said if I told anyone—told my pa 'r Agnes 'r Otto 'r Milo, he'd kill me. Said he'd kill them, too. His mind was affected from lookin at them pictures in them White Slavery books. That sortin room at the mill is fulla that stuff. Well, my nerves was shot. Then Otto says marriage would cure me. 'Oh yeah?' I said. I was ketchin on ta his ways by then. But he sweet-talked me some more. Said he'd never get me in the family way. Sure, he *promised* he wouldn't get me caught until Jesus made my nerves stronger."

She slams the iron down, shoves out her dentures like the drawer of a cash register—click—and gulps them back in. She thumbs her nose. "Shit. I *bleeved* him. I was *dumb!*"

—*Dumb. You have no idea how dumb, Mamma. Dad, too. In my civics book there's a diagram: Men are grouped like a set of dominoes: Professional, Business, Labor. It stabbed me like a knife in the belly. Turn the page, another diagram, another set of dominoes: Education: college—high school—grade school. Another knife in the belly. I was so sick I couldn't look up from my book. "White collar. . .blue collar," the teacher was saying. . .labels, labels, Dummy, for all the layers of society, just like labels for all the layers of rock. "Privileged: Underprivileged." The words were roaring in my ears. I couldn't answer the teacher's questions. . . my eyes were stinging with tears. All day, all week, I was in the bottom of a deep pit with Casey and Milo and the whole dumb family.*

Mamma is grinning like a witch. "Agnes! If I could do it all over again, I'd let Agnes have him. She had her cap set fer him. By rights, she shoulda married him; she's closer to his age. She's ten years older'n me n Otto's two years older'n her. When he come along that railroad track—oh, Agnes won't admit it—but did she *change!* All of a sudden her skin cleared up n she was fulla pep. Boy, you'd think she'd took a *tonic.*"

—*Agnes, too. Cora, too. All of them DUMB. I'm asham-*

ed of them; ashamed of my shame. Especially towards Dad. "Evolution?" he sneers. "Dear Little Sister, 'The blind are leading the blind' in that there school of yours!" I've stopped arguing with him. After I saw that diagram, I stopped. I just go on reading my biology book. The thorns of my ambition stab him. He waves his Bible at me. His voice goes strident. "Satan is working awful hard!" I refuse to look up from my book. "Science!" he croaks. "Piffle!" "Poetry!" he screeches. "Piffle!" I cannot look at him anymore—that boney face on that skinny neck like an old birdcoop on a pole . . . all those piffles flapping out of that mouth—

"Fifteen years old, don't even weigh eighty-five pounds. Girl, you've got no idea how I *worry* bout you."

—I have to crawl up out of that pit . . . fly up and away from all of you. I used to think painting would be my wings. Now my pictures have turned to words . . . and words will be my wings. I am a poet.

"Talk, talk, talk, what good does it do? You don't listen." She looks up from the ironing board to see the blonde head still bent over the notebook. "Did Cora tell you bout Nellie, that other girl in her office? Boy, there's a good girl fer you. No lipstick. No high heels. Hair so plain. Knows her Bible. She don't *preach* it. She *lives* it. Calls on the shut-ins ever Sunday. Cora told you, didn't she?"

Willo jots in her notebook: *"My mother has a new atomizer in her brain. She squirts me with a reek called 'Hannah' . . . another reek called 'Nellie.'"*

"Oh, well, I can't put an old head on yer shoulders." She screws a finger into her nose and pretends to flick a booger at Mina.

The pristine daughter ignores it. She writes in her notebook. *"I give you A for trying, Mamma."*

All week Cora has been sewing a red taffeta formal for a dance at the high school. She doesn't dance. She doesn't have a boyfriend. But Hannah, the girl from the office where Cora has started to work, has persuaded Cora to go with her "just to watch."

Saturday after supper Cora takes the rollers out of her hair, and Mamma helps her tussle it into a billow of curls. She puts on the rustling red dress and some lipstick and sits on the sofa waiting for Hannah. They are going to walk to the school together.

Dad looks up from his WATCHTOWER. "Going some-where, Cora?"

Cora gets up and looks out the front window.

Mamma says, "She's steppin out with a chum."

Dad stares at Cora's rump. "Going to a party, you mean?"

"Something like that," says Cora, without turning around.

Dad clears his throat. "A *dance?*"

Mamma says, "It's some kinda doins at the school fer the lum—the lum— What's that word, Cora?"

"Alumni." Still looking out the window.

Mamma makes a scribbling motion with her finger. "That means them that graduated last year or a coupla years ago git together n sing n talk n have some ice cream. I think it's real nice."

Dad clears his throat. "You think there will be *dancing,* Cora?"

Mamma says, "Maybe there will be some, but Cora don't know how ta dance. Her n her chum are goin just to be— well, sociable."

Dad lays the magazine on his knee. His eyes are nailed to Cora's rump. The lower part of his face drops, and the lips part in a long horizontal slit. "Why, Cora, this may be the most important night of your life."

Willo, who is doing homework at the dining room table, looks up from her notebook.

"Don't start that, Otto," Mamma says. "She never had any fun in school. Never went to the prom. Now in the office she's just gettin a little confidence. Why, she *oughta* go out with young people."

Dad shakes his head. He sighs. He picks up the magazine and looks at the page again. Then he starts breathing hard, as if he's running. The magazine in his hands is trembling. "Cora—your daddy—is informing you: —This may be—the most—important night—of your—life."

Cora walks over to the other window. Her lips are pressed tight.

Dad slaps the magazine down onto his knee. "Cora! Dear Sister!—You have—just a few minutes—to make—a choice: Who—will it be tonight:—God or the Devil?"

Mamma says, "Fer Christ's sake, Otto, you must've knew all week somethin was brewin. You shoulda spoke up sooner. Now her chum is comin any minute."

Dad slides out of his chair onto his knees on the floor. He's breathing so hard it sounds like asthma. "Hadn't we better—pray on this—Cora?"

Mamma says, "Oh, leave her alone! She ain't goin out with a *fella.*"

Dad raps the floor with his knuckles. He stretches his lips in that baboon-grin. "Dear Sister!—Did you hear me? —I said—Hadn't we oughta—pray on this?"

Willo feels herself turning ill.

Cora blinks her eyes. She says to the curtain, "I prayed on it already."

Dad's face has turned gray. He's wheezing hard.

Mamma looks scared. "Otto! Them WATCHTOWERS have affected yer mind."

He hammers the floor with his knuckles. "You foul-mouthed woman!—You've *worked*—and you've *worked*—to turn my daughters—against me!"

Mamma has turned pale, too. "Cut it out. You'll bring on a heart attack."

The wheezing sounds like a bicycle pump. "Dear Sister—Cora—won't you—get down—on your knees—with your daddy?"

Cora is frozen at the window.

He pounds the floor with his fists. His eyes pop out of his face like two spring onions. "You may never—get this opportunity—again, Cora! Who will it be:—God or the Devil?"

Cora is sniffling.

Mamma looks out the window. She tries to speak quietly. "Otto, don't get all worked up. Her chum will be here any minute."

He tries to slow down the breathing. "I'm not worked up." That baboon-leer. "I'm just trying—to discuss a very important—matter—with my dear daughter."

Cora's shoulders are shaking.

"Wait on the porch, Cora," Mamma says.

The palms slap the floor like a tomtom. The lungs pumping. The face greenish. The neck throbbing. "Woman! You'll answer for that!"

Willo feels sick. She tiptoes up the stairs.

Cora does not move from her spot. She just stands there shaking.

Mamma whispers, "Yer *crazy*, Otto. You must be goin through yer change o life."

Cora is sobbing. The taffeta dress is shushing.

Hannah is clattering up the front steps.

Mamma says, "Shall I go to the door, Cora?"

Cora wrenches the knob, the door opens, and she nearly jumps out onto the porch. She slams the door behind her. She's talking with Hannah.

Mamma rasps to Dad, "Why, yer *crazy!*"

He waves the magazine towards the closed door. "Cora"

81

he moans. "Oh, Sister! —It's your last chance! —Make your choice—Cora!"

The door opens, and Cora rustles back into the house.

Hannah clatters down the steps and away down the sidewalk. From the upstairs window, Willo sees that her formal is bright blue taffeta. She's wearing silver sandals.

Cora's face is greenish. It's soaked with tears. Her eyes are little black beads. She marches into the closet and takes off the noisy dress. Upstairs, Willo can hear it talking back... can hear the coat hangers protesting. Then Cora blows her nose and walks out into the living room in a clean striped housedress.

Dad smiles like a man having his picture taken. He hands her THE WATCHTOWER. "Blessed Sister, Jehovah has the most marvelous, matchless message for you." He smacks his lips on those *m*'s.

2

In the senior high school, which is enormous and loud as a factory, Willo pines for Frederick Sinclair.

Noon hours, instead of mingling with the rich mob in the cafeteria, or with the poor mob in the bag-lunch room, or with the fast crowd in the corner drug store, she stands at a hall window on the fourth floor, nibbling raisins, gazing out into the tree-tops, which are turning the color of a bonfire. Wearing either a baby blue cardigan or a violet one, and a gray skirt, with that whitish hair streaming nearly to her waist, with a white rose bud carefully placed on top of her books, gazing out that window and sighing, she imagines herself as a princess in a tower, and with every breath, she wishes for a second blond god of a teacher, a Galahad or a Lancelot, to rescue her from this loneliness.

To the boys rushing down the hall, the princess is not exactly apparent. What they do perceive is more of a celluloid angel-doll stuck on top of a Christmas tree. These boys are not drawn to angel-dolls, nor is Willo drawn to sweaty, guffawing boys.

She has attracted one gaze, though. For a month, one pair of eyes has been following her everywhere. In homeroom, in English class, in biology class, a squinty gaze is always on her. It makes her nervous. She tries to hide from it, but when she looks up, it is still there. These squinty eyes are set in a broad flushed face; and under the hot face, a thick neck; and under the thick neck, wide shoulders that draw the man's shirt tight at the seams. The inhabitant answers roll call to the name of Margaret Peterson.

At the fourth floor window, Willo prays every day that this Margaret Peterson will not find her here, yet she knows it is only a matter of time. And sure enough: Here comes that tomboy, swaggering heavily down the deserted hall as if she's pedaling the floorboards. She pedals over to the window, plops her books down on the sill next to Willo's books, slicks back her short brown hair, and says, "Hi."

"Hi," says Willo very flatly, and she pretends to be reading something in her book.

"Hey, have you seen the movie at the Uptown?"

Grateful, for once, for her family's strictness, Willo answers, "I'm not allowed to go to movies."

The big fist raps restlessly on top of the books. "Come walking around the block then," says the growly voice.

Willo can find no excuse, and to her dismay, she is drifting down the hall with this zigzag walker so close to her that her big bust keeps bumping Willo's thin shoulder.

Out in the sunshine, where the others are standing around on the sidewalk and on the grass, talking and laughing and shoving and pummeling and smoking cigarettes, Margaret points across the street to a shiny red roadster. "That's mine. Want to go for a spin?"

Willo's hands are icy with dread. "No thanks."

The tomboy picks up a gray rock and hurls it against the curb. The rock explodes into gashed halves, glowing salmon-pink inside.

The next morning, Margaret strides through the locker room full of babbling tenth grade girls and finds Willo standing in her homemade slip.

"I demanded a transfer," she gloats. "Now I'm in *all* your classes." Those narrowed dark blue eyes hover like two bees over the pair of timid touches made by the buds against the childish slip.

Blushing, Willo turns her back, and the lumberjack savours the ivory hair sliding like water over the sharp little shoulder blades; she slicks back her brief hair with that quick elastic gesture, like a dog licking its chops.

* *

That same day at noon, now wearing man's slacks and a black leather jacket, that swagger advances towards Willo at the hall window.

"How about it?" Margaret grins.

"How about what?" Willo hears herself saying in a brave little voice.

"A spin in my car."

"No thanks."

The big hand shoves the zipper of that jacket up and down, up and down. "Jeez! This is one day I don't want to go home. My parents are finishing their divorce."

All that afternoon, and all the next day and the next, in all their classes, Margaret Peterson is prancing around, waiting to walk to the next class with Willo. . .prancing and looking anguished, like a hound holding up a thorned paw.

One day after school, as Willo is walking home, that red car careens up to the curb beside her and screeches to a stop. "Get in," Margaret growls.

Willo shakes her head and goes on walking.

Margaret leaps out of the car. "Then I'll walk with you."

They walk along the sidewalk together, the big bust in that black leather jacket punching like a boxing glove against the frail shoulder.

"The divorce is final," says Margaret. "My Mom owns the motel in Craig Harbor. My Pop owns the Buick place in Bronson."

Willo knows of nothing to say but "Oh."

The lumberjack kicks at a bracken fungus on a tree trunk, and it splatters on the sidewalk like entrails. "How about calling me PETE?"

"The answer to my prayers!" says Mamma. "Looks so healthy. Ain't a bit stuck up. She can take you places in that nice car."

Cora, hunched over her sewing machine, wets the end of the thread in her mouth. "Wow! That snazzy red roadster."

Dad smiles enigmatically over his Bible, and Mamma explains: "He's so glad you ain't chasin around with the boys."

PETE: Looming like the statue of liberty.

Every noon they sit, the lumberjack and the doll, in that parked car and talk.

"You know what?" says Pete. "When you read your poem in class, I said to myself: She's a *genius!*"

"I'm not." Willo suppresses the smile that says *I am.*

Then for a while, Pete, who initiates all the conversations, tries the impersonal, more formal, approach: "Will the war ever come to this country?"

"Maybe. Maybe the school will be bombed," Willo says solemnly.

"My father was a lieutenant in the last war. He was shot in the leg."

"My father was too old to be in that war."

"Your father is nice," Pete says. "You look like him."

"He used to be nicer. Now he's too religious."

"I wish my parents were religious."

"I wish my father would find something else to occupy his mind—like literature or science."

"I can't stand my mother," Pete ventures between big bites of ham sandwich.

"I can't stand mine, either," confides Willo, nibbling her raisins.

Pete bounces her fist on the steering wheel. "My mother is never home; always chasing around; always swindling someone." She munches her chocolate eclair.

"Mine is always at home, always scrubbing the floor, always accusing my dad of something," says Willo, nibbling an apple. She is surprised at how fluently this misery spills from her lips.

Pete thumps the steering wheel. "Jeez! I can't believe that old bat is your mother."

Willo feels herself waft up like a genie out of an ugly jug.

"Does she always blab about her *nerves?*"

88

"Always."

"Why don't you run away?"

"Someday I will."

"My mom is the opposite of yours. She's glamorous," says Pete. "I don't want you to meet her. You'd like her better than me."

"No I wouldn't." It's so cozy to talk in this elegant car every day—so natural. Saturdays and Sundays Willo misses it.

One noon Pete says, "I know a keen place for a picnic."

"I don't want to be late for class."

"We won't be late." Pete slicks back her hair, deliciously. "Trust me."

They cruise past students in parked cars. . . past houses and stores. . . and all of a sudden they're out in the woods.

"Lovers' Lane," Pete laughs, and she parks the car. She slicks back that hair again, turns to Willo, and those indigo eyes narrow on the fairy girl like shears. "I have a present for you," she growls.

Flustered, Willo looks down into her lap.

Pete unscrews the ruby Girl Scout ring from her finger and slips it onto Willo's engagement finger, where it dangles like a bracelet.

"I can't wear it," Willo protests.

Pete transfers the heavy ring to the thin little thumb. "Sure you can. We'll wind some string around it."

—*It looks like a bumblebee.* "I can't wear it, Pete."

The mannish thigh presses so hard against the delicate thigh that Willo springs alive like starched organdy under a hot iron.

Pete draws Willo's hair around both their heads, like a curtain, and kisses.

"No!" whispers Willo.

Pete keeps kissing.

"No!"

"Don't be afraid," Pete laughs, and she kisses again.

89

—I've been CHOSEN, Willo thinks. *By God or by Satan?*
Feeling like a Madame Curie, she searches in the library for
the parts to this riddle: The big dictionary: SEX. The ency-
clopedia: LOVE. The biology section: ENDOCRINOLOGY.
The chemistry section: POSITIVE AND NEGATIVE
CHARGES.

For English class, she writes a theme called *"My Secret."*

*When we drove out to the woods...out to that
field of flowers, my life was a flat sheet of white
paper. Then something strange happened. Something warm stained the paper all colors of the rainbow. The four corners all flipped up. They curled
and curled towards the center, and a sharpness
snapped them all together. When we rushed back
from the woods, my new life was whirling like a
pinwheel.*

"You've changed!" said my mirror.

"You're different!" said my friends.

*This new life keeps whirling and whirling. It's
beautiful, but the whirling hurts. I wish it could be
still again; not flat and white, maybe. The colors I
can stand, and even some curling. But I would like
to be still again, like a flower.*

Please! Stop the twirling!

After class, the spinster teacher hands back the paper,
privately, to Willo. She has marked it with an A. "Don't
worry about this secret," she says to Willo. "You're a poet.
Concentrate on getting a scholarship to a faraway college."

Back to the library: The poetry section: She sneaks like a
mouse through the books.   *...I cannot live with you/It
would be life/And life is over there behind the shelf/...So
we must keep apart/You there, I here/With just the door
ajar/That oceans are/and prayer,/And that pale substance,
Despair!* —Emily Dickinson.   She nibbles like a mouse at
cheese in a trap.   *—whose happiest days were far away*

through fields, in woods, on hills, he and another wandering hand in hand, they twain apart from other men. —Walt Whitman. *—Others have held their tongues. So shall I.* —A.E. Housman.

Night after night, the poems wander, octave by octave, through her insomnia, and her face takes on the stricken look, the rapt look, of someone who is exploring a peripheral music.

Pete keeps laughing at her. "Don't *worry,* darling. We're not *crazy!* My Mom is a happy homo!"

Kissing was their springtime. Lying together, in the Craig Harbor Motel, whispering, sighing, in this elaborate web of wanting, other lips grow frantic for kissing...and the ripe burning bud, like an electric button, shoots Summer into their luminous limbs and right off their fingertips.   More and more and more   until Willo is afraid of so much magic.

"No!" she says once more, and she hardens herself to study for that scholarship.

"Yes!" says Pete, and her kisses bash that hardness open like the rind of a melon.

—Oh, wait for me, Mr. Sinclair!

*   *

Hoping that her narrow-minded family will pinch her out of this riddle, Willo tells them: "Pete is not a nice person."

They turn blank faces to her.

"What I mean is—she's *wild.* "

"She don't run around with boys, does she?" Mamma asks.

"Does she drink or smoke?" asks Cora.

"Has she started wearing rouge and lipstick?" Mamma asks.

"No, not those things. She doesn't study. She gets D's. She sasses the teachers."

"Haw!" says Mamma. "You're a sissy. You're stuck up

about them A's. You need a tomboy to toughen you up."

Willo tries again: "Pete steals hubcaps."

"Tell her to stop," says Cora.

"Sure. Don't *you* steal them, that's all," says Mamma.

"Pray for her," says Dad.

"What I mean is," Willo says, nearly crying, "Pete is *strange*. She's like a *boy*. Not just a *tom*boy, but a *boy.*" Still those three blank faces. She blurts, "We're *in love.*"

Silence.

Then Mamma says, "That can't be."

Cora purses her lips and goes on sewing.

Dad sucks his teeth. "Piffle. Puppy love."

For her birthday, Pete gives Willo an expensive Swiss watch. It gains ten minutes every hour. They return it to the jeweler for repairs. . . . Back on Willo's wrist, the watch again gains ten minutes every hour. Pete wears the watch: It loses two minutes an hour. . . . Back to the jeweler's. . . . Back on Willo's wrist: The same story.

"It's trying to tell us something," Willo says.

Pete shudders. "It's crazy."

Back to the jeweler's. Back on Willo's wrist. Back on Pete's wrist. The same story.

"It's a clue to the riddle of US," Willo muses; "a kind of electromagnetic—Oh, I lack the vocabulary! A kind of numerical version of our—*energy.*"

"It gives me goosepimples," Pete whispers. "Don't talk about it." She licks the words off Willo's lips, chews the words off her tongue.

Still Willo's mind whirs like a hummingbird over this intricate flower of PASSION and TIME and ??? —*Please wait for me, Mr. Sinclair.*

After two years of twirling, Willo can hardly eat or sleep. Again, she approaches her family: "I can't make this Love stop. Please may I see a psychiatrist?"

"A *what?*" says Mamma.

"A psychiatrist: a doctor for the mind."

"You crazy?" says Mamma. "You wanna be put in the sylum?"

Mina's eyes fill with tears. "If someone doesn't help me, that's where I'll end up."

Mamma turns that bruised gaze on her. "How can you put this on me—just when I'm going through my change of life?"

Cora scowls over her sewing. "It's that Buick that's to blame."

Mamma grins and thrusts up her finger to show she has a bright idea. "I'll have Agnes tell the judge. We'll have a warrant swore out. Then that tomcat can't chase ya."

Behind his Bible, Dad clears his throat.

Willo wrings her hands. "I don't want punishment. I want help."

Dad looks up from his Bible and smiles. "Jesus Christ is the only psychiatrist you need."

"That's the kinda talk that'll put us all in the sylum," Mamma says. She gets up and rummages in the cupboard. "I'll fix that hot-ass." She places a butcher knife and a bottle of turpentine next to the front door.

Dad smiles almost blissfully. "Little Sister, do you need any more proof that we are living in The Last Days?"

Poor, pretty, and hemorrhaging poems, Willo has been offered five scholarships. She has chosen the college farthest from home.

Pete, who has preceded Willo to the campus town to select an apartment, tells the landlord: "I'm twenty-two years old. I'll be looking after my kid-cousin; she's eighteen."

Thus in a large anonymous-looking brick building a mile from campus, a neatly printed label: *Margaret Peterson, Willo Von Musson* appears on one of the mailboxes in the entrance hall.

—*Nothing noteworthy about that label,* Willo reminds herself. *Two female cousins living together in wartime.* To her parents and her sister, she writes: "*...I'm sharing an apartment with two girl-students: Marian is a sophomore from Iowa. Barbara is a freshman from Minnesota...*" "They need an illusion," she tells Pete. "The truth would kill them." But will the neighbors accept an illusion? She worries. Is it obvious to other tenants who encounter them in the halls that they are locked in this symbiosis? Is each a confession of what the other lacks? Pete is five feet seven inches tall, one hundred and fifty-two pounds, a hulking ox with stiff reddish-brown hair and narrow eyes and rough skin, always in slacks and men's shirts and men's jackets. She swaggers along, slouched, scowling at the floor. Willo, five feet three inches, ninety-three pounds, with white-blonde hair over her shoulders, holds her head high, walks primly, smiles obligingly.

Another aberration they must conceal from neighbors: Their first week here, Willo faints in the grocery store. The next week, she faints in a restaurant. "Food in public places has haunted me all my life," she tells Pete. Pete is exasperated at such cowardliness. Then the exasperation gives way to a kind of cheerfulness: She's indispensible, a placenta to this frail creature. Smugly, she shops alone for food.

It's the masculine-feminine aspect that most likely hits a stranger in the eye; yet beneath the surface there's a surprising criss-cross: Pete, who looks so burly in those loose male jackets, is hiding those very large breasts. In shame, she keeps them squashed like buttocks inside a corselet-like bra and covered with a high-neck T-shirt. Willo has never seen those breasts, nor will she ever see them. She only feels them pressed like hard male muscle against her own rose buds. . . does not even dare to remark that on the drying rack in the bathroom, her own bras look like pairs of eyeglasses next to Pete's soup bowls. . . . And it is Pete, not Willo, who is laid out in agony every forty-five or fifty days with menstrual cramps. Spartan, she refuses medication, even aspirin, and lies humped and moaning on the floor like a dog that has been struck by a truck and left in the gutter to suffer. . . . Every twenty-seven days, like a quick moon, Willo menstruates without pain. . . with no discomfort except one night of insomnia, followed the instant the bleeding begins, by the only two nights of sound sleep she ever knows. —*Like the watch,* Willo muses. *We're ticking away in our concentric orbits in a code I'm not yet smart enough to decipher.*

They clash over food. Pete loves to cook, loves to eat. Proudly she bakes a meatloaf, bread, oatmeal cookies. Willo picks at the feast like a finicky cat.   Pete bakes cheese soufflé and chocolate cupcakes. Still Willo picks. "Eat! The wind will blow you away!" Pete growls.   She cooks a pot of spaghetti, bakes an apple pie. Still the finicky cat. Pete tries spooning it into her, like a baby, and Willo vomits. Then, pale and tense, she flees to the college library, where she remains until it closes late at night. When she returns to the apartment, Pete is laid out on the sofa, sluggish as a gorged lion: She has gobbled all the goodies.   Willo stands at the refrigerator, drinking two glasses of milk. "You'll get sick!" Pete scolds. "You'll become anemic!" Willo nibbles a handful of raisins. On her ravenous days she will eat a tuna sandwich and an apple.

Pete scolds her, too, over her studiousness. Late at night, early in the morning, Willo is *always* at her books and notebooks. She checks and re-checks every assignment, dares not admit even to Pete that she sits always in a back seat, quaking for fear she'll be called on in class; hence must heap all her skill into her written work.

After a while, Pete says what Willo was fearing she would say: "Why, if I studied as hard as you do, I'd get all A's, too!"

"Anyone would."

"So why slave? What's the point?"

How can she tell Pete that every breath she draws tells her: *It is dangerous to be dumb?* "For a long time, I've known I have to walk a tightrope from the apes to the angels."

"That's crazy."

"Maybe." How else to explain it? "My cousin Maybelle was running fast with a torch. When she died, it felt as if she flung the torch to me."

Neighbors, overhearing their conversations, would suspect nothing. Both voices are female. Pete's is lazy and rich as butter. Willo's is tense and feathery. Pete laughs sometimes, cries a little, and sings—when she is *blue*—silly little Girl Scout songs: *"Oh, I wish I were a little cake of soap! Oh, I wish I were a little cake of soap! I'd go slippery slippery slidey over everybody's sidey. Oh, I wish I were a little cake of soap!"* Willo does not laugh or cry or sing.

Out of boredom, Pete takes a job welding in an aircraft plant. But the long hours of manual labor do not change her into the man. She is still the self-sacrificing one who will continue to cook and wash and iron and scrub floors. She will spend large chunks of her wages on Willo: one week a pastel cashmere sweater; the next week, a delicate skirt. She will drudge late at night over the sewing machine, taking in the seams of the skirt until it is exactly right for those slight hips. Willo will always remember to kiss her and say, "Thank you for the pretty sweater." "The skirt fits perfectly. Thank you." "You've made the bathroom all gleaming again!"

The masculine-feminine bond is frail compared with this mother-daughter bond. Each girl is merely moving in grooves that were carved deep into her early in childhood. Willo has always been the aloof princess served and scolded by a coarse, martyred woman; in fact, by two martyred women: her mother and her sister. Pete has always been subservient to a glamorous mother, who was usually away from home, achieving. She has been housekeeper and cook, too, for a busy, burly father who had wanted a son.

There is a brand new flavor, though, that neither girl has ever tasted in her family: Week-ends Pete drives them to the beach. For hours and hours, the two of them, arm in arm, walk the sandy shores of Lake Michigan. "Oh, Pete, this is beautiful!...Thank you, Pete....Thank you," says Willo, who has been transformed—flag of sunblessed hair flying in the wind, face sunblessed, too—into the American coed of the films.

Pete tells her: "When I was eleven, my father gave me a new Buick. Sure, *eleven!* I looked like a boy of fifteen. By the time I was twelve I was driving all over the place. The police never once stopped me. I'd go to the movies by myself, to roadside stands and fill up on hotdogs and rootbeers and Hershey bars and ice cream. Then I'd go to the beaches. I'd walk and walk and walk and watch all the beautiful girls. Over and over I came back to this one beach—summer, fall, winter, spring—and I'd stand on this cliff and look down into the wild water and I'd say to myself: *I'll give you until age eighteen. If you come back here when you're eighteen, without a friend, then you'd better weight your pockets with stones and drop yourself into this lake.* And I meant it."

Willo snuggles up to her. "What an awful loneliness, darling."

"Now the loneliness has ended....Another thing: this damned atheism. I'd love to be religious, but religion is so stupid."

Willo, who has been bludgeoned into atheism by her father's preaching, seduced into it and out of it and back into it again by her professors, says, "I've been reading MARIUS THE EPICUREAN. In it, a handsome young man, Flavian, is dying of an incurable illness. His friend, Marius, says to him, 'Will it comfort you to know that after you have gone, I will come here often and weep for you?' And Flavian says, 'Not unless I be aware and hear you weeping.' "

The anecdote slips onto Pete's need like a wedding band onto a finger.

Sometimes they encounter a man or a boy who lassoes Willo with a look of longing. Then Pete always tightens her arm around her pretty prize and gloats. Willo gloats, too: It's really Frederick Sinclair's arm, or the arm of that ever-present dreamman who is nearly like him, far more than Pete's arm, that shields her always from these yokels.

So the flaws of the week are rinsed away by these walks and talks on the beach. Back in the apartment, Pete brushes and brushes that long scarf of chiffon hair...plays that thin little body like a flute.

"You have a magic touch," Willo sighs.

"I'm pampering you. I'm making sure you'll never be satisfied with a man."

"Taurus and Gemini," Willo muses. "Maybe it's a magic combination."

"May first and May thirty-first. You know something? I can't even stand to be separated from you by thirty days."

"Then let's make May fifteenth Our Birthday."

They seal it with a kiss, and for an instant an irridescence seems to halo them.

The magic has its price: In her free hours, Pete stalks Willo on the campus. Finding a professor bending over her shoulder, smiling at something in her notebook, Pete is scalded with adrenalin. She cannot rest until she has found his car in the parking lot and bashed the fender. . . . Then one day, an alien tube of lipstick between the cushions of the sofa enters Willo's sight with one blink that leaves her eyes for the rest of the day two colorless slots.

One Saturday in June, Pete watches Willo open an envelope, take from it a brief message: ". . . Your scholarship has been renewed. Congratulations!" All day Pete witnesses the golden girl wearing her honor vividly as an orchid from a secret lover. Pete sulks, grumbles about the drudgery in the factory.

"You could enroll in college next fall," Willo says.

Pete taps her fists on the the table. "You know me and books."

"You could be a phys ed major."

Pete bangs her fist on the wall, kicks the door, and departs.

—*It's that bust. To her, it's a deformity, like a hunchback . . . shameful as my terror in grocery stores and restaurants.*

When Pete returns late that evening, a heavy residue of bitterness still clings to her.

Willo cannot go home for the summer; cannot, she knows, ever go home again. The illusion-game has taken root: She has come to view her family as a social worker might view them: underprivileged, ignorant, pathetic. She sends them cheerful letters ("My apprenticeship in fiction," she tells Pete) about the wholesome Barbara and Marian; about the wide-lawned tree-shaded campus. She sends them smiling photographs of herself; sends them birthday gifts—nightgowns, slippers, gloves; thanks Cora, abundantly, for the homemade potholders and the aprons edged in rickrack. She has found at last the remote role she believes they have always wanted for her: the fairy godmother.

The dean of women, who has been watching this aloof little stranger, calls Willo into the office. She's a middle-aged woman with blue-gray hair and a big missionary-smile. "A talented person should contribute to the group!" she beams. "You ought to join a sorority."

Willo allows herself to be "rushed" by these girl-groups. "Rushed" is the right word for this assault upon her emotions. Her hands turn to mittens on the teacup. That knuckle rises into her throat. Her teeth lock. The walls are watching her. The carpets are watching her. The lamps are watching her. These privileged sisters are watching, baffled, her nigger-performance.

She has to excuse herself and hurry home, where, after many hours in Pete's arms, her flutterings settle, like a covey of quail returned to safety.

One by one, the faculty approach her: "Join the poetry club." "Be our guest at the Philosophy luncheon." "Try the modern dance club."

Again, Willo submits to alien maneuvers. It's as if an austere nun is being baptized in a river by the holy-rollers ....And again: It's as if an exotic jewel is being passed from hand to hand to hand to hand, until it loses its lustre.

The professor of psychology calls her into his office. "Why should a lovely girl act like a recluse?" he asks. He is fortyish, married, jowly, and kind.

She describes her torment in social groups, tells him about vinegar-mouth mother and sermonizing father...about the bead curtain.

"Phobic," he concludes. "You need psychoanalysis, and that's expensive."

The professor of sociology, also middle-aged, bald, and kind, has a try: "You're different," he says. "I want to help you."
She unveils for him the window-peeping nights of her childhood.

He listens, spellbound, to the bemused voice; notices the shoulders delicate as eggshells showing through the voile hair. "Come often," he says.
On the fourth visit, she spills the truth about Pete.
"It's the damned war," he sighs. "When it's over, your prince will come, Rapunzel."

Their kindness opens her . . . coaxes into her wakeful nights that peripheral music she explored in high school. . . . One by one, the professors of everything from psychology to ethics to drama receive her essays and her term papers—Walt Whitman, A.E. Housman, Sappho—all sleek and damp and glistening—Oscar Wilde, Gertrude Stein, Shakespeare—like wild things winged by a nimble night-prowler.

"A fascinating mind," says the professor of clinical psychology. "But people don't earn a living writing poetry. Have you considered a profession?"

"I've been thinking a lot about that. For my class in childhood psychology, I've been playing with the kindergartners." Her face lights up like a messiah's. "They're more like poems than anything I've ever found."

"What on earth do you mean?" he laughs.

"Last week, when I was observing a class, the teacher asked: 'What are some of the nice things that grow on trees, boys and girls?' The pert little girls were quick with their answers: 'Apples!' 'Cherries!' 'Pretty leaves!' 'Flowers!' The little boys didn't offer much. The teacher prodded a shy little fellow. 'What else grows on trees, Jimmy?' Without looking up, he answered in a little low voice: 'Sticks.' "

"That's poetry?"

"That's poetry."

When they are twenty, Willo says to Pete, "I want a child."

Pete says, "Poetry is your child. I'm your husband. Isn't that enough?" Willo broods on it. When they are twenty-one, she says, "More than anything in the world, I want a *child.*"

Pete, who has given six years of devotion, is growing tired of this *prima donna*...tired of her phobias, tired of her ambitions, tired of that embroidered language, tired of this silent reproach. She has begun to look elsewhere: In the factory, she has been watching a calm-faced brunette, freshly widowed by the war.

In April of her senior year, the dean summons Willo: "We've given you every advantage," she says. "You refuse to grow up. We could expel you for—for living with that—that horrid—*person*—but it would be a shame to lose our only *summa cum laude*. However, we *must* remove your name from our employment file."

The psychology professor shakes his head. "You're ingenuous. You've told all the wrong people."

The sociology professor sighs. "Wipe the dust of this city from your feet.... Why don't you try Hollywood?"

Willo watches the fly on the warm window wringing its hands.

"This is no place for Alice-in-Wonderland," the WAVE recruiter had warned her.

Willo had gone on filling out the application form.

"The war is almost over. There's nothing left but hospital duty."

Willo had continued to fill out the form.

"Under, you're eight pounds under the minimum weight limit."

Willo had gone on writing.

"Surely a gal with a bachelor's degree—" When Willo did not look up, the officer had shrugged. "They'll cut off that pretty hair."

Thus, in a naval hospital school just outside Washington, D.C., Willo finds herself existing, without valence, among seventy-one barracks mates out of the factories and the department stores and the offices and the mining towns and the churches of Ohio and Indiana and Pennsylvania and Brooklyn and West Virginia and Kentucky...seventy-one young women, uniformed like wrapped bars of soap, confiding in one another: "When my Jimmy was drafted, I thought I'd go nuts."..."I didn't think they'd make you march while you were having your period."..."Personally, I believe...." "...and then I had to slap his face!" In the mess hall, at calisthenics, at mail call, a briny face like Pete's face is always watching her...at bed check, at dog watch, at the commissary, in the lab...always watching...and always Willo salutes their secret with the averted eye.... "THIS IS MY BELOVED? Oh, that's that dirty book."..."Go have the chaplain punch your T.S. chit." "Come on now, on the double!''

Willo classifies them into ethnic groups, into somatic types, into degrees of masculinity and femininity, into Freudian stages, into regional idioms, into shades of Puritanism...like pinning a collection of insects, almost autistically, onto a board.

Poet, she soars above all of them. Nigger, she can barely swallow milk and mashed potato at their table.

The four months of lectures and films and demonstrations and tests on ''Nursing the Wounded'' is just a grapevine swing into this sudden scene in technicolor: One hundred and forty-six marines (''Don't push, Ladies!'' calls Brooklyn. ''There's enough for everyone!'') with fresh scars like wads of pink gum and older scars like strands of stale gray gum... all of them prone on clean sheets, awaiting backrubs from these patriotic girls. They look more like rashers of bacon than men.

In that corner, skin-graft cases resembling fakirs and pink balloons. Over there, amputees looking and smelling like old saddle-stitched luggage.

''Just when it's my turn in brain surgery,'' says Pittsburg, ''they serve macaroni for lunch.''

''I've found a pretty good way to stand it,'' says Kentucky. ''I play like it's Halloween every day.''

An odor rises from these men that makes Willo feel faint. It's not the sour odor of boys rushing from gym class. Nor the stink of male tennis shoes in the classroom. Nor the putrid odor of Milo after the D.T.'s. Nor the pungent scent of creosote on her Dad's skin. This odor is different. It rises from their beds like heat waves from a pavement. It smells not of live flesh but of moldy, rotting canvas and moldy leather and rusty metal. Not the exciting odor of virility, but a stale, tepid odor of an inanimate presence.

—*Don't be persnickety. Join in the banter. Think of them as cartoons. You're reading the colored comics, with stink added.*

104

She sleeps fitfully, dreams again and again of groping, with a baby-spoon in her hand, through weeds and snakes and centipedes and spiders...of digging and digging through tangled roots and clay with that bent baby-spoon...looking always for tiny blue cups. But the roots are not roots. They're veins and arteries and tendons, and the blue objects turn out to be not cups but nodules and cysts and bruises and toenails and eyes.

As if the dreams are warnings, she escalates the CHEER in her letters to her family, escalates the gifts from the commissary—jackets, leather coats, shoes.

Saturdays she forces herself to dip, like a strip of litmus paper, into the U.S.O. where the jukebox toots "DON'T SIT UNDER THE APPPPPLE TREE WITH ANYONE ELSE BUT MEEEEEEE!" The mob of young men, all turned by sailor suits and haircuts and coca cola and shyness into yokels and bumpkins, call her "Blondie."

She excuses herself from dancing: "I have to write a postcard."

SOME ENCHANNNNNNNNNTED EEEEEEVENING YOU MAY SEEEE A STRAAAAAANGER ACROSS A CROWDED ROOOOOMMMM

She excuses herself from ping pong.

"Hey! Blondie's writing *another* postcard!"

The litmus paper comes out bright pink.

She yearns for a learned man, a handsome man, a protector, a friend, whose language of precision and beauty will dive like an otter into this deep waiting.

In the hospital, there is one intern of privileged profile and cadenced gait, but he only yaks about baseball and sailing and "those punks." All day his jargon lids sleekly onto the prosaically-grooved nurses, who accompany him through the mutilations calmly as mechanics through a junked-car lot. This intern, and even his nurses, also call Willo "Blondie."

Day after day, slim as a peppermint stick in her striped uniform, masqueraded in an angel-smile, Willo massages

bristly shoulders with bright blue alcohol, totes, like a re-
verse-waitress, jugs of foaming urine and steaming pans of
excrement...is marionetted from one end of the ward to the
other by that chorus: "Blondie! Blondie!"...all the while
watched with jungle-eyes...awaited with tattooed anaconda-
arms...as she signs each buttock with an exclamation point
of penicillin.

Out of this marathon, her gaze calls HELP!

And the cry is answered by a chaplain. "You look as
though you're about to cry," he says, smiling a little. He
looks something like Tyrone Power.

"It's for myself I could cry," Willo says, "not for these
men, and that fills me with shame."

He laughs. "Walk down the hall with me. Tell me about
this shame." He is also a marine, also emblazoned with a
scar—his, a gorgeous flash from temple to jaw.

"I keep hoping I'll wake up some morning a Clara Barton
or a Florence Nightingale or a Walt Whitman. Instead, I'm
more and more the art connoisseur cringing through a gallery
of grotesqueries."

"What a refreshing honesty. I've been telling them all
along that girls should not work here. It's work for older
women, or men....These men are not men, Willo. They're
guerillas who have spent two to four years in fox holes. Shall
I request that you be transferred at once to The Dependents'
Ward?"

White-robed, white masked, she waits with a little warmed
blanket in her hands to receive from the ends of opalescent
undersea-looking umbilical stems—babies—a whole series of
them: rose-colored, cream-creased, compressed from their
journey, looking worried at the white-walled world.

The chaplain, Father Vincent, comes often to watch
through the big window.

"My task," she tells him, "is to transplant them from the
plant to the animal kingdom. I call it 'a pilgrimage of Pity.' "

He shakes his head. "I can't tell whether it's atheism you

106

are voicing, or Calvinism.''

She shrugs. ''I can't believe—I suppose I have never really believed— there is a God who cares for us.''

This Jesuit meets her evenings in his office, ''not really for *instruction,* Willo; just for some plain talks.'' As he lights his pipe, his hands tremble.

She likes to think it is from her emanations, but he explains: ''That's my gift from Okinawa.''

''All I really know about Catholicism,'' she says, ''is that phrase: *'Kyrie Eleison.' ''*

''Esthetics again.'' He smiles. ''Tell me about—this disbelief.''

She flits from Schopenhauer to Spinoza to Sartre.

He talks about Aristotle and Aquinas and Augustine and warns her away from ''that beautiful devil, Plato.''

''Plato? I like his cave, with shadows.''

''Be careful. Shadows are tricky.''

''So is logic. What is this—Zen?''

''Butterfly!'' he scolds. ''You flit from one to the other.''

''That's the way I learn.''

''That's the way you *avoid* learning.''

Week after week of these talks. Still she cannot *believe.*

''All these theories have made me willy-nilly,'' she complains. ''I feel like a thread that has come loose from the needle. What I want more than anything, and I suppose it's plain lazy, is to be thrust right through the eye of that needle. . . and for the needle to pull me into Faith.''

''Ho! You've never heard of The Communion of the Saints?''

She shakes her head.

He tells her. It is midnight when he finishes.

''It's beautiful,'' she says. ''Here, for now, with you, it seems true.''

''Come next Friday,'' he says.

She does. And the next Friday. And the next.

He talks sometimes of himself. Of his boyhood and youth:

107

"I was a loner, Willo, like you." Of the war: "I walked for months among banks of Japanese corpses. I grew indifferent. I suppose one has to in order to carry on." Of the future: "I want to go to China. There's the real challenge."

Warmed by his charm, she feels the tale of Pete rising repeatedly to her lips, but she bites it back. *—Don't be like your mother, your shameless mother who in the presence of a stranger will plunge her bucket down into bathos and haul it up asquirm with woes.*

"It's Friday night," he is saying, his hand shaking in his tobacco pouch, "a starlit Friday night. The other girls are out with men, at the dance, at the movies. You puzzle me, Willo."

"I'm not sociable." Her clasped hands in her lap shaking, too. "In fact, the transfer to the dependents' ward saved my life. You see—" letting that bucket plummet—"I have a block about eating in a room with other people. I can only eat when I'm alone—in the little kitchen off the nursery of the babies' ward."

"Ho!" he laughs, the smoke haloing his handsome head. "Did you know that a certain sect of cloistered nuns, the Carmelites, always eat alone in their rooms? You're in excellent company, Willo!"

Ann Arbor: an old university town in late June: green grass, massive maple and oak trees, roses, large Victorian houses...heat shimmering off the pavement. Graduate students, mostly men, mostly G.I.'s, some solitary, some in pairs, all of them loaded with books, stroll from large brick building to large brick building. Fans hum, typewriters buzz. Conversation is sparse and serious. The carillon clock drops its *doon doon doon* onto the humid air.

High on a hill at the edge of the campus, in the white-washed attic of a pointy gray house, bent over a notebook, her hair drawn up into a psyche knot, is Willo. Like the men, she is here on the G.I. Bill of Rights.

"Here is your chance to unburden yourselves of that autobiographical material," the professor of creative writing has told the seminar of eight students. "At the end of the term, the author of the best manuscript will be awarded a scholarship for the following year."

Willo writes:

SNOW FALLS ON FLOWERS

snow   snow
I've never seen so much snow:
forest and field and farm souffléed in snow,
Snyder's Funeral Home like a huge wedding cake;
pink roses, blue larkspur wearing white bonnets;
all of us white-veiled by the blizzard
that Valentine's Day you married Death.

Maybelle. Wild cousin. Ripe sixteen.
Bride. I caught your bouquet.

What I mean is: I had already memorized you:

109

That summer you were fourteen and I was twelve
you pendulumed back and forth in that swing,
back and forth before me, like a hypnotist:
your lacquered lashes swooping up and down
up and down over those chicory blue eyes, like
bird wings   your amber mane galloping
that cologne swarming   that pout like a
pink ladyslipper   those breasts brimming
in that thin blouse like two dollops of ice cream
in a glass bowl   those consonant knees
those assonant toes   that sassy butt
flash! that pout opening: "Apples peaches pumpkin
pie Screw a hundred boys before I die!"

    You were a hive of rhymed couplets
    which I memorized—easily!

Those hot nights I couldn't sleep, I'd scoop
your glamour into myself as one scoops ice cream
into a bowl.   I'd heap your libido into myself
as one heaps fresh fruits into a basket.

All fall, all winter, in dreary school,
I'd chant to myself: *Apples peaches pumpkin
pie   Let me look like Maybelle before I die!*
And my listening vulva would blossom like an orchid.

    Oh, label me Lesbian if Lesbian means
    learning to love myself through first
    loving you.

    snow   snow   snow
Snyder's Funeral Home a huge wedding cake
pink roses   blue larkspur wearing white bonnets
all of us veiled by that blizzard
that Valentine's Day you married Death.

    ". . . kept fast company. . . caught a bad disease
    . . . . What did I tell you?. . . died a dog's death."
    prick prick   prick prick
    My mother vaccinated me.

It didn't take, *Maybelle.*
I went right on swiping you.
With sheer concentration, I'd inhale you

through all my senses   puff out my pencil-
proportions with orbs of voluptuous pink
warm my ice-blue eyes to sapphire and drape
them with movie-star fringes. Then, wandering
through the house, I'd meet in a mirror
that puny pastel girl. *The mirror lied.*

I'd recoil into my chrysalis, where the moist
yearning would ferment once more:
Apples peaches pumpkin pie—
and I'd pump pump pump pump that skimmed-milk
self into Creamy Fifteen.
It was easy.

Then tolling across my mother's worried face
came the thought my father slipped into a sigh:
"I declare! That's *Maybelle!*"

> Beautiful bride, I caught your bouquet:
> Always in summer, I turn cold:
> Snow falls on all the flowers.

GRIT

> "Think of someone worse off n yerself,"
> snaps my mother.

>> I droop on the couch.

> "And wipe that look off yer face!"

>> I try to go blank.

Brandishing a mop,
she thrusts her face into the doorway.
She looks like the puppet Punch.
"If there's anything I can't stand,
it's a *baby.* "

>> She retreats to the kitchen.
>> Wham! goes the pail.
>> Splat! goes the mop.
>> The theme for today:
>> TENDERNESS IS TABOO.

Fumes of ammonia leap towards me like a noose.
Bang. Whomp. Swat.

    Cora, my older sister,
    brushes by the couch.
    Out of the side of her mouth,
    she says, "Think of jewels."
    Then she goes out the door, to school.

The Punch-face pokes around the doorway again.
"I wish you had just *half* of that girl's *grit.*"
it huffs. "She's been twice as sick as you, for
three days; threw up from the soles o her feet;
cleaned up every mess by herself. Her face is as
yellow as butter, but she goes to school, anyway."

    I wilt.

"Yer thinkin of yerself!
Think of someone *else!*"

    She pops back into the kitchen.
    More ammonia. Another mother would
    be laying a soft palm on my forehead,
    offering pale tea or orange juice.
    I should be glad she doesn't try to soothe me.
    Her hands are like alligators. (*"When I was*
    sixteen, I asked fer some lemon hand cream for
    Christmas, and my brothers pissed in a bottle
    n give it to me. Ha. I laughed. I can take
    a joke.")

Re-enter Alligator:
"Why, where would *I* be if *I* thought
about myself? In the sylum, that's where,
or in the grave. What would *you* do if *you*
had my laxeration floppin between yer legs
all the time, *huh?* That's what I've had to
put up with ever since givin birth to Cora."

    I've heard this a hundred times. I picture
    a cubed steak, of moderate size, flapping from
    her crotch. Her big bloomers accommodate it.

Exit, Alligator, to the kitchen.
Sounds of huffing and puffing and of the mop

bludgeoning the cellar steps.

Somewhere, nuns are saying their beads.

She calls out: "Dr. Tenbrink said:
'I don't know how you stand it, Mrs. Van Zandt.
You could sue the doctor that left you in that
shape!'"

A chair topples.
"But I don't think about my pains.
I think about Minnie Huyser. She's nearly
seventy. Her organs are hangin almost to her
knees. Think of *that!* Someday they'll pull
the bladder right outa her!"
Splat.

> I picture a wad of chicken parts
> on a purplish thong, like a pendulum,
> tolling away Minnie Huyser's days.

Another noose of ammonia.
The toilet gulps down the pail of mop water.

> (*"Yer no good! What'll I do with you? Huh?*
> *Shall I throw you away? Huh? Aw, wipe*
> *that look off yer face. It's just a game!"*
> Memories of playful baby-days.)

Now the odor of Fels Naptha soap.
My head throbs. My eyes sting. My throat
feels "laxerated." The washing machine,
in the cellar below me, growls with its
hugged prey. The wringer squeals.

Re-enter Punch.
She thrusts a glass of water at me.
"I spoil ya. Cora got her own, always."
She points to her temple. "See that?"

> I see nothing.

"Bumped it on the corner o the cellar door.
Isn't it red?"

> I nod.

"Soon it will be a lump—purple, green, blue.

113

I'll forget about it. Ha!''

> That *look* has come over her face.
> I brace myself: Here it comes:

"I hope n pray you don't turn out like yer
Aunt Marie—layin there cryin in that sylum.
Hell, a nurse oughta slip her a dose o somethin
to give her a *real* bellyache n make her clean up
after herself. Give her sumpin *real* ta cry about,
huh?"

"Think of Aunt Ida. Her with a tumor like a
grapefruit in her side n other like a bunch
o grapes in her tit. She goes right on workin.
Yer cousin Freddie: hemorrhages from his nose
like cranberry sauce. He goes on drivin that truck.''

> —Her speciality, in technicolor, like a
> slide show: Uncle Case: skin disease like
> raw hamburger all over his neck...Aunt
> Elsie: goiter like a hen's egg...Aunt
> Agnes: wad of fur the size of a cantaloupe in
> her appendix ("An fer years, her pa *told* her
> n *told* her not to keep kissin that cat!'')

"Think of Uncle Casey's sinus trouble:
Why, to look in that man's handkerchiefs,
you'd think he'd blowed out his *brains.*"

> *Diamonds...Diamonds...*
> Sikes told her once of a carnival where he saw,
> among other heroics, a man pushing his nuts in a
> wheelbarrow: elephantiasis. *Pearls, opals, garnets;*
> *ropes of calm jade, cover that wheelbarrow.*

"And don't forget Uncle Milo: the doctor in the prison
hospital told him drinkin is a *disease.*"
She taps her forehead. "Is it swelling?''

> I nod.

She lunges at the curtains, shakes them:
testing for dust. Knocks a picture askew
on the wall. It is Jesus in the Garden of
Gethsemane praying to God to call off Good Friday.
She's getting hopped up now. This sublimation-stuff

114

exhilarates her. "And the doctor said: 'Why, Mrs.
Van Zandt, if you don't have that laxeration
operated on, you'll not last another five years!'
That was when you was born—leven years ago. And
here I am, cleanin the house. You know *why?*
Because I think of OTHERS!"

She snatches the Hoover.
They whiz around the room together, like a
dance team. "Sadie Morton!" she spurts.
"Think of poor Sadie Morton!"

> Sadie Morton: Dead of consumption last year.
> *Sapphires, emeralds; a wreathe of them on
> your grave, Poor Sadie Morton.*

She's glowering at me.
Has that babyish look seeped back into my face?

"I don't know what will become of you, Girl.
Just like yer father. Just like his sister Marie.
Three sissies."

> I turn my face from her, waiting for five-thirty,
> when my father's mournful glance will sanction
> my misery.

She slams the Hoover into the closet.
Her glance re-evaluates my face.

> C minus?

She points a pistol-finger at her calf.
"What'dya do if *you* had legs like this?"

> I make myself look at that bunch of marbles
> in her stockings.

Jabbing that gun-finger: "What'd *you* do, huh?"

> Shoot it?

"Speak up. What would *you* do if you had these veins?"

> *Wear slacks?*   I shake my head, woefully.

A smile twitches at her lips.

> I'm up to C plus?

"I don't give them a thought. I think of others.

Right now, you know who I'm thinking of?"

I shake my head.

"Hank Plow. Did I ever tell you about Hank Plow?"

I nod, but too faintly.

"Hank Plow had his arm tore off in the cutter at the
papermill. Gangrene set in. . . ."

*A garland of rubies around your green stump,
Hank Plow.*

"Then Hank's brother, Ernie, he had this terrible
Accident—"

I lie there, imprinted, her *tabula rasa.*

Those colored slides, which have rendered me
catatonic have filled her with a helium. Billowing
with borrowed sufferings, she seizes the step-ladder.
"I've a good mind to wash the ceiling!" she sings.
She mounts the rungs: *Minnie Sadie Casey*
Halfway up, her red Aryan hands take a swipe at
the beige lampshade: *Marie Dad me*
"My lump's turnin green now, isn't it? Ha!"

She soars to the ceiling
and scrubs the stains from her heaven.

RISKY LANGUAGE

Long exiled from Lesbos,
I wonder if my flesh still chants
the lavender litany. . .
still slurs the syntax into violet:

he? ho hum

he? she they

She I WE

After such declension,
how will it link proper nouns
into compounds?

116

Maybe Mr. Past Imperfect
will conjugate my bluff.

Maybe Mr. Him Humdrum
will become my accusative.

Maybe Mr. Red White Blue
will inflect my tongue
into the anthem of lies.

Maybe Second She
will reflex me into
the lilac idiom.

Or maybe—just maybe--
Prince Prism
will leap down from Olympus,
and translate me
into a rainbow of thanks.

For three years, in that whitewashed attic, the poems have boiled out of her brain. For two years, she has won the scholarship. Now the boiling subsides to a simmer. She unwinds the psyche knot, brushes her hair, and descends from the hill to walk among her colleagues on the campus.

It's summer again.

In the basement room at the end of her street, a new student, a crewcut chemist in a holey T-shirt, scowling over a page tapestried with bonded hexagons, looks up and watches her pass his window. He notices the banner of banana-blonde hair, the biscuit-bosom carried primly atop the notebook tray of books; notices the non-sway of her hips. Compared with the diligent schoolmarms returned for a summer of further diligence, this girl looks bright.

Next time he sees her, she is barely visible on the porch swing. She looks up from her book, and through the trellis swooning with red roses, he says, "Hi. Would you happen to have a can opener?"

On his second visit to the white attic, Clay chuckles: "A box of crayons?"

"I'm illustrating a book of poems I'm writing for children."

"And a Sears catalog?"

"I send gifts to my family."

He laughs. "I like your little whispery voice. You talk just like Marilyn Monroe." He inspects the shelf above the hotplate. "Peanut butter, saltines, Pet Milk, apples, dates. No wonder you're so tiny. How about a sauerbraten dinner at The Old German?"

"I don't eat out." She tells him about her phobia.

He lifts an eyebrow. "A poet's kink, I suppose. Never mind: You'll be an inexpensive date." He scoops her into his arms. "My three-year-old niece lives on peanut butter and apples and milk. I'll bet you taste like her."

She ducks her face into his shirt. "I don't do this, either." She tells him about Pete.

Still hugging her, he laughs. "This is going to be a strange summer." He describes his fiancée far away in California: "Nancy: dark, French, voluptuous, rich, sexy, spoiled." He rocks her, kisses the top of her head.

"This is the first time I've ever stood like this—with a man."

"What does it feel like?"

"Protective."

He rubs his jaw over her forehead.

"And scratchy."

"I'll be damned. This *is* going to be a strange summer."

The carillon doles down its cadenced doons.

"I've had it with isotopes," he tells her. "Let's go canoeing."

Out on the calm river, she tells him, "The last man I talked with was a priest—nearly four years ago."

"A *priest?*"

"A Jesuit. He told me about The Communion of the Saints."

"You fell for that?"

"I did."

"Why, all that bosh is just an old Medieval *wish!*"

"A wish? I suppose you're right." She adds sheepishly: "I believed it only briefly."

In languid phrases, he hurls hierarchies of Western values into fjords of doubt, and she watches them bob up, precariously, in reverse order.

"I wish I had a brother like you," she tells him.

"That's the classic put-down, but I guess you're too naive

119

to know it. Well, for this summer, I'll be your brother. I can hardly believe it. How on earth can I make Nancy believe I spent a platonic summer with a little lesbian?"

"You can give her my love."

September, at the little depot, where he is waiting for the train that will take him back to California and Nancy, he kisses her goodbye. "Hey!" he whispers, "What a luscious kiss. What does this mean?"

"It means you've changed me."

"That breadbox nailed to your windowsill beats my damned refrigerator," says Ben. He's a big bewhiskered psychologist whose smile, adorned with one large buck tooth, suggests the satyr within. He strums his guitar for her and improvises a song: "I used to be a melancholy Jewwww! But now Juuupiter has moved into Aquarrrreeeeeeusss—" He bounces with the melody as if he's in a trampoline. "—and Jung is giving me a tollllerannnnnnce for ammmbiguuuuuuity!"

In his ramshackle kitchen, he spreads out pimpled and carbuncled sausages and bloated dill pickles, grasps a giant phallus of bread in his armpit and saws off four chunks.

The pupils of Willo's eyes dilate like those of a cornered kitten, and she flees down the stairs.

He catches her, hugs her in big hairy arms, and listens to her trouble.

"Ha!" he laughs. "I'll bet it's a Dutch phobia. The Dutch are such a *private* people. Come, watch a Russian Jew eat!"

He carries her back to his kitchen, where she witnesses the bravado of his feasting. He throws back his head, guzzles red wine from the jug, gobbles bread and meat. He opens and closes the door of the refrigerator with his foot...tosses a bar of candy to her: "Halvah, to take home with you, my shy little kid."

On her next visit, they dance to his Jimmy Yancey records. He draws her hair up over his head, like a hood...over his face, like a veil...draws it towards the ceiling, where he

120

pretends to fasten it. "Rorschach hair!" he laughs. "It's a chandelier. . . . Now it's a birdcage."

Far into the night they dance, she, standing in stockinged feet upon his big feet, massaging his stallion-back with slow fingers, giggling as his toenails click through his holey socks, like a dog's, upon the bare floor. Their sleepy kisses grow stormy.

On his bed, his hard hoofed kisses surprise her nipples, and her flesh begs for more of this galloping maleness. She opens wide wider for a cucumber a corncob grasps this nub of a rubber-sheathed playmate, who wriggles inside her once, twice, and withdraws and leaves her baffled slot blinking.

"There!" he beams. "Now you know a man has something a lesbian lacks."

"Yes!" she sighs, cupping her sandpapered face in both hands: —*whiskers.*

Sam, another psychologist, another Jew, is fascinated with her hair. On his bed, he makes a tent of it over his dark head. "My new Weltanschauung!" he whispers. He's also fascinated with her eating phobia. "Something to do with hating your mother, I'll bet; same root as the lesbianism. I don't know enough yet to help you. All I know is that I long to eat you!" Playfully, he gobbles her thin arms, which he calls "spaghetti," her thin legs, "noodles," and "turns on" her tiny tiddies: "little radio."

A dark, stocky little man, he lifts her, twirls her all around his room, rejoicing in her lightness. "You make me feel like a lion! a tiger! a bull!"

He tosses her back onto his bed, where he starts to eat her all over again. This time it's dessert: ". . . two little custards, two raspberries. . . ." In a frenzy of exuberance, he fucks her.

"Big Eraser," she names him. "A few more times like this, and you'll rub out all my lesbian memories."

*   *

"My name is Naomi," a small, pretty, dark girl addresses

121

Willo as she crosses the campus one day. "I audited the creative writing seminar last term, and ever since I read your Maybelle poems, I've wanted to tell you how deeply they moved me."

A week later, in her apartment, looking chic in an apricot-colored cashmere sweater, Naomi confides in Willo: "I'm frigid. Would you believe it?" Her cheeks flushed, her hazel eyes flashing, she brushes the crisp black curls back from her heart-shaped face. "My husband is an intern in neurosurgery. He knows everything there is to know about erogenous zones; yet our sex life is nil." She glances at Willo, and seeing the fair face calm and receptive, she continues: "The summer I was twelve, my brothers tied a rope from a limb high up in a large tulip tree in our back yard. We played pirates and all sorts of adventuresome games that involved sliding down that thick rope." She giggles musically and looks out the window. "The friction between my legs gave me the most delightful sensations. I couldn't get enough of that rope-sliding. Well, my mother caught on. She seized me in one hand and that rope in the other, and she whipped me. In the fall, she sent me away to a convent school. And in the convent—Lord! I must have had a healthy little pussy!—during classes I'd rub myself ever so slyly against the seat of my chair; I'd cross my legs tight and rub and rub. I'd almost achieve that delightful sensation, but not quite. Well, I guess the wriggling and rubbing became automatic. I did it without realizing, and one day, a nun hauled me out of the study hall. She marched me to the kitchen, right to the refrigerator, and handed me an ice cube. I can still see those glassy eyes, that accusing face, can still hear that cold, cold voice: 'Go into the bathroom, and place this on that mosquito bite between your legs. Hold it there until it melts.' I obeyed. Every day, before study hour, every night at bedtime, I got the ice cube treatment. It was routine as brushing my teeth." Tears glisten in the curly black lashes. "It worked. I'm frigid. My poor husband has tried everything, and I'm just a marble statue."

"It's a sad story," Willo says.

"I thought you might help me."

"I?"

Naomi looks out the window and toys with her curls. "I've also read your lesbian poems."

Willo is nonplussed.

"I thought you could teach me."

"Oh, Naomi, I'm sorry. I'm past all that."

Naomi reaches out and takes Willo's hand in hers. "Please."

It's Willo's turn to blush. "I can't, Naomi." She looks down at the small hand holding hers. "You're so—*dainty.* I'm attracted to—when I was attracted, and I'm sure it's all gone now—to a few big burly women. I can't imagine a physical relationship with a woman as feminine as myself."

"You mean you're *passive* in sex?"

Willo nods. "Passive. Plain. Quite conventional, I guess."

The musical giggle. "Lord. I imagined you were a sort of—acrobat."

"If I'm an acrobat, it's with words only." Willo looks at the ceiling, and like a spider letting itself down on its own spun thread, she says, "I might write you a pavane for a dead pussy...something about the nun who was a taxidermist... or The Rope-Lover...or the hex of sex...."

Naomi gives her a pretty little fox-smile. "I won't let you off so easily. If you won't sleep with me, could you do the next best thing? Sleep with Ned?"

"Ned. Your husband?"

"Yes." The fingers play provocatively with the curls.

Willo stands up. "This is getting silly, Naomi." As she puts on her coat, she sees the other girl, for a second, as a man must see her: coy, seductive, determined.

The sweetheart-face emits a musical, "Please! Ned is good-looking. He's read all of Proust and Thomas Wolfe."

So: Willo finds herself walking through the arboretum with Ned, who looks something like F. Scott Fitzgerald. They talk quite comfortably about Proust and Wolfe. They giggle a lot, and climb into bed. He winds her hair, like a rope, around her neck, saying, as if he's reading lines from a Hollywood script: "Sweetie, you make me feel sadistic."

With matching phoniness, she replies: "You make me feel masochistic."

He leans on his elbow, and with a self-conscious finger, charts her erogenous zones, or what he has been taught in some medical class are every woman's erogenous zones. After considerable charting by the clinical finger, their two anatomies confront mechanically as a pencil and a pencil sharpener.

Walking back to her attic room, more like a patient from a dentist than a mistress from a lover, she thinks: *This must be how a prostitute feels. Maybe it's how Naomi feels. I'm lucky Ned is not my first man. Else I'd bounce off him like a child's ball off a brick wall, and right back into lesbianism.*

"Please!" Naomi keeps pleading. "You're helping us. Ned's father died before he was born. He was reared by his mother and his aunt and his grandmother."

Willo tries a second time: Still the pencil and the pencil sharpener.

The shoddiness is soil for her fantasies.

"I'm very neurotic, too," Willo confides to Naomi. "I have this dreamman—tall, blond, very virile and very kind, whose kisses will poultice out all traces of my lesbian years, all eating phobia—whose charisma will umbrella me and our two sons forever from the drenching dullness of the conventional world."

Naomi laughs. "You want to be shielded from the conventional world by this soap opera male? You're chock full of inconsistencies. Well, Ned knows a lot of psychiatrists. I'll ask him to introduce you to a tall, blond one."

So, like a prostitute expecting to be paid for her services, Willo goes to bed again and again with Ned to earn the tall blond god. Six more times she lies there, a map for his finger; a chart of erogenous zones.

Then, for a New Year's Eve party: the tall blond psychiatrist: six feet four, about one hundred and fifty pounds of twitches and giggles.

Willo leaves early, with "a headache." She whispers to Naomi, "I guess I mean I want psychiatric help, not a psychiatric date."

Naomi kisses her on the cheek. "That's what we all want."

Willo hastens to the university health clinic, where she is allotted three half hours a week for reciting her catalog of conflicts to a pallid resident, whose mumbled "fellatio"... "cunnilingus"... "coprophagic" send her scurrying to the big dictionary in the library.

Then an old friend is standing in Willo's room, leafing through her drawings and her poems for children. "Little Lesbian," says Clay. "You'll be psychoanalyzed and having kids of your own before I will. Nancy has married another man."

In his basement room, which is as low as his mood when he first took it, she comforts him. His ceiling pipes are fuzzed with dust. "Spanish moss," he calls it, that sifts down upon them on the creaky cot beneath. She winces.

"You're too Dutch for my pad!" he teases her.

Dutch, yes: For his birthday, she washes by hand, and darns, a whole drawer-full of reeking socks.

"Honey!" he gasps. "Those are not my socks. They were left in that drawer by the syphilitic creep who had the room before I took it!"

125

Into this blitheness pops a chubby pink bald man in owl-glasses and a pressed suit and a striped tie, bearing an embossed briefcase. Willo cannot believe her eyes.

"What's a nice girl like you doing with those Beatniks?" he chirps.

She cannot believe her ears.

On the bench outside the library, flicking his fingertips across her fresh lesbian poem, as if brushing away crumbs, the pink bald man declares: "American is ruining you. You need to learn Zen-discipline in Japan."

He walks her home, and she finds herself inviting him to her room, where he sits on the edge of her spindly chair, clutching his knees, his shoulders drawn up to his ears, his round face blushing out of his chest.

—*He looks like Humpty Dumpty.*

He averts that owl-gaze from the rusty hotplate. "No radio, Willo?"

"I can't stand noise."

Now averting that owl-gaze from the Sears catalog. "And so few books?"

"I'm not a scholar. I'm a poet."

"But a poet needs to *read.*"

"It's all inside me. I spin it out, like a spider."

Two parallel creases arch over his left eyebrow, like a double question mark. "That's narcissism. That's bad."

—*Has this troll come to guard my talent?*

At the door of the library, dressed like a banker, still carrying that embossed briefcase, the Kewpie-man beams: "Willo! I have two tickets for José Limon Saturday night."

At the door of her seminar, smiling like sunshine: "Willo! Two tickets for Dylan Thomas Friday."

At the door of her house: "Two tickets for The Oxford Players doing *King Lear* Sunday afternoon."

So woefully smitten, so pitifully priggish. People are beginning to tease her about him.

"Who's your duke?" Clay snickers.

"What's with your Victorian gentleman?" Sam grins.

"Saw you with Daddy Warbucks again," says Ben.

"His name is Melvin Sanders," Willo tells each one, defensively, like a mother protecting a peculiar child. "He's a graduate student in Asian studies."

Yet she warns herself: *Get rid of him.*

"That lesbian poetry you dislike," she tells Melvin. "It's true. I was—maybe I still am—"

He blushes. That squeamish look returns to his face. "I don't want to hear about it."

"And I have this phobia about eating—"

"There's a Bergman film playing downtown. I'll hail this cab, and we can get in at the beginning."

Blushing and blushing, Melvin says, "I've never had a woman-guest before. I don't know what the management will think."

The Lincoln Hotel. She has never seen anything like it: three walls lined from floor to ceiling with books. Moss carpets. Velvet drapes. Sumptuous leather chairs. A wall of Japanese masks. In an alcove, a gnarled tobacco-colored ivory cross bearing a pale ivory Christ. A shelf full of cameras.

He pours her a glass of sherry, puts a Mozart record on the phonograph, and phones for dinner.

"This university is provincial," he says, his voice lower than she has ever heard it, his speech slower. "You ought to live in Kyoto."

More sherry. More Mozart. Willo begins to feel cozy.

"I've been thinking—you ought to study haiku under a master, Willo." His tone calm, almost benevolent.

The dinner is wheeled in. The waiter lights two candles, pours pale wine into tall goblets, and exits.

Melvin sips the wine. Willo imitates him. She sees herself mirrored in the four silver domes over the four platters on the table between them; sees, beyond the silver domes, beyond the candles, Melvin: so still, the small eyes in his round face almost Oriental: the lush lips wide and rosy as a tropical flower.

—*Now he looks like a buddha.*

He lifts the domes. Steam. Aroma. Rice. Creamy, pastel foods.

—*It's like a Hollywood movie.*

He begins to eat, fastidiously. She imitates him. It seems to her it is the first time in her life she has ever enjoyed eating.

They can't stop teasing her about him.

"What's he carry in that satchel?" Clay laughs. "Dildoes?"

Ben takes a guess at the contents: "National secrets."

She tosses her blonde mane, flippantly: "Money."

Dinner at the Lincoln Hotel again. Mozart, Schubert, Beethoven, Bach take the place of conversation.

After a while, she asks politely, "Do you have any brothers or sisters?"

He takes a long drink of chablis. "My two brothers died of polio when I was nine."

She quickly sips her chablis. "I'm so sorry. And your mother? your father?"

"My father died of a heart attack when I was ten. My mother died of cancer when I was eighteen." A sip of chablis. "It's all right. Each time, I went on as if nothing had happened."

—*Passed to me like a file card of statistics.*

The Lincoln Hotel again: His face is yellow as the ivory Jesus. He scarcely eats. His forehead on the left side is furrowed with deep wrinkles.

"Are you not well?" she asks.

"It's this headache." Scarcely moving his lips.

She stands behind his chair. "Take off your glasses." Her thin, cool fingers make largo movements across his forehead ...slowly, dreamily, as if she's drawing a landscape of lakes and valleys. He sighs. Her fingers begin to make little tapping movements across his temples, over his ears, down the back of the neck.... "Loosen your tie." His shoulders are soft, pliant, not stallion-shoulders, like Ben's...not the alligator-shoulders of the battered marines...but voluptuously flesh-ed, velvety, like a seal....Her fingers dance back up the soft neck...resume the tapping at the temples, and she murmurs as to a child, "I'm touching the pain...I'm coaxing it into my fingers. It's nipping and thrashing. It's a dog. I've got hold of it...such a wild, wild one! Let's open the window and let him leap out. There. He's landed in those bushes. He's so *wild!* He's running away."

"Kitten!" he sighs. "You've missed your calling. You're a *healer.*"

Beethoven pulses and throbs and swells until the whole room is filled with robust health. They eat their dinner hungrily.

When it is time for him to walk her home, as he is helping her on with her coat, he holds her by the shoulders. His small dark blue-green eyes are like tadpoles in the pools of his thick lenses. He presses her gently against his Santa Claus paunch, and smiles. His big rosy lips are the bow on this strange gift.

After the next visit, she tells him, "We must stop seeing one another."

His grip on her shoulders is strong. "Why?" Above his head, the jaundiced Jesus is glowering from the cross.

"Because you're Catholic."

129

His arms enclose her in a teddy bear hug. "As soon as I met you, I stopped going to mass."

"I don't trust sudden conversions."

"It isn't sudden. I've been reading Zen for years. Mass was just a sick habit." The big bow lips on her.

"What a lovely way," she sighs, phonily, "to convalesce from Catholicism."

But it's no laughing matter: "I can't sleep. I can't study. I can't write poetry," she tells the psychiatrist at the clinic. "It's a torment, like the old lesbian love."

The psychiatrist frowns. "You mean he looks like the ex-woman-lover?"

She averts her gaze from the bald psychiatrist. "No. He's—bald."

A long silence. When she looks up, she meets the coldly appraising eyes of the psychiatrist, and she blushes.

"What are you thinking?"

She looks into her lap. "—that all my life I've avoided—pitiful men."

"Why?"

"I don't want to be trapped."

"Go downtown and see *The Blue Angel.* You are just like Marlene Dietrich."

Melvin keeps smiling and smiling. "Psychiatry is the hoax of the century. What you need is Zen. . . . Let me take you away from all this."

3

Bending together into the October gust, Willo and Melvin Sanders, married five minutes ago by a justice-of-the-peace, head home. Each is aware of the thin, brittle circle of gold around an unaccustomed finger.

The carillon bell dips a moan out of the bright blue sky. A late rose weeps its red petals into the street, and with each step, Willo thinks—*Goodbye, Dreamman. . . . Hello, Husband.*

"I'm afraid you won't feel married," Melvin says. In his gray Stetson and his slate-blue wool chinchilla coat, he's like a figure straight out of a haberdashery.

"I wouldn't feel married with any other kind of ceremony." In her new hooded gray coat, which is too large for her, she looks like a nun.

They had agreed that the standard church ceremony was OUT. A home wedding, she assured him, was OUT, too. *"My house is a scrubbed shanty,"* she told him. *"My mother talks like a roustabout. She sleeps with my sister instead of my father. He identifies with Saint Paul."* Melvin accepted it as a part of her impish humor. But even a civil ceremony, they learned, is not entirely private. It requires a witness. Here it became awkward. Melvin has no close friends, and he considers Willo's new friends Beatniks. After fretting all week, (*Bridegroom's nerves,* she called it, and advised herself to be the calm one) he selected a man in his political science seminar, an ex-buddy from army intelligence. He was waiting for them at the courthouse: a solemn crewcut man of military bearing, and right after applying his signature to the marriage license, he departed briskly. Willo thought—*It's furtive, more like an abortion than a marriage. . . but don't think about it now.*

She links her arm into Melvin's. "I've never been to a church wedding. I've never once dreamed of the white gown and veil and flowers, as girls are supposed to do. A wedding is just a mold into which unimaginative girls pour their emotions—and parents pour their money."

Melvin makes a little grumbling sound.

Willo has all but memorized these streets, these Victorian houses, with rooms stashed away like books on the shelves of a library. Up there, in that big gray house, where the rusty breadbox juts from the windowsill, dwells Ben, still grinding away towards his PhD. *"Veronica Lake and Winston Churchill"* Ben labeled her and Melvin. *"—except Veronica doesn't have that poignant smile, and Winston doesn't have those Mayan lips."* She laughed it off. *"The pederast!"* Ben growled. *"Melvin is only three years older than I,"* she said. *"He looks older because he's bald and plump and because he's had a very sad life."* Ben persisted: *"Are you sure you're not marrying your father?"* *"My father is skinny and poor and uneducated and a religious fanatic."* Ben winked. *" 'Inside every fat man lives a skinny man.' "*

"We should have taken a taxi," Melvin whines.

"The walk will give us a good appetite."

"Home to a bottle of Burgundy and *filet mignon.*"

"That's ceremony enough."

—Goodbye, Ben.

Across the street, in that brick duplex, Ned and Naomi, still married to each other, both in psychotherapy now. *"No church wedding? Good for you!"* said Naomi, and she gave them a gift: a book of poems by Rilke in which she had circled: *'Religion is the art of the uncreative.'* Naomi helped Willo select the blue velvet dress she is now wearing, took in the seams on her sewing machine, and insisted that "for this one occasion, at least" Willo wear high heels. *"I could never walk in those,"* Willo groaned, and she purchased blue flats. The chic Naomi laughed affectionately: *"They're the next thing to gym shoes. You always manage to look like a hybrid ballerina-refugee. . . . Well, you couldn't have found a better husband. Melvin will take care of you. He's so placid, so self-contained, so rich,"* Naomi gushed—*"so mysterious, so absolutely different from all the blue-jeaned kooks—"*

"That orchid is going to be crushed under your coat," Melvin says.

"I'll put it into a bowl of water when we get home. It will revive."

"I doubt it."

—Goodbye, Naomi.

In that old house on the left, somewhat renovated with sky-blue paint, lives Sam. *"That Sanders dresses like a Babbitt and talks like one, too,"* Sam told her. *"I know. Among the verbally elite, he's pitiful." "Pitiful?"* said Sam, who had been in a seminar with Melvin. *"He's the most cynical guy I've ever known."* Cynical: That was not a word Willo ever used. She thought it meant: *Wise, knowledgeable, aloof, above the crowd.* She put the word away on a top shelf in her mind. *"Melvin has attended six universities in four countries,"* she told him. *"That impresses you? How many PhD's does he have?" "None. He says degrees are just a status symbol." "Ha. He must be very rich. You're marrying a sugar daddy." "I want a patron,"* she confessed. *"I want to be freed from earning a living. I'm too shy to get a job, too encumbered with phobias. I'm a poet, and only a poet." "I still think if it's a patron you want, a protector, that chubby Libra-guy is too lazy for you."* Sam, like Ben was immersed in some wizard called Jung, who believed in horoscopes. *"You'd do better with Aries or Aquarius,"* Sam teased.

The carillon bells are bleating. The trees are weeping their leaves in the wind. The two figures bend more sharply into the gust.

"I'm really worried about that orchid," Melvin whines.

—Fuss fuss. "Some things are supposed to be ephemeral."

"Put it in the refrigerator as soon as we get home."

"A tall blond psychiatrist?" Sam said. (She had brought up the subject when he had grown over-zealous about his

135

Eraser-mission.) *"Aryan? Alter ego? Seriously, though, 'The Best is Enemy of The Good.' I wonder if this fantasy-man is a kind of mirror wedged between you and the real men of flesh and blood and flaws. I wonder if he's a veneer over your left-over lesbian feelings?"*

—*Still a lesbian?* She wondered: *Was marrying a dumpling-man a camouflaged way of marrying a woman?*

—*Goodbye, Sam.*

There, down that street a mile, the canoe house and the river. *"I'm marrying him for his Zen,"* she told Clay. *"Zen? Schmen. I'll remember that the next time I want to hand a woman a line."* *"I admit I don't understand it very well,"* she said. *"All I can do now is to flaunt the word and a few phrases, like a STOP sign every time an ardent Christian tries to haul me into church. Meanwhile, it lays in wait, like a fire extinguisher, to be used in emergencies for us and for our children."* Clay probed: *"Zen? There has to be a better reason for marrying him."* *"All right. He's an orphan. I'll have no trouble with in-laws."* And she told him about Melvin's multiple bereavements. *"That figures,"* Clay said. *"Poets love Death."*

—*Goodbye, Clay.*

What she had not said to any of them was: I'm marrying him for SEX. Maybe when Ben mentioned the Mayan lips, he was telling her he had guessed the sensuous adventure. She would not have guessed it from that first shy kiss or from those first Santa Claus hugs. For weeks, this lovesick virgin filled her with disgust—and pity. At last, coldly, like a nurse assigned to a case to alleviate fever and swelling, she lay back on his couch and guided his hands, like puppies, through the tissues of her lingerie. His kisses started moving through her like a ghost down cobwebbed stairs. She was astonished. He was Lover Supreme....Night after night, on his bed, sometimes on her bed, he would knead her and knead her, from shoulders to ankles, like a cat making a cloth into a bed... and his plump furred torso would cushion her razor-blade hips until she found herself comforted...spellbound as a

136

child being rocked to sleep by a parent reciting *The Three Bears*. *tried this chair and that chair and this bed AND HERE SHE IS!* Her whole physiology would ripple into a rapture of applause over and over better and better each time. And he would spread her hair, ever so tenderly, over her breasts, like a shawl and after sleep, through this flaxen shawl, he would kiss those breasts awake. *—Dreamman, could it be more savage with you? More tender? More yin and yang?*

A scarlet dot appears on Willo's sleeve. Another late rose is weeping. There, to the right, high on the hill, watching like an eye through the crimson treetops, the window of the little white attic. *"Ivory tower,"* Melvin called it....Once he tasted sex, he was an addict. He stalked her, would not let her out of his sight. *"We could have a divine marriage,"* he moaned. *"If I invest my money wisely, we can travel indefinitely; live in any country we choose. Please! Let's turn my year of research in Japan into a honeymoon." "Marriage is a momentous step,"* she told him. *"Go alone. Give me the year to decide."* What she meant was: *Give me this last chance to find that dream-psychiatrist....*No sooner had he departed than her former lovers rushed to her as to a drowning girl. She threw back their pejoratives, one by one, and chose to sink in solitude. Her hauteur surprised her. Melvin had inoculated her against all these others. She was addicted, too. She would wake in that little white attic aching for his warm furry body...the valved membranes of her funnel taut and throbbing, like an habituated instrument that waits the live plunging hammer to pound it into music....Sleepless, she would torment herself with the fantasy that a Japanese girl, petite and responsive as herself, had slipped into the rent she had gouged in Melvin's feelings by refusing to go with him. Jealousy, like pneumonia, drained her of all inspiration to write poems. *—I have all the penalties of passion,* she told herself, *and hardly any of its joys.* She nearly drowned in self-pity. Then she hauled her misery, once more, to the clinic, where this time a middle-aged Jewish woman doctor requested a photograph of Melvin. *"The classic suckling face!"* she exclaimed. *"Are you awfully maternal?"* Then the woman was transferred to another city, and Willo was assigned to a suave Princeton man whose glance wandered from his wrist watch to the golf clubs in the corner: *"Of course this kind of therapy doesn't help you. You need psychoanalysis, at least two years of it. Can you borrow twenty thousand dollars from this rich lover?"* She fled across town to the veterans' hospital, where a secretary gave her pages of forms to fill out...waited weeks for the letter: *"Miss Von Musson... we have no facilities in this hospital for women.... You can apply for admission to the hospital in Oakland, California...."* She paced the floor. She had become a disembodied nervous system, fluttering, shivering, clawing itself to tatters. She yearned to be insulated from this destructive introspection, needed to be embedded again in that cushion of seal-flesh. Only then, it seemed, could she eat again, and sleep.

"That *filet mignon* is the best-looking steak I've ever seen," Melvin says.

"Good." —*He's trying to be cheerful.*

"Come back and guard my solitude," she wrote to Melvin. She awaited a Zen-transformed man, but a month later, he stood at her door less like a buddha than a bulldog. The twin question marks glistened in perspiration. Pity, more passionate than any Love, filled her. Pity made a deep nest inside her, and she said to herself: —*I'll let him deposit his griefs in me, and my warmth will hatch them, and one by one, they will fly away.* Her cool fingers stroked away his headache and tossed it out the window. She asked about Zen. He showed her a few colored slides of Zen temples, Zen monks, Zen gardens, such as any tourist might bring back. *"Didn't you learn zazen?"* she asked. *"No. Zazen was for you to learn. I did research on economic problems."* Words failed. Lips, tongues, nipples, valves, hammer spoke a better language. Like a couple of larvae that sense the shortness of their sunny season, each fed ravenously on the other. He

138

moved from the Lincoln Hotel to a furnished apartment, the entire second floor of a large new house surrounded by large trees in which a pair of mourning doves cooed quietly all day. The landlady, who lived on the first floor, wanted a reliable tenant to occupy the place while she spent a year in Europe. *"We're all but married,"* Melvin sighed in this brand new bed. *"Let's make it legal."* She searched the relationship for The Enemy: *"Are you sure you accept my lesbian past?"* *"As far as I'm concerned, it never happened." "It did happen. I was 'married' to Pete for four years."* He laid his fingers on her lips. *"Nonsense. It was a girlish crush. That doesn't count." "I worry that you will be embarrassed by the nausea that overtakes me on social occasions,"* she said. *"Nonsense. A cocktail or two will solve that problem." "I'm still uneasy about drinking." "That drunkard-uncle of yours frightened you. My style of drinking is middle class." "You're such a gourmet,"* she continued. *"Do you mind that I can't cook?" "I'll buy you a shelfful of cookbooks."*

"The neighbors will never believe we're married," Melvin says.

"No one will believe it, I suppose. I'll write to my family tomorrow."

"Just so we believe it."

—*Oh, Dreamman.*

"Are you sure you won't revert to Catholicism when we start raising the children?" "Positive. Zen has cured me, absolutely, of all traces of Christianity." She mistrusted his aplomb. *"That would be a remarkable achievement,"* she said, feeling her way towards what she most dreaded. *"Hardly any human being can do that." "It can be done,"* he assured her. —*Is that what you've done with those four deaths?* she thought, but instead, she asked: *"Are you sure you want children?" "Yes! Two girls!" "Why girls?"* He all but ate her face with kisses: *"I can't get enough of your beauty."* She came up for air, laughing: *"I want two sons."* He refused to search for The Enemy. Optimism coated him like a layer of pink icing. *"But there must be things about me*

you don't like," she persisted. *"I don't like your infatuation with psychiatry,"* he conceded. *"You won't run to a psychiatrist as soon as you hit a snag, will you?" "If you can help me, I won't seek a psychiatrist." "You're so ingenuous; of course, I can help you." "What else about me don't you like?"* The wrinkles above the left eye: *"You don't intend to keep turning out that sobsister poetry, do you?"* It was her turn to slather on the pink icing: *"I'm not much of a poet. I can hardly keep prose on its toes." "Good. I thought that in your zeal to write, you might neglect the children." "No! Children ARE poetry.... Will you give me lots of help in caring for them?"* Again he ate her face, her throat, her shoulders, with kisses: *"Lots!"* Dread filled her again: that file card of four epitaphs. *"I keep trying to picture you as a little boy,"* she ventured. *"That's silly. Take me as I am now." "I can't help wondering what you were like. You're so bookish now. Did you ever play?" "Sure! I was a perfectly normal boy."* Doubt, like a red light, showed on her face, and in a moment of courage, she asked: *"Do you have any photographs of yourself as a boy, and of your brothers and your parents?" "None." "Not one?"* Again, the red light flashed. *"All right,"* he said. *"Of the five in my family, I was The Sore Thumb." "I can't believe that. That's just the guilt-ridden evaluation of the sole survivor of great suffering." "Aren't you the Romantic! I was a peevish kid. My feelings were always being hurt." "By whom?" "I can't remember." "It's important. Who gave you that name 'The Sore Thumb?' " "It's not important." "It is important. Maybe someone in your family was your Hair Shirt." "Don't be silly. I was just born sensitive. Everyone hurt my feelings, except my mother. But that was long ago. Zen has wiped it all clean." "Do I remind you of your mother?" "Not in the least. My mother was red-headed and heavyset and not the least bit flighty.... You seem so impressed by those earnest PhD's. Maybe you'll find my way of life lazy. Actually, it's a Zen-style: wu wei. That means relaxing, not joining the rat race, taking one day at a time." "Wu wei."* She savoured the word. *"I like that. It sounds—ripe."*

Scowling, both of them, against the harsh wind, they turn up the street to his apartment, which, with the addition yesterday of her typewriter, her formidable manuscripts, and her skimpy wardrobe, is now THEIRS....It comes into view, behind the brown-leafed oak trees: a big squarish house, gleaming white, with four dormer windows rising out of the roof in front.

"Those birds again," Melvin says.

Willo follows his glance up to a center dormer, where the pair of mourning doves is huddled in the corner out of the wind. She flits up the outer stairs, and he chugs along behind her. He unlocks the door, and they cross the threshold like any married couple coming home from work. Their shoes tread across the spongy carpet as if they've treaded across it for years.

"Your orchid is bruised," Melvin scolds. "I told you."

—*Oh, Dreamman.* Meekly, she removes the flower from her shoulder and looks a long time at the soft contours delicately tabbied with tan. The flower is all throat, a mutely mewing kitten. She places it in the refrigerator.

He takes two new cut glass wine glasses from the cupboard and sets them on the table.

"How like you," she says.

"How *bourgeois* you mean. Please smile."

Her face, verticals all day, splits into horizontals, like an obedient venetian blind.

"That's my Sunshine," he says. He kisses her.

Soon his steak is bleeding all over his plate. She turns her back on the sight and waits for hers to burn to a cinder.

He says, between chews, "You're not going to nag me the rest of our lives for a honeymoon, are you?"

"Honeymoon? We've already had a long one."

"I mean a real one."

She shrugs. "Who needs that?"

"I do. Taste your wine."

Eyes stinging in the smokey kitchen, she allows him to place the charred steak on her plate. —*Be brave. Eat your mis-steak.*

That carillon clock starts bailing buckets of melancholy out of the darkened sky. She goes to the window...glances down the street: *Dreamman?* Only the mourning doves. She closes the drapes.

Melvin pours more wine and places a record on the phonograph: Beethoven's Ninth Symphony.

Six-thirty. The hands of the clock kiss and scissor off the day.

"I hafta count the cars," she says, her hooked finger jabbing the November rain.

"Count the cars?" Willo asks. "Why?"

"I hafta!" she snaps. Her head pumps to assist the finger. "—fourteen, fifteen, sixteen—"

They stand shin-deep in wet snow, hunching under a renewed squall—Mamma, Cora, Willo, and Melvin. The uncles and aunts are straggling away from the fresh grave.

"But why?" Willo whispers as she takes an elbow to steer her mother away.

The scrawny woman wrenches herself from Willo, grabs at Cora. "Now I lost *count!*" The finger finds the place in front of her face and resumes the poking; the head pumps more earnestly. "Twenty-three, twenty-four, twenty-five. Sikes n Agnes always count the cars, an' if I don't know how many, they get mad."

Willo dares not look at Melvin. She dares not look at Cora. Mamma has been babbling nonsense all day: *"Cancer o the throat: brooded. Brought it on hisself." "Take yer husband to a restrant. He stinks o the mustard. I don't know how ta set a table fer the rich."* The soggy flakes of snow are chilling all their shoulders, but no one dares to pull away this widow, counting and counting like a retarded child.

The cars are twitching like starlings out of the slushy cemetery. Willo looks down at the wet chrysanthemum.

"—thirty-four, thirty-five, thirty-six—Oh, I *hope* I got it right!"

A toad-man stumps towards them. It's Sikes made even more top-heavy by hat and cigar. "Hey! Git in the car,

Kate!"

Mamma turns a startled face and starts flopping towards him like a simpleton. "Thirty-six? No, maybe thirty-seven?"

"You *crazy?*" Sikes snarls. "Agnes got nine. You was countin cars from *another* funeral." He looks over his shoulder at the smooth-faced Melvin, screws his finger to his temple and hisses, "Poor soul."

Willo stands still, looking down at the wet chrysanthemum. It seems to look back at her. Then she trudges with her husband and her sister to the car.

Mamma and Sikes make skating motions toward the flivver, where Agnes of the ochre jowls and cinder eyes waits with soggy old Milo and coffee-colored Casey.

—Like Goya's portraits of lunatics, exactly.

Then Mamma is wrenching herself from the flivver and floundering towards Cora and Willo. "Agnes says I oughta go with my daughters!" she hollers.

Installed in the back seat of the big car, the widow clamps her gaze to the driver's back. All day, amazement at her son-in-law has overshadowed grief for her husband. At least four times she has whispered to Willo, *"He looks just like a doctor. . . . Don't kid me: He MUST be some kinda DOCTOR."*

—Well-dressed? Reserved? Plump? Do those add up to a DOCTOR in that demented mind?

"I spose you never heard a Jehovah's Witness preach a funeral, Melvin." Her voice clawing at his mild face. "Me neither. I never been in a church. Not once. Ain't that awful? I'll go ta Hell, won't I? Well, it's not my fault. No one took me when I was a kid. I wanted to go more'n once, but no one took me. We was too poor, too low, shamed of ourselves. Otto he never went to church neither. Read the Bible constantly. I spose Mina's told ya. But he hated churches. Hated Cathlics. He read them AWAKES and them WATCHTOWERS sometimes, so when the end come, Cora and me didn't know what to do. So we got that Jehovah's Witness to preach the funeral. Was that all right?"

"That was sensible," Melvin says, warily.

Mamma leans towards Willo and whispers, "See! Just like a doctor!" She plucks at Willo's sleeve. "His fingernails!"

—So: Clean fingernails equals doctor. Mamma, how can I address myself to such abysmal ignorance? What I've been wanting to say all day is: I think I'm pregnant. It's a little too early to tell. The gynecologist allowed me one tranquilizer, only one. If I seem impervious, remote, it's to protect my baby.

"Otto he had no schooling. Eighth grade. That's better'n what I had. My mother died when I was five. Guess Mina told ya. I was too nervous to learn in school. Had to get out to work when I was twelve." Still clawing at that buddha-face. "Them with money, them with schooling, they can't understand."

Cora tugs her sleeves down over the red rash on her wrists. "Sixty-five pounds. Starved to death. You wouldn't have known him, Mina."

—That phrase has buzzed out of her big acne-scarred face at least four times today, like a lone wasp out of a forsaken hive. No, I wouldn't have known him, Cora. In the coffin, he looked like a praying mantis. . . . I'll put the image away. . . take it out later, when it is safe.

Mamma's face wags from side to side, from window to window, as if she's looking at scenery. Her thin lips twitch.

—Here's the wind-up.

Mamma stares at Melvin, then away, then back at Melvin.

—Here comes the pitch—

The red finger spurts towards Cora. "There's my *jewel!*"

Cora's spongy face soaks up the compliment. Through two reddened slits, her beady eyes wait for more.

The red finger spurts again. "Cora she knows her Bible. Boy, she could preach a funeral that could stump a lotta people!"

Cora bows her head and pulls demurely at her sleeves.

Wag wag wag goes that skinny face, like a dog shaking its prey. Twitch twitch twitch go those lips. "Sure! Cora could stump a lotta them educated people, but she don't wanna. She's bashful.''

Silence.

The mean face ducks, then comes up, cleansed. The Garbo eyes turn to Willo. "Dad was good to youse girls, wasn't he?''

"When we were small," Willo says, "he was a very good father.''

"Never once hit youse girls. Never cussed. Never drank. Never made youse girls work.''

Willo takes a deep breath. "He was kind.''

The Garbo eyes gaze out the window. "Yeah. Very kind. Then his mind went bad, poor soul.'' The misty gaze wanders back to Melvin's cheek. The gruff voice scrapes gently. "I feel bad. We never did much fer Mina. Never helped her with her schoolwork. We didn't know how. All that studying, all them scholarships, she had to do that all by herself. Not a soul ta help her. It musta been awful hard. We did things fer Cora—bought her a sewin machine, a typewriter, nice bedroom furniture. Fer years we didn't ask a cent fer room n board. We didn't give a cent ta Mina after high school. I feel bad. Many's the night I laid awake my heart achin fer her. Dad did, too. When she got married last year—no weddin, no nothin—Agnes said, oh everbody said: 'No wonder.' Gee, I felt bad. She was like a—*stranger.*''

—*I was born with a caul.* "I didn't need your help.''

"She was a poet," Melvin offers.

The foreign-sounding statement glows for the old woman like an absolution. At last she has clawed open that slit. Now she leans back, her eyes sucking at Melvin's plump pink cheek.

—*Little do you guess, old beggar, that he has been whispering to me all day: "Let's get out of here." My first time home in eleven years, and your theme hasn't changed one bit.*

"My brother Milo," she is nattering, "he's goin ta paint the house fer us. Cora picked out the paint, like in LADIES' WAY. What's that color called, Cora?''

146

Cora says to her lap: "Bermuda pink."

"Yeah. He's goin ta start on it soon as the weather warms up. I never did like that old gray color."

—Old Candle, you'll be lit up the rest of your life on the widow's little pension. Daddy, oh my Daddy. The tranquilizer will not bolster me much longer. Melvin's gracious manner may buckle any minute. Best to depart while these two are still mistaking our courtesy for compassion.

Willo bids them goodbye. No handshakes. No kisses. Just a wave to that vulture and its side-kick in the doorway of that sagging bungalow, which will soon be reborn, bright pink as an infant.

They drive through the slush of the dismal city...pass the papermill...Casey's shack...the railroad track where Daddy prayed and preached for more than forty years....

—Daddy, oh my Daddy, I see you walking along with that dinnerpail under your arm. Daddy.

Now they are nearing the crossroad that leads to the cemetery.

—That chrysanthemum is calling to me. "Please, Melvin, take me back to the grave."

"You've been so calm. Don't spoil it now."

"Only for a minute. Please!"

"No! You can't do that to the baby." He speeds past the crossroad as if he's tugging her out of quicksand.

—You have not coped with Death, Melvin. That makes two of us. She swallows her tears.

"Travail" is the right word for this pregnancy. While they are waiting for her odyssey of complications—nausea, tumors, peritonitis, surgery, and more nausea—to end in a small plaque in the cemetery, or worse, in a toadish freak, eight months have passed, and a Caesarean; on her thirtieth birthday, Willo is saying: "Am I on a euphoric drug, Melvin, or is this actually the most beautiful baby I have ever seen?"

Melvin wrinkles his brow.

She kisses the tiny pink head. "I want to name him Lieb."

"That's ridiculous."

"But he's so beautiful—like a poem."

"Nonsense. He's a boy. Name him Max."

Home from the hospital, Willo's infatuation with the baby escalates. To Melvin, she seems like a tigress, who keeps hauling her kitten away from him, away from everything, into the other room.

Displaced, bored, he dreams of impressing her with that postponed honeymoon to some exotic island.

To nourish this dream, he puts aside the Zen for THE WALL STREET JOURNAL, and within a month, he has fed a large chunk of his savings to Wall Street, which, with a swish of its dragon-tail, swats them out of the university nest, and dumps them into that humid swamp, Washington, D.C.

Dazed, Willo says, "I never wanted to come back to this awful place."

Equally dazed, Melvin replies, "I never wanted to be a *civil servant*....But it's temporary—just until investments straighten out."

Melvin returns to their tiny apartment each evening from the jangle of typewriters and the maze of statistics and the wrangles of traffic like something that has been rushed to the emergency room of a hospital.

Willo must stroke his forehead, knead his neck and shoulders, to unleash the angry dog.

"Those jerks at the office!" he mutters.

She must bring him a tray of *hors d'oeuvres.*

"That ass Eisenhower!"

She must bring him a glass of wine.

"That ass Nixon!"

She rushes in with a tray of dinner.

"Those dopes next door!"

She brings him homemade cherry pie. Then Max cries.

"Don't pick him up!"

She picks him up, anyway, and carries him out into the living room: a miniature buddha who, with small dark blue eyes, watches his father eat the cherry pie.

"You hold him all the time," Melvin grumbles. "You spoil him."

"I need to feed him and bathe him and rock him to sleep. *Then—*" she bargains, "I'll give you your massage."

And she does: neck, shoulders, back, legs.

"Don't stop now!" he moans. "It's just beginning to feel good."

After a while, his strong kisses suck up her feeble ones like milk through a straw, and in her scarred pelvis, frail as a doll's wicker cradle, she rocks his NEED to sleep...night after night: this ritual of repairs to restore the sybarite to that box of civil servants...to keep the bachelor from nipping at her child.

—*Tomorrow,* she tells herself, *or the day after...or the day after...I'll take a nap or read Zen or write a poem.*

But tomorrow, and the next day, and the next, the red-headed neighbor children clamour and cough in the hall... cry and fight on the stairs...knock on her door and stare at

149

her with pale Orphan Annie eyes, and breathe upon Max through sudsy green nostrils. And Willo, the tigress, snatches up her baby and takes him for long, long walks in his carriage.

"It's outrageous," she tells Melvin when he comes home. "Those children live on potato chips and chocolate milk."

"I nearly slipped on the stairs," he sighs. "There was a pink plastic crucifix all sticky with gunk."

Behind the curtains, they watch the big pumpkin-headed, beer-paunched father come and go in his plumber's truck. As he enters the building and as he exits, he always spits into the magnolia tree, like a male dog watering his territory. They watch the fat salmon-haired mother lumber out to slap a child who has wandered into the street.

"Her big bare legs are autographed with a varicosity from each baby," Willo whispers. "They all look like jack-o-lanterns."

"It's like living in a Belfast slum," Melvin sighs. "We'll have to move." And he pours himself a drink and turns up the phonograph.

The evening of his first birthday, the teething Max is fretful. Rocking him in the nursery, Willo reaches for the flashlight; shines the beam on the ceiling. *Off, on. Off, on. Blooming like a moon.*

The crying stops.

Off, on. Off, on. Lovely moon.

Willo places the tiny thumb on the switch and slides it up and down, up and down.

The thumb commands; the moon obeys. Max is mesmerized.

Melvin's bear-shadow blocks the door of the nursery. "Willo! Stop that at once!"

"Stop it? He loves it."

"Stop! He must learn right now: *A flashlight is not a toy!*"

The tiny thumb continues to make the moon.

"Stop that!" Melvin whines. *"A flashlight is not a toy!"*

"Melvin! Anything that amuses can be a toy."

"No! It's the most important lesson he can learn: He may touch his own toys. Everything else HE MUST NOT TOUCH!"

"That's the formula for creating a *prig*. I want to teach him that the whole household—including this flashlight—is his toy."

Melvin wipes his throbbing forehead. He sighs. "That's the formula for creating a *brat.*"

Far into the night, the enchanted one-year-old, in the lap of his mother, makes the moon with his thumb.

The obstetrician, shaking his head over her seamed pelvis, warns Willo: "If you want one more child, your last chance is right *now.*"

Over his third bourbon, Melvin says, "Let's have a pretty little daughter."

"I wanted to wait another three years. If we have two babies, I'll need a great deal of help from you."

Melvin gives a boozy smile. "I'll play and play and play with a pretty little daughter."

"You think a female, if she is pretty, lands sunny-side-up, don't you?"

"Of course. Look at you."

In sweltering August, Willo bears a blond boy.

"Another beauty," she says to Melvin.

"But don't name him 'Lover-Boy.' "

"Max," she says, "This is Tad."

Max slides the scene into his navy blue Tartar eyes: *a head wobbling on her shoulder...the face on backwards....She keeps tasting the ear....* He snaps his thumb into his Mayan mouth.

It's the same chorus all over again: the mew at midnight, tearing her, nude, from Melvin's embrace...her nipples, as

151

she runs, raining loudly on the linoleum...Melvin wilting into peevish sleep...and now Max mewing, too. By dawn, both babies mewing and mewing and Melvin growling for all that she can GIVE.

Willo snatches repeatedly out of her drowning:
"Could we have a little picnic next Sunday, Melvin?"
"I guess so. Pack a good hamper."
Sunday he has a migraine.

"Next Sunday, Melvin, a walk along the canal?"
"Sure. Fine."
But on Sunday he says, "It's too muddy."

"If only we could move out of this apartment."
"I'm thinking about it, Honey. I keep reading the newspaper for ads."

"I've been wondering, Melvin, should we go back to the university?"
"Back to your Beatniks, you mean?"
"They were not Beatniks. They were all serious PhD candidates."
"Back to your status symbols, you mean."

"Melvin, I read in the POST that there's a Zen monk in town—"
"Forget it. He's a phony. Rub my back. Have a bourbon. Listen to Schubert. That's Zen."

"Max is jealous. If you could feed Tad—"
"What do you think I am? Some kind of queer?"
"Then could you play with Tad in his sandbox, or push him in his swing?"
"Don't be *silly.*"

"Sometimes, before we were married, you broiled steaks, Melvin. Could you do that again on the week-end?"
"Bachelors cook. Husbands don't."
"What a silly rule."

He does not answer. He goes on reading his novel.

"Melvin, I need to see a psychiatrist."

"I don't want to hear that silly talk."

"I'm losing my enthusiasm for the babies. I need some kind of help."

"I've told you: Psychiatry is the hoax of the century. Bourbon is better."

She sighs. —*You warned me, "Sore Thumb."*

Melvin, reaching out of his drowning, says, "How about a week-end in New York—dinner, theatre, and shopping?"

"The babies. What would we do with the babies?"

"Willo, we've been invited to a cocktail party."

"I can't find a baby sitter. Go alone."

"Willo, we've been invited out to dinner."

"I have no middle-class manners. Go alone."

"You're stir-crazy. Learn to drive a car."

"I can't. I need to see a psychiatrist."

On and on, this tic tac toe.

By age three, the sturdy, handsome Max will not touch a crayon to paper, as Willo has demonstrated again and again, but he melts the crayons in the oven and on the hot air vents: "See, Mommy!"

He snaps his phonograph records in half, like hardtack: "See Daddy!"

Behind his book, Melvin mutters, "Something's wrong with that boy, Willo. Can't you discipline him?"

Willo sighs. "He's bright; he's virile; he's *experimenting.*"

Max pees a bugle out of the bathroom window onto the sidewalk below: "See, Tad!"

He drags the toaster and table lamp around by their cords, like dogs on leashes, and pushes plugs into an array of outlets: "Ouch!"

"Is that what you want, Willo," Melvin says, "The Noble

153

Savage?''

"I like him to be *inventive*. If you want him to be something else, play with him."

Melvin turns up the phonograph.

Tad sends the toilet paper yipping from its reel into the chortling gobble of the flush. He squeals and claps his hands at his accomplishment: "See! See!"

Melvin tries to enclose himself in a bourbon-bubble.

Finding him asleep in his chair, Max plugs the string of Christmas tree lights into his nostrils.

Melvin does not laugh. He does not spank. He folds whatever he feels inside himself, where it ferments into a monstrous headache.

Standing behind his chair, massaging away the headache, Willo looks out the window, where the red-headed children are all climbing on the sagging chainlink fence.

"They look like chunks of cheese on a wire grater," she says, "I wish they'd grate themselves away."

"Stupid Breeders," Melvin sputters.

"We've become regular Haters. It's terrible for us; worse for the children."

"Rub above the ears. . . . It's the sick society. We have to get out of it."

As the Christmas season approaches, Willo writes a few cards to a few friends. *"Red hair, mustaches of green snot: I must guard my children from the neighbors,"* she writes to Naomi and Ned.   Then, ashamed of her bitterness, she recalls the face and the voice of another kind of Catholic, the Jesuit who was once so helpful to her in that naval hospital just outside this city, and she writes to him: *". . . Remember the time when I pitied every baby I touched? Now I pity my own two babies. . . ."*

Late in January, Father Vincent's response comes in a blue

envelope from Korea: *" 'Wild persimmons: The mother eating the bitter parts.' A poet named Issa said it better than I can. I've asked the Carmelite nuns to pray for you, Willo. "*

Early in February, Melvin stirs like a groundhog. "I'm tired of living in this dump. I'm tired of working with those knuckleheads in civil service. What do you say, Honey, to a go at foreign service?"

Willo, who is draping wet laundry on a tall drying rack, looks up through a festoon of diapers. "I thought when we came to Washington, it was for only a year—two, at most—before your investments started paying off again."

"They're not paying off. We're not exactly rich."

She looks at him as if he's jesting.

"Don't look at me with those big innocent eyes. I said we're not as rich as you think we are."

Still those mirror-eyes.

"I fed you a line."

"A line?"

"You know: In fraternities they always tell you how to get a girl: *'Feed her a line.'* "

"No. I wouldn't know. I've avoided fraternities and sororities."

"You've always avoided reality. Now you'll have to start facing it: I've accepted a job with the C.I.A."

"C.I.A.?"

"Central Intelligence Agency."

"But—back at the university—isn't that the one they used to call 'Catholics-in-Action?' "

"Your Ivory Tower Liberals called it that. The salary is twice what I'm making now, with promotions in sight. The work is a cinch."

She shakes her head.

"Don't be naive. It's *—slightly* clandestine but that doesn't mean we'll be in any danger. My assignment is London." He smiles smugly. "I'll tell you another thing: You know that trip I made to Japan? The trip that should have been our honeymoon? That was for C.I.A., on contract. They paid me a fabulous salary for a very small amount of work.''

She shakes her head again. "London? I feel—lost. What's expected of me?''

"Not a thing.''

"Mommy! Come see!'' calls Tad.

Willo hurries to *see:* With his yellow Easter bunny, he has turned the toilet into a jack-in-the-pulpit.

"Look, Mommy!'' calls Max.

Willo looks into his room, where he has turned Melvin's old turntable into a merry-go-round for shoes and blocks and crayons.

Back to the laundry, Willo says to Melvin, "But as your wife, don't I enter a new role?''

"Oh. Well, discipline those boys. Don't write any more of those neurotic poems. We're semi-diplomatic people now. Our 'cover,' by the way, is 'State Department.' ''

Through the festoon of diapers, Willo sighs, "I'm *summa cum laude* from Skid Row. I'm a freak in suburban Washington. What would I be in London?''

Melvin places a record on his phonograph. "In a huge house, with a charwoman and an *au pair* girl and a nanny, you'll be a queen.''

"I can't do it.''

"You can. In London, everyone buys Miltown over the counter, like aspirin.''

The Bartok beats against the walls like sleet.

While Melvin stokes his salestalks with museums and theatres and bookstores and Soho and Chelsea and Stratford-on-Avon and embassies and Paris and Rome and yes, *Miltown,* and while Bartok and Hindemith swell inside her skull like a sinus headache, Willo strings one clinker day to the next and the next and the next with nip after nip of cooking sherry.

—Carmelite nuns, all I want is a haven where my tots can ripen slowly, like poems.

In the London house of thirteen rooms and thirteen fire-places, Melvin sits in the drawing room, under an afghan, like a baron, listening to the hi-fi, drinking Scotch, leafing through a stack of maps: France, Italy, Spain. "Honey, this job is a junket!" he says.

Her back to him, Willo is sweeping out the hearth.

"You're always toiling. I wish I could help you."

"You can: Take the children to the heath."

"They don't need help. *You* do."

"They need to be taken to the heath or the park. That would help me more than anything."

He pours himself another Scotch, puts another record on the turntable. "I'll help you if you can suggest something sensible."

"The fireplaces are a mess. Can you help me carry the ashes out to the bin?"

He winces. "I don't have any work clothes." He sips the Scotch, unfolds a map. "Let's plan a trip to Paris."

Willo scowls over the ashes. She diapers Tad. Takes Max to the toilet. Bathes them. Gives Tad his bottle. The Stravin-sky saws at her nerves.

"It's ridiculous the way you slave over those boys," Melvin says. "Two weeks after they arrived in London, the Baxters left their three children with a nanny. They toured Paris, Rome, Spain. They say Spain is a paradise."

Max is pulling at Tad. She takes him into her lap, too. "Melvin, I'll bet Max would love to wrestle with you on the floor."

"Wrestle? What kind of nonsense is that?"

—Didn't you ever wrestle with your brothers? "Play like

157

lions and tigers. It's stimulating. I learned that in child psychology class."

"That's the best reason I can think of for not doing it. Psychologists are a neurotic bunch." He turns up the concert. "Let Max listen to this Bach. That's stimulating. That's the difference between you and me. You're a Calvinist; I'm a Buddhist. Why, if I were you, I'd have a charwoman to tend all these fireplaces and do the laundry, an *au pair* girl to buy groceries and wash dishes, and a nanny to take the children to the park."

"Our *au pair* girl was helping me a lot."

"Now, Honey, it's for the best that I made you dismiss that dyke. Anyway, we can't have a German living in the house. It's bad politics. Get a Danish girl, or a French one, or Swiss. The Baxters have a gorgeous Swiss girl. She takes the children off their hands all the time."

Willo kisses the heads of her boys. "I'd no more delegate the rearing of my children to another woman than I'd delegate the writing of my poems to a hack."

He takes a long drink of Scotch. "I never dreamed you'd turn into Supermom. Kitchen table full of fingerpaints . . . blocks all over the floor . . . that hideous sweet potato climbing all over the windowsills . . . that swing set an eyesore in the garden—this place is like nursery school, not a home for two dignified adults."

"I keep telling you: Small children need plenty of stimulation."

"They need *discipline.* A big old nanny wouldn't let them run around naked, laughing at their bodies."

"They *enjoy* their bodies."

"You've read too much of that pervert, Walt Whitman."

—Careful: Your Catholic mother is showing. "I love Walt Whitman. He's Zen-like."

Melvin takes another long drink. He raises the big map high to cover his face. He lets Stravinsky do the sawing for him.

The children are struggling for her skimpy lap. Tad cries,

and she pushes Max aside. Now he slumps on the floor, sucking his thumb. "Melvin, I'm sure Max would like to sit in your lap."

"Don't be silly."

"Or help him build a garage with his blocks."

"Max is fine. Take a Miltown."

An hour later, Melvin says, "Now you look better, Sweets. I hate to see you getting things so distorted. Everything is fine!"

She carries the children to the nursery for their naps. Then she wilts, exhausted, on her bed.

Melvin follows her into the bedroom. "Think about something pleasant," he croons. "Think about going to Spain. Think about going to the theatre next week to see Lawrence Olivier. . . . Mostly, think about buying a new dress and wearing it to the cocktail party at the embassy next Friday night."

"Those are not pleasant thoughts for me."

"That's a sick response, if ever I heard one."

"If it's sick, then let me see a psychiatrist."

He kisses her. "I won't listen to such silly talk. I didn't mean SICK in that sense. I've overcome a lot of my shyness just by going to the office and to cocktail parties. You can do the same."

She starts to cry.

"Stop that. Crying won't help."

"Please. I do need to see a psychiatrist."

He says very slowly, very patiently, "I've told you: I've read all the latest literature on the subject. Psychiatry is *passe.* 'Mental illness' is largely chemical. It's cured by medication. Take another Miltown."

She obeys. Half an hour later, he pulls her body to him and takes it with great pleasure, like a necrophile.

The next day, Sunday, Max and Tad squabble ceaselessly, like lion kits, over the last scraps of her love. By afternoon, she pushes them both off her lap. They sit, thumbs in mouths, forlorn as refugees. . . .

"Please!" she implores Melvin. "Every Sunday the heath is full of fathers romping with their children."

He smiles mildly over his book. "Those effete Englishmen."

"They're not effete. They're—"

"When the boys are a little bigger, you'll see what a stimulating companion I'll be to them."

She sighs.

He hands her a book. "Read this. Learn about *wu wei*. It will cure you."

"THE WAY OF ZEN. I tried to read it yesterday, and the day before. I can't. I'm too frazzled to concentrate."

"Make yourself concentrate."

She shakes her head.

"You don't want to help yourself. You want a psychiatrist to do it for you."

"I'm in a deep pit. I'd like an expert to reach down and give me a hand. Then I might start helping myself."

"Forget it. If you went to a psychiatrist, I'd lose my job."

"That's hard to believe."

"You'd better believe it: No sickees in The Agency."

Willo takes another Miltown. Then she wanders and wanders through the huge chilly house. . .feels her arms hanging heavily at her sides, like baseball bats. . .sees, as from a distance, as a window-peeper might see, Melvin, Max, Tad . . . .—*We've come to look like that family in that Charles Adams cartoon.* . . .She wanders into the bathroom for another Miltown. The face she sees in the mirror is alien; no, not alien. It's her mother's face, her father's face, caged in an educated restraint.

"I'm half an inch from suicide," she tells the neighborhood physician.

"Give me your husband's phone number," he says...and through her thick stupor, she hears..."It's Miltown-addiction...I'll stay with her and the children until you arrive." He dials another number...talks...writes a name and address on a slip of paper. "This psychiatrist will see you as soon as your husband can take you to him."

He sits on the floor between Max and Tad. "What a fine set of blocks. Can you build a garage?...Such a chilly November fog....You don't have these in America, do you? ...Good. Now, can you get a little van...a 'truck,' you call it...and now a little car?..."

An hour later, Willo slumps beside a grate of coral coals and gazes towards the blur of a psychiatrist who sees a wilted waif in a sparrow-colored coat, her dimmed hair misered into a knot, her skimmed-milk hands drooping from wraith-wrists...also, her penguin-built husband, with the look of a man whose watch has gone on the blink.

Willo murmurs, in that Miltown-monotone, "I'm thirty-four, mother of two little boys. I'm empty. I can't...—*give* them anything...anymore."

The psychiatrist nods, and Melvin sees a very tall Nordic, who looks almost like—Matt Dillon...grave, hushed, slightly stooped, as if in apology for so much virility.

The psychiatrist says, "Come four times a week, Mrs. Sanders, starting tomorrow, Wednesday."

The smoke from his pipe curves out to her, wreathes her, coaxes her into focus.

Wednesday:

Lying on the couch, substantial as a paper doll, she speaks, and her voice lapping lapping lapping like water against an old rotted pier post, brings him the flotsam: "My mother is like a retarded child....My father was a self-styled evangelist. They quarreled incessantly....My sister is a spinster with long sleeves over psoriasis." Her chapped fingers, clenched on the sweater between her small breasts, are the fingers of an old pedlar unloading a knapsack of trinkets no one has ever bought. "I left them for a lesbian."

"You click off this information so stoically," he says, "like a schoolgirl reciting a lesson. I wonder where your feelings are?"

Friday:

She lies on the couch like a bound insect waking in a web...watches through the bowed window the bare tree twigs clawing at the gray sky. "I'm so tired. I have nothing more to say."

"You seem exhausted," he says from somewhere behind her. "Maybe you've come here to rest."

She watches, through another bowed window, the clouds drifting. Like an insect waking, she hears the fire humming in the grate. "I'm so tired of sweeping ashes out of fireplaces."

He listens to her voice, faint and hoarse, like the voice of a child who has been crying for a long time.

Slowly, she turns her gaze to the warmth, watches the flames—salmon-colored—caressing one another...a coral one hugging an orange one...listens to their language, like a lullaby.

"You're too frail, far too frail, to be a Cinderella," he muses.

She listens to his voice...a voice akin to the voice of the hearth.

"...yet you're something like Cinderella, something like Rapunzel. I have the strongest feeling that you've come to me straight out of a fairy tale." He watches her hands clench.

"...perhaps a fairy tale I've never read or heard...."
—*Dreamman? Prince? You've come too late.*

"You'll tell me about it bit by bit." The voice—kind beyond all other voices—that voice wraps her, warms her, nourishes her for Monday.

Monday:

Her hands clenched between her breasts, she addresses her grievances to the windows: "I cannot find a sitter imaginative enough for my children.... That pretty *au pair* girl is always on the phone with her boyfriends....Melvin criticizes the meals...the housekeeping...my grooming."

"We can't find a sitter imaginative enough for our children, either, and our last housekeeper stole all our winter coats."

"Really?" Her hands open as if to catch a ball, then snap shut again. "And I'm always too tired to go out, to cook, to—"

"My wife is always tired, too. Every week-end I shop for groceries and do the cooking."

Her hands open again. "Now who's telling whom a fairy tale she's never heard?"

He laughs. "The war changed everything here. A New Age has dawned. Maybe it hasn't yet reached your country."

January:

Her bungled bun of hair is released and lolling in flaxen crayon lines around her little cat-face. "Ben and Sam and Clay were starting to heal the lesbian kisses." Her voice shimmers a bit. "Then came Melvin. His kiss was a Venus fly-trap...." "...my mother's little blue dishes...now that ache has turned to hate." Her fingers on her sweater are almost lambent...."My father....He...." She dabs at unshed tears. "He was just a praying mantis in a box under a wet chrysanthemum. I never said goodbye." She wipes again at unshed tears.

Departing, she beholds his blond handsomeness outrageously haloed in the light from the bowed window behind him, and she turns tense as a tinker toy. "I'm afraid I'm just The Little Match Girl."

February:
   Melvin mutters, "Does that doctor have an orgone box?"
   "What's an orgone box?" Willo asks.
   "Never mind."
   "An orgone box? I'll ask him."
And Melvin watches her skip off to Olympus for yet another session with Apollo.

April:
   He who in November was a tall gray blur has become a Viking in a crewneck sweater, and she who was a sparrow has become a hummingbird-girl, too vibrant for the cage-couch.
   She flutters one day into his lap.
   "Your parents gave so little of this," he says.
   She snuggles. He strokes her arm.
   "I have four children at home," he says in that voice like a lullaby. "Are you asking to be my fifth, Willo?"

May:
   She is beautiful.
   Rooted, at his command, like a lily, to the brown couch, she issues invitations in fragrance and gesture. "What I feel for my husband is but the flicker of a firefly compared with the skyrocket that rises in me when I enter this room. I long for a baby...yours...a beautiful blonde daughter named Skye."
   Pipesmoke and voice caress her: "Isn't it *you* who longs to be re-born?"

June:
   "Maybelle...Maybelle...a little bell in my heart keeps tinkling MAYBELLLLLLLLE!"
   He listens raptly to her mournful tone.

"The last time I saw Maybelle, there was a snowstorm, and she was in a coffin...and this icicle in me keeps dripping and dripping....I wrote her a poem 'Snow Falls on Flowers' ...but still the icicle keeps dripping and dripping and the bell keeps tinkling MAYBELLLLLE! and the snow keeps falling on all the flowers...."

He says quietly, at the end of the session: "When you get home, look in the mirror. I think you will see Maybelle."

July:

Ever-audience to this drama, Melvin's narrowed eyes above his button-nose seems to be sighting over a double-barreled gun.

Mornings, watching her flick his black wire hair from her mashed nipple, as one flicks a spider from a rose bud...slip her heart-shaped seat into lacey pants, as one slips a valentine into an envelope....Evenings, watching her return on the park path, her hair jubilant with pipesmoke, as roe lavished with milt....Nights, watching her sleep shift from Writhing to Smug...soothing his insomnia with reading, his eyes keep splitting the word "therapist" into "the rapist."

August:

Glowing umber from his Algerian holiday, his chest a smoulder of sandy hairs through his thin shirt, he is too much for her. And this so-slim Willo, in violet sheath and matching heels, this exclamation point of ladylike longing, pleading with wet eyelashes against his throat is too much for him.

"Willo, Willo," he whispers, "we have work to do."

Re-planted, once more, on the couch, she shields her begging breasts with gold leaf hands.

His plume of smoke shields them better.

"You don't know me," he says. "I'm an illusion."

"I know that I know the YOU of you." Her scent drifts back to him, like milkweed seed, and clings.

September:

Tough and taciturn now, he is the warp through which she weaves her swift satin shimmers.

"You and I are two searchlights," she says. "Each carves a crown of light out of the darkness. Must we always intersect at one point only, then lean out into separate nights?"

No answer.

"The Zen monks say we Westerners eat the menu, not the meal. Do you suppose they mean psychoanalysis?"

No answer.

When, on parting, she turns a zither-glance upon him, (*I know that I know the YOU of you.*) he turns a metronome-glance upon her. (*You don't know me. I'm an illusion.*)

October:

He says, very slowly, "Lately, when you come and go, you no longer look at me."

It is her turn to be silent.

"What comes to mind?"

She squeezes her hair.

"Surely," he says, "the professional distance—" slowly, like a surgeon probing for a splinter "which I must maintain...must be...as painful for you...as it is...for me."

"Maybe."

"In three months, you'll be leaving the country, terminating treatment long before you are strong. I'm wondering... are you already packing your feelings away into that trunk?"

"Maybe."

"When you arrive in America, write to me. Rules of this profession forbid me to write back, but since you'll be terminating against your will, and since your husband may not permit you to resume treatment in America, by all means, write to me as often as you wish."

When she rises, she takes him back—every inch of him—into those large lavender eyes. "You're still the grandest tiger in the jungle."

November:

"I had this wonderful dream," she smiles. "I was sitting in your lap, and I slipped my hand across your chest and lifted up a rib, a flap, like a fish's gill...."

He watches her fingers play like a harpist's through her chatoyant hair.

"—and I reached in and took into my hand a big soft lung. It was round and fragrant, like an orange or a tangerine. And I peeled back the thin membrane and sucked a slice and ate it. Oh, it was so succulent, so delicious!"

He listens to her voice, almost like singing.

"...and I peeled another slice...and sucked it...and ate it...and another...and I ate all night."

"Yes. You are such a thirsty waif, such a hungry waif. Yes."

December:

Who would have guessed that one corner of this old city would turn into that haven for her two noble savages?

Max's kindergarten teacher says: "He climbs. He yells. He builds. He reads. He paints. He writes. He counts. He sings. He fights. He's full of beans!"

Tad, enclosed with the tabby cat in the garden of late roses and still-later wisteria, molds sand and mud into a paradise of lumps, and with a stick he scratches TAD   TAD   TAD all over his domain.

In Hampstead Heath, Willo roams hours and hours and hours with the two of them. They picnic like monkeys in the big beech trees, gather a treasure of conkers and smooth-split flints   and race one another lickety-split to the oldman vendor for warm little bags of chestnuts.

"Sixpence, thank you, Laddie...and sixpence, thank you, Laddie," he tweedles, like someone out of a nursery rhyme.

His glowing old cart is as magic to them as that hearth of her rendezvous is to her.

January:

In a pub across from that guru's tower-like office, Melvin

167

sips ale and reflects upon the muddle. He has learned that preceding Willo's visit to this sacred cell, there is another—banjo-hips gift wrapped in shining jade slacks, lime jello-bosom brimming, flame hair wafting across the ripe pout .... Then Willo, clicking along on those absurd high heels like a little wind-up doll. And following Willo, by ten minutes, a lusty Latin with snorting nostrils and yum-duff, also gift wrapped. So. This parade of fulminating females inhaling from Him their zillion kilowatts of zing.

Sipping his fourth ale, Melvin reflects on the price he has had to pay for this zing: No more covert assignments for him. No more junkets in foreign capitals. He will be assigned now to a desk job in Washington: Eight hours every day, month after month, year after year, of dull, dull research.... Even there, he will be watched for signs of indiscretion...his wife will be watched for evidence of instability. The price of falling in love with a little blonde who wrote silly poems.

He sips slowly, trying to eke out the ale to match the exit of the Latin.

The doctor notices that she has grown remote again. Maybe it is his turn to talk: "You speak sometimes of Zen. Are you familiar with this little story? Two Zen monks were walking in the heavy rain down a muddy road. They met a beautiful girl, dressed in a lovely kimono. She could not cross a wide puddle without soiling her gown. The first monk lifted her in his arms and carried her across the mud. All that day, the second monk sulked in silence. At night, when they had settled down in a temple to sleep, he snarled: 'You know we monks have vowed not to touch a woman.' 'I put her down on the other side of the puddle,' said the first monk. 'Are you still carrying her?' "

February fourteenth:

On the couch, her arms crossed, she talks stiltedly of the snowstorm and the slippery streets.

He watches the fingertips pressing into the sleeves of the sweater.

She draws a deep breath and says, almost formally: "At the end of a Brecht play, someone says, 'A thing belongs to the one who loves it.' "

"You don't have to use the words of another writer today."

The fingers press harder. "What I mean is: When I leave for America tomorrow, you'll go with me."

"You're a poet. You'll sublimate a lot."

She glances at the bowed window, where the snow is whirling. She glances at her watch.

"I'm waiting for my Little Match Girl."

She looks at the hearth. "The coral coals have turned into pink roses."

"Pink roses. Snowstorm." He watches the fingers grasp the thin arms. "Valentine's Day."

She watches the snow converging abundantly upon the window pane. Her face turns to the second window: the snow is converging upon that pane, too.

"Where's my Little Match Girl?"

Slowly, as if dreaming, she rises and looks beyond him to the third window of whirling whiteness. "Look: We're in the heart of a great chrysanthemum."

He rises, too. He holds her hard. "Hello, Bright Bird," he says, "and goodbye."

4

The new highway is a raw seam across the lush Virginia landscape. Cars and trucks and motorcycles unzip it with the helps of pain.

A dark, handsome woman who looks like Patricia Neal crosses the lawn from the house next door. "Ah'm Beverly Cain," she says, not in the rich molasses voice that Willo expected to drip from such a face. "Yawl been overseas? Gosh, I can't wait to see yer loot." The whanging voice of blue jay.

From the boxwood hedge, her three sons, crew-cut, slung with guns, stare at Max and Tad.

"Ah'll tell yawl what yawl oughta do," Beverly whangs. "Take yer kids down ta Roanoke first weekend you're free. There's an old train there, and the kids ride on it for a dime each. Then the Indians come runnin outa the trees an attack the train, an' the kids shoot em with these guns. You oughta hear the hollerin!"

The three scalped gunmen appraise the two foreigners, who gaze back at them out of generous frames of English hair.

"My three—the youngest, specially," Beverly continues, "they jest can't wait ta go back ta Roanoke."

Her husband, she tells Willo, is a dentist. They came up from Georgia a year ago.

Across the street: woman who resembles Susan Hayward. "Our kids are terrifically *creative,"* she beams, as her two girls and a boy on the porch hook together the plastic do-dads of a do-it-yourself kit. "They're advertised on T.V. You'll have to get one for your boys." The cigarette-scented com-

173

mand barks out of her pretty face. She beams again at the children: "They're *so* creative!"

Willo smiles politely. —*Creative? Don't you mean 'industrious?'*

On the *cul de sac,* a Radcliff mother petitions to entice a few Negroes into the school: "We don't want our children to be deprived of the interracial experience."

Willo smiles, hopefully, at the genteel inflection.

"Sign here," she commands.

—*Is this a subtle brand of slavery?* Willo wonders as she smiles timidly and signs her name.

In their absence, the London women bloom vividly. Though she encountered them only casually on the heath and in buses and in shops and the theatres, and only a bit intimately in Max's school and at the embassies, she misses their unlaquered hair, their intelligent faces not masked in cosmetics, even their unshaved shins and armpits...misses their natural strides in large flat shoes...misses, most of all, their diction, drifting like dulcet music out of their faces.

One by one, the neighbors show her their houses: wall-to-wall carpets...gleaming kitchen-factories...two television sets, or three...always one in the tiled 'rec room'...encyclopedias: "A real buy at the supermarket. Better get a set for your kids before they're sold out." Two sleek cars in every double garage, like a shark and a whale, which, when revved up, give off the reek of overfed pets.

She makes a mental note for her first letter to London: —*Everywhere, all up and down the street, Acquisitiveness lies like an elephant upon the consciousness of the people.*

"We don't read books," Max says gravely. "Just some words on cards. The teacher won't let me write script, as I did in England. That comes in third grade."

Willo hears within her dulcet voice of Max's London teacher: *"Can you tell me, Mrs. Sanders, why they teach*

174

reading and writing in America as if they're such a chore?
Here, we think they're jolly fun!''

At show-and-tell, the teacher says to the silent Max: "I'm sure there are many things here that you didn't have in England. Just think about it and tell us some."

Max says, "Kennedy and Nixon...and television...and hot dogs...and bubble gum...and guns...and station wagons...and Hawaiian punch...and guns."

Often on Saturday night, The Agency cocktail party: The men, like Melvin are all attired in those charcoal gray suits and diagonally-striped ties and black horn-rimmed glasses. All drinking bourbon on the rocks. All beeping the same jargon. All batting the namby pamby joke, the namby pamby laughter, back and forth, like ping pong balls.

—No tall blond Englishmen musing about fairy tales. No whiskery Ben exhalting "the tolerance for ambiguity." No T-shirted Clay cartwheeling through isotopes and medieval dogma. No playful, probing Sam. This is just a box of dominoes.

The wives, mostly bovine, several—even a gray-haired one —are pregnant. They are all smoking   smoking   smoking ...chug-a-lugging those bloody Marys...praising their parochial schools: "Those nuns are *strict.* That's just what we need."

They issue smiles, like tendrils, towards this petite newcomer who does not smoke...who barely sips her sherry... who smiles back like a frightened child.

"You'll have to learn to play bridge, Willo!"

"You'll have to learn to drive a car!"

"Stella has seven children. Mary has five. I have six. You'll have to catch up, Willo!"

Their smiles, their commands, surround her like a chain link fence.

Sundays they escape for a walk along the canal. It is

175

bordered on the berm side with locust trees and willows and grapevines, and on the near side with chicory and pink clover.

"Look," says Willo. "Together, those two colors are lavender."

Goldfinches, bluebirds, mallards, pileated woodpeckers ...sycamores and tulip poplars. And fungus   and more fungus.

"Here's a mushroom just like half an apple!" calls Max.

"Here's one like a bun!" calls Tad.

"I've found one like marshmallow!" calls Willo.

Melvin hustles them onto a tickertape of kodachrome.

Willo hoards them into thoughts for that letter to London: —*My love for you overflows into flowers and into my children and to Jack Kennedy, who is an American version of you....*

"My feet hurt," Melvin mutters.

"Mom! Here's one like lemon custard!"

Across the Potomac, delicate as a blown leaf, skims the chiming of bells.

"What's that?" calls Max.

"Bells," says Melvin, "from The Sacred Heart Convent."

"What's a convent?" Max asks.

Willo answers, "A Catholic school for girls." —*Catholics: Willo will write in that letter: My love/hate mechanism spins them like a centrifuge and separates them into different layers*—

Melvin glowers at Willo. "I said: *My feet hurt.*"

—*and the layers are utterly polarized: At the bottom, those tepid creatures at The Agency; at the top, Kennedy, The Prince.*

"How much farther, Willo?" Melvin whines. "I've finished the film."

—*Love, hold me a little longer.*

176

It's a rainy Sunday afternoon. Tad and Max are engrossed in a marble game of their own invention. Tad kneels in the hallway at the edge of the living room. Max kneels fifteen feet away from him at the far corner of the living room. Between them stretches a five-inch strip of wooden floor, like a road, bounded on one side by the thick carpet, on the other side by the baseboard. Max rolls a marble down the strip to Tad. Tad rolls one back to Max. Max rolls two marbles at a time. Tad rolls back two. Four marbles pass one another on the road. Then eight marbles. Sometimes they click or crash. After a while, twenty marbles are humming along the wooden strip.

The brothers have been playing this game for weeks. *"Rorschach marbles,"* Willo has explained to Melvin. *"One day they seem to be cars, then ships, then migrating birds; some of the time, just marbles, I guess."*

Willo takes increasing pride in these growing sons. At six years, Max still looks like an English schoolboy. He is sturdy in build, ardent in coloring: pink skin, auburn hair, dark blue eyes, Mayan lips. A vivid face. A baroque boy. He looks much like his father, speaks with his mother's imagery, which he has graced with the English lilt.

At four years, Tad is elfin; his features are trim and neat, except for the extravagant billow of blond curls. A pastel boy. He looks like his mother, and like his mother at that age, he loves nothing better than to draw pictures with his crayons. Willo loves to hear him chatter to her as he draws ...or better yet, to consult his big brother: *"Is this O.K., Max?"*

"My two sons," Willo wrote yesterday to London: *"A*

pleasing balance: the assertive and the compliant; the vivid and the pastel; Baroque and Doric. Yang and yin. Facing one another like two buddhas.

Midway between the two buddhas, on the carpet, is a third buddha; or more of a jug than a buddha; the gray tabby cat, Madame Wookey. Her eyes travel back and forth, back and forth, like the eyes of someone watching a game of tennis. She is taut with predatory instinct.

Willo looks around the room. Lining glass bottles with a brocade, revealing their inner mysteries are radish seeds sprouting on damp blotters. In the corner of the room are six grapefruit halves drying into bird-feeding bowls. The turtle snoozes in the terrarium. Fish swoop in the aquarium. So cozy to Willo. So annoying to Melvin.

The hum of the marbles has grown to a roar, like traffic. Behind his newspaper, Melvin clears his throat. *"Longsuffering mother,"* he told Willo last week. *"You tolerate the cacophony of those marbles far better than you tolerate Schoenberg or Hindemith or Schubert."* *"It's true,"* she said. The London psychiatrist had laughed: *"You're a most indulgent mother; that's exactly what I'd expect of someone with a Leo ascendant."* She had taken it as a joke, just as years ago she had taken Ben's and Sam's comments on horoscopes and their enthusiasm for someone called "Jung." Now she is beginning to wonder: *"Who is this Jung?"* she asked Melvin last week. *"I've looked in the library for Jung. He's not even listed in the catalog."* Melvin had replied: *"You can be glad he hasn't infiltrated this country. He's that Swiss weirdo who believes in flying saucers."*

Behind his newspaper, Melvin is scowling. "How long does this game have to go on?"

Willo says, "Boys, after about two minutes, can you start to play another game? Dad's ears need a rest."

The marbles continue to roar. Two minutes. Three minutes.

"Time is up!" Willo calls.

The roar accelerates to a crescendo. Marbles collide, crash, crackle like fireworks. Out of the side of the newspaper, Melvin casts Willo the accusing glance: *They never obey you.* She shrugs: She knows that.

Slowly, theatrically, just as the curtain of a stage is raised, the newspaper is lowered. Melvin's arms reach out like menacing limbs. His fingers curl into talons. He issues an ogrish grunt. "Dragon!" he growls. "I'm a dragon!"

The boys glance up, startled.

Glowering, Melvin swells up out of his chair. . .rises slowly and spookily like smoke from an oily fire.

"Eeeeeeee!" the boys shriek.

The cat scoots.

The monster lumbers towards the boys. They flee. He pursues. "Urrrr!" he grunts. "Dragon!" They hide. He seeks. In the closet. In the shower. Under the bed. He flashes out of a corner, pounces upon his prey, bundles it in furry arms, bites it. "Urrrrr."

Willo is spellbound.

Squealing and squealing, the boys pounce upon plump, panting Papa. "More! More!"

When they are eating supper in the kitchen, Madame Wookey meows at the table. She scorns the proffered meat. She scurries to the living room. She does not want OUT. She meows some more. Then she plants her butt on the carpet, faces the wooden strip of floor, turns again into the jug, with only the eyes moving back and forth, back and forth.

"She's been hypnotized by that marble game," Willo laughs.

No sooner have the family resumed supper in the kitchen than from the living room comes the hum of a rolling marble . . .another marble. . .another. . .humming along the wooden strip. It's Wookey: With her paw, she has resumed the game.

"What a marvelous day!" Willo says, after the boys have gone to bed. "You were just like a Kabuki dragon."

"I was mean," Melvin says sheepishly. "I can't believe you really enjoyed such meanness!"

"I did. You were openly mean—playful."

He chuckles. "I was so *mad* at those boys."

"They knew it. Open anger gives a *relief* that hidden anger doesn't give. Open anger is so much healthier than—*indifference.*"

Sunday after Sunday, Max and Tad try to provoke their father into playing Dragon again.

He will not: "I have a headache. Leave me alone."

Willo sighs: —*Have I slain the dragon?*

They are wakened by a small cough at their bedside. Willo opens her eyes to see Tad standing like a little ghost beside her.

"I have a sore throat," he whimpers.

He receives the instant embrace of his mother; from his father, a bearish groan and a swiftly turned rump.

Willo kisses the hot forehead, then takes Tad to the kitchen, where she gives him a spoonful of cherry cough syrup. She leads him into the moonlit living room, wraps him in the afghan, and lifts him to her lap in the rocking chair.

Madame Wookey, aroused from her basket in the laundry room, patters across the floor and leaps into the small crevice between their two bodies. Tad lays his hand on the furry head.

"Does a veterinarian have to know how to play Musical Chairs?" he quavers.

Willo kisses the curly head. "No."

"That's all I want to be—a veterinarian. So why do I have to go to kindergarten?"

She lays her cheek on the fluffy head. "It's the law in Virginia that every child must be in school by the time he's six years old. You could have waited until next year to enter first grade when you're six, but we thought it might be better for you to have a year of kindergarten first."

He snuffles his clogged nose.

She sighs. The whole truth is that all last summer she kept saying to Melvin: *"He's too young."* And Melvin kept countering with: *"Other kids go to school when they're five."* *"But Tad will be five scarcely two weeks before school opens. That's an immature five, especially for a boy. I've*

181

worked with kindergartners, and I know many boys would be better starting when they're six." "You were blacklisted from teaching," Melvin huffed. "I doubt that you're a competent judge."

A spasm of coughing shakes Tad's thin body.

Willo pumps the rocking chair into a soothing rhythm.

So Tad went to school last September...threw up the first day...caught cold after cold...and again, Willo pleaded with Melvin: "I know he's too young. One more year at home, and he could rest and gain some weight and grow more stable—" "One more year of pampering would ruin him," Melvin insisted. "I won't have a son of mine starting first grade when he's SEVEN!"

A feathery little cough flies from Tad's lips. "I can't even tie my shoes," he whimpers. "I'm the only one that can't tie my shoes."

"It's my fault, Tad. I neglected to teach you."

"I'll never learn. All I can do is make one loop. I can't ever 'member what to do with the other string."

"It's my fault, Tad. When you're feeling better, I'll teach you."

"I won't learn. I can't even zip my coat."

"When you're over this cold, when you're feeling well again, you'll learn."

He coughs. "I can't even make an 'S' right."

With her foot, she escalates the lullaby motion of the chair. "When you're feeling better, it will come to you."

"No, it won't."

She rocks so vigorously that Madame Wookey's claws grip her knee. "Everything seems difficult when you're sick. Let's think about something pleasant...like your big bold drawing of the snowman that Mrs. Bertram pinned up on the bulletin board for Visitors' Day."

Sitting there in that kindergarten room yesterday, next to Beverly Cain, with her eyes fastened on that picture, Willo, nevertheless, could not help seeing, out of the corner of her eye, William Cain coughing cracker crumbs all over Tad's pale little cheek. *"William has been going to Sunday School ever since he was three years old,"* Beverly beamed. *"All my kids did. See, that way they get used to being away from their mothers and being with other kids."*

Willo sat there, enduring, while the plump Mrs. Bertram thumped the piano into a sound of thunder, and with her gold tooth flashing, belted out "The Farmer in the Dell!". . . enduring the squeaky singing of the children. . . their clapping . . . that clapping going rat-a-tat-tat. . . enduring that many-headed monster of coughs and sneezes revolving around her spindly Tad. . . enduring the sight of Mrs. Bertrams's fat arms, at the end of the song, raised in exaggerated joy. . . feeling Tad flinch at the sight of the big wet armpits. . . .

Willo pumps the rocking chair into deepening dips through this choppy sea.

As if he has been reading his mother's thoughts, Tad whispers, "When William draws a person, you know what? He makes the eyes—" He extricates his hands from the cat and the afghan and places two forefingers on his forehead. "—he makes two dots way up *here.*"

Willo kisses the pale fleece. "How *gross.*"

"Yeah." His hands, weak with outrage, flop back to the cat. He snuffs the clogged nose and coughs again. Then he thrusts out his hands and splays the fingers stiffly. "And when William draws the hands—gee!—they look like *rakes!*"

"I know. How ugly."—*Ah. This chorus all over again: the suffering of the artist at the mis-perceptions of the commoners.* "I saw one good picture, beside yours, yesterday. It was of a girl raking leaves. Who drew that?"

"Kitt."

Her heart quickens. She recalls Kitt. A civilized little girl with merry dark eyes under a mop of dark brown curls. "Someday when you're over this cold, shall we invite Kitt to come here and play with our clay and fingerpaints?"

The delicate hands droop forlornly on the afghan. "No. When we're standing in line for recess, you know what Kitt does?"

"What does she do?"

He coughs. "She always yanks the earflaps down on my cap—*real hard!*"

Willo strokes the pale curls. "But there are *some* nice children," she persists, as she pilots him through this choppy patch. "What's the name of the girl who gave you that big cherry lollipop for Valentine's Day?"

"Pam." He folds his hands benevolently.

"Yes, Pam." She rocks so zealously that the seasick Wookey disembarks and jumps to the sofa, where she tucks herself up neatly; and from this platform, she glowers at the aggressive Rocker.

Tad's eyes close...and with a steady dipping motion, Willo navigates this Vulnerability through the turbulent months ahead: She recalls Pam from last summer...*in the neighbor's yard...after that birthday party...Pam, high in that beech tree, her pink ruffled pants blooming like a peony and Max and Tad on a limb below...conferring and giggling and gazing up at that peony...the laughing Pam throwing leaves down into their faces....*She rocks and rocks and plans the invitation: *A new box of crayons and big sheets of colored paper...and cupcakes and juice....*She rocks and rocks and rocks towards this cove called "Pam."

They are wakened by a flash of light.

Melvin, in his pajamas, is standing across the room with his camera. "That big kid dangling off your little lap; I couldn't resist."

Tad whimpers, and Willo scowls.

"It's six-thirty. Sorry if I woke you. What's for breakfast?" The light flashes again, and the camera clicks. "He's as big as you are. If it turns out right, this shot will look just like Michelangelo's PIETA."

Lying in bed one summer night, Willo says, "That's a remarkable slide show you gave us this evening."

"Those of Max's birthday party are excellent, aren't they? I'll have duplicates made for Wendy and Pam," Melvin says.

"Good. Their mothers would appreciate that. Wendy in her hoola hoop looks like a Degas ballerina."

"Isn't she pretty? And Pam blowing the soap bubbles—how about those?"

"Mmmm. Those are idyllic." She places her hand on Melvin's shoulder. "And that sort of silhouette shot of Tad; he looks so slender, so remote, like a candle lit with that aura of pale curls."

"Those girls are darling. I'd like to photograph them some more."

"And such a poignant one where you caught Max's disappointment with his phonograph."

"That's realism for you."

"I can't help wondering: Are you sure you don't have any pictures of your brothers stored somewhere?"

"I'm sure."

"Not one?"

"Not one."

"Do our boys look like your brothers?"

"Max does." His voice guarded.

"Which one?"

"Like Lee. Exactly like Lee."

"Lee was the younger one?"

"Yes." The lips scarcely open. "Five years younger than I." The shoulder tense.

"What was Lee like?"

185

"Cute. Brilliant. A real performer."

"And the older brother?"

"Nelson."

"What was Nelson like?"

"A very nice guy. A good athlete." The lips almost sealed.

"And our boys don't resemble him?"

"No. Not at all."

"Did you have good times with Nelson and Lee?"

"Nelson was my pal. He was always standing up for me." The words hurrying ahead of the breathing like sandpipers caught in a sudden surf.

"Then when you were five, Lee was born. Did you play with him?"

"No. He was always in my mother's lap, or riding on my father's shoulders, or riding piggyback on Nelson." The words urged through closed teeth.

"It must be hard to be displaced."

"It wasn't that." The voice lodged in the throat. The shoulder like a stone.

"It must be hard to be the middle boy."

"It wasn't that."

"What was it?"

He reaches out to the radio and turns on the eleven o'clock news. She keeps her hand on his shoulder, like a poultice, during the news; slips her arm around him and gives the full length of her body to his side. His heart is galloping with the past as it has never galloped with the present. . . . He turns away from her.

Willo lies awake far into the night, her hand cold as a glass lense, her whole body cold as a metal camera that contains a coiled strip of still-life.

"Look!" calls Max. "The inside of this log is red as beefsteak!"

"My vivid son grows more vivid every day," Willo wrote in her letter to London last week.

"Come!" Max yells. He scuffs another damp log. "This one is orange as salmon."

Tad's fleecy head shows faintly through the rain-wet bushes. He does not turn in response to his brother's command.

"My pastel son grows more pastel," she wrote.

"There's a huge bracken on this tree—Oh, come see!" Max calls. "It's like a wooden salad bowl!"

The glow of pale curls dips towards the ground.

The underbrush crackles, and Max peers through. "Stones!" he scoffs. "You dodo! You've been collecting *stones* all summer in Arlington. Why don't you find something better to do in West Virginia?"

"Don't let Max be so bumptious," Melvin has been scolding her. She waits for Tad to defend himself. Silence.

"Stones are full of mystery," she offers. "Some contain fossils. Some contain gems." *"You're so pedantic with them,"* Melvin has also scolded.

Tad remains stooped.

"Tad has grown sad," she wrote. *"All winter his head lolled like an aster on a damaged stem; he carried that assignment of Roman numerals as if it were chiseled on a granite slab; my baby, at seven, scarred from school."* Willo lays her hand on the froth of curls. "Let's see, Tad, this one may be a fossil. Isn't this the print of a leaf?"

He does not answer. *"He's withdrawn,"* his teacher had

reproached her. *"He daydreams. He'll need speech therapy and remedial reading. By the way, is his father overseas?"*

His father is back in the cabin now, doctoring a headache with gin and tonic and THE WALL STREET JOURNAL and FINANCIAL TIMES and THE CHINA QUARTERLY and eight books on Zen and a collection of works by Camus and by Sartre. *"The radio report says it's going to rain again today,"* he warned them when they left the cabin. When they turned to say goodbye to him, he was invisible behind that stack of books. *"Melvin continues to be a Cipher,"* she wrote in that letter.

"Let's find a big flat rock where we can eat our lunch," she says to Tad.

It's Max, of course, who finds the rock, next to a brook. She spreads the food on the surface—hard boiled eggs, cheese, apples, raisins, peanuts, lemonade. Max grabs an egg and peanuts. Tad wanders off to the brook, takes off his Keds and wades, thin-legged as a crane.

"Something's gone wrong with Tad," she told Melvin last winter. *"The pediatrician didn't mention anything was wrong,"* Melvin said. She persisted: *"He scarcely eats. He sleeps poorly. He seldom talks. He's stopped drawing pictures. How can we help him?"* Without looking up from his book, Melvin said: *"Don't let Max be so bumptious."* —*Isn't that just like you?* she thought: *Turn down the exuberant one. Not: Turn up the discouraged one.*

Max is gobbling the eggs and the cheese. Tad is the timid animal who cannot eat in unfamiliar surroundings. *"All your devout mothering has just reproduced your own hang-ups,"* Melvin sneered.

Volleys of advice from the neighbors: *"You ought to join the Cub Scouts." "You ought to take those boys to Summer Bible School." "You ought to learn to drive a car; take them to the swimming pool." "Their father ought to take them to a baseball game."* YOU OUGHT TO: that Puritan refrain. She took driving lessons: ten, fifteen, twenty...flunked and flunked and flunked. *"My brain lacks the circuits,"* she sighed. Melvin took the boys to a baseball game. All three came home with headaches. The front window, like a T.V. set, showed fathers, all up and down the street, tossing balls to their boys; fathers and sons leaping with basketballs; fathers helping sons to ride two-wheelers; fathers and sons hitching boats to cars and driving off for a weekend together.... "Could you read them a story?" she asked Melvin. He tried; ten minutes: *"It hurts my throat."* —*Didn't your father ever play with you? Don't you remember what it was like to play with Nelson?* she wanted to ask. Instead, she said: *"Both our minds lack the circuits for a suburban summer."* Hence this August retreat into the mountains of West Virginia. But even the three-hour trip here warned that this was not going to be a panacea: *" 'Luray Caverns!' "* Max read on a sequence of signs. *"Oh, that's what I want to see!" "You don't want to see that junk,"* Melvin sniped. With determined cheer, Willo said: *"Yes, we do!" "I saw all the caves when I was a boy—even Carlsbad Caverns. You've seen one, you've seen them all." "YOU saw them,"* Willo continued, still on a playful note. *"WE didn't."* Melvin sped past the last sign. *"You haven't missed a thing,"* he growled.... She tried after that to point out the beautiful trees and the interesting old houses, but the faces of both boys were locked in scowls. Once more, the old porcupine had shot his quills into his sons.

A bright orange streak spurts across their view.
—*Oriole?*
"Wow!" says Max. "I thought that was a flower flying."

"A precocious boy," Max's teacher had told her. And just as Willo was beaming agreement, the teacher frowned: *"He hugs and kisses Wendy in the cloakroom."* —*Good!* Willo had thought: *He has a friend.* Then Wendy's irate mother on the phone: *"I'm afraid Max picked up some bad habits in that far-out English school."* As if it were contagious, Pam's angry mother on the phone: *"Ahm afraid Tad knows too much about guhrls. We don't want Pam to play with him, but we sure would like to take him to Sunday School—"* Willo had

received these reproaches stoically as a cat picks up burrs in its fur, but in the night, she has gnawed at these burrs: —*This aura of radiance that was kindled at that London hearth... that can find no hearth in Melvin... has it beckoned to my sons? "Melvin, I'm afraid the boys echo my tensions. I'm with them too much. They absorb all my attitudes. They need your more objective influence. They were so pleased when you started to teach them to play checkers." "Nonsense. You project your pleasure into the situation. They were bored stiff."* A few weeks later: *"Melvin, I need to see a psychiatrist again, just a few times, maybe." "You'd better get unhooked from that ridiculous fad."* And a few nights later: *"Melvin, I thought you said under Kennedy The Agency is becoming more HUMAN. I'd feel so much better if we could take the boys to a counselor, just for a check-up." "More HUMAN doesn't mean they're pampering the families of ex-spies and broken poetesses with psychotherapy."* So it has gone all year: Her supplications: His refusals. This tug-o-war.

She sighs. *LOVE, BE WITH ME NOW.*

A second orange spurt: *like a struck match* —or, she smiles: *like a flower flying.*

"You cannot step twice in the same river!" she calls to Tad. "A thousand years ago, in Greece, a man named Heraclitis said that."

A vague smile twitches at his lips.

"Because the water is *moving!*" Max hoots. "It's always *changing!* That's why you can't step twice in *exactly* the same river!"

"Right!" She tosses the word into Tad's cupped gaze.

"Don't let Max be so bumptious." As if it were merely the *brother's flamboyance that has dimmed Tad... not the father's sulk... nor the mother's loneliness... nor the teacher's platitudes... nor the neighbors' prudery... nor something genetic from one of those brothers or that father or even that mother whom Melvin keeps buried in silence....*

Max has gobbled three-fourths of the lunch. She puts aside some lemonade for Tad.

Sunlight blooms through the leaves. *—LOOK: WE'RE IN THE HEART OF A GREAT GOLDEN MEDALLION.* Tad tiptoes up to her, points towards a twitching clump of mountain laurel.

Sniffing, dabbling. . . twenty feet from them—a raccoon.

"It smells our lunch," Willo whispers.

The three of them arrange bits of apple and peanuts on the rock nearest the water. Then they ease quietly up to a higher rock. . . from which they peer down like eagles.

The raccoon enters, sniffs, takes the apple to the edge—to her baby. Two babies. The boys giggle.

After the raccoons have left, they emerge. Tad drinks a long draught of lemonade.

Above them the sky is a clean blue swath. A breeze rustles the sassafras trees.

"Look!" calls Max. "The trees are clapping their hands!"

Tad turns a reverent gaze to the trees. He takes another draught of lemonade.

—Yes, I'm a tigress. My only cure to our ills has always been to lead these two out into a wilderness-haven. She basks a long time in the heart of that great medallion, while the boys gather stones and shells and flowers.

When the sun is going down, they turn, bulged with treasures, towards the cabin.

That squab-silhouette is waiting at the screen door.

—My tall and tawny Love, you filled the whole doorway.

"Guess what, Dad?" Max calls out. "We saw a raccoon and babies. Their faces, gee! They looked like they were wearing great big black sunglasses!"

Melvin scowls. "Willo, don't you know we could all get hepatitis from those shells?"

She helps Tad arrange the shells on the porch. They wash their hands at the pump.

Melvin rattles the ice in the glass of gin and tonic. "It's late. I'm hungry." He sloshes the drink. "What a gross chair. It's given me a backache. That rinkydink lamp has given me a worse headache."

A whippoorwill calls. Another one answers him. Twilight.

At the table, Melvin keeps grumbling. "This hillbilly food knots my stomach."

Willo notices that Tad is lapping up his beans like a Campbell Soup kid.

The whippoorwills call. Back and forth. Each to each.

"I wish we could have a raccoon," says Tad.

" 'A thing belongs to the one who loves it,' " Willo tells him. "A German playwright named Brecht said that."

Tad grins.

Max says, "Ho!"

Melvin casts a sneer, which she translates: *pedantic teuton.* He rises from his scarcely-touched meal. . .walks back to his chair. . .and sinks away behind the four stacks of books.

—Four tombstones?

"I wish those raccoons would come to our cabin," says Max.

"Maybe they will," says Willo. "Why don't you two put a few peanuts and an apple outside your bedroom window?"

In bed, after the boys are asleep, Melvin says, "You seem chipper here in the boondocks. Is that what you want: to go back to being Poor?"

"I'm comfortable with simplicity."

"I despise it. I'm freezing. You're so warm."

"You've been sitting still for days. I've been hiking."

"The sheets are clammy."

She gets up and finds a soft, flannel blanket, which she tucks around him. Then she crawls back into bed and hugs his buntinged form close to her.

"God, I hope *someday* we can have a *civilized* vacation," he sighs. "Put the boys in a good camp, and just the two of us go to Paris, Rome, Copenhagen. Investments are paying off. We don't have to hole up like Thoreau."

"You should have married a middle-class girl."

He nuzzles her cheek, reaches for her breast.

192

—My big cranky baby, will you never be weaned?

The lush lips nibble at her throat. . . taste her nipples.

—Orphan. Jealous, guilty orphan.

He thrashes out of the bunting and pulls her up onto his seal-belly.

— You keep begging me to heal you.

He pulls aside her gown, and she guides his swollen organ into her warm slot.

—Sore Thumb. I am only the nurse who does her dull, dull duty.

Sitting with Melvin on the screen porch late one hot night, Willo says, "I wish I had handled Wookey's funeral better."

"What do you mean?"

"After we had buried her under the dogwood tree, I talked about her body decomposing into chemicals that would nourish the roots of the tree, and the roots sending the nourishment up the trunk and out into the limbs to the flowers, and the flowers transforming the food into beauty, and the beauty giving us pleasure each spring, the flowers and their scent attracting bees, the bees helping the flowers make seeds, and the seeds making new trees, and the new trees giving shade and beauty and comfort forever."

"That's a pretty good sermon."

"I wonder if it was. After I went into the house, the neighbor children came into the back yard, and for a while they all stood around the grave, talking softly. Then I heard them calling our children 'eggheads'...scoffing at their version of the cat's destiny...flaunting *souls,* tooting that Baptist heaven....Later, when our boys came into the house, their faces were full of tension. They scarcely touched their lunch, and they went separately to their rooms. They've avoided me all evening. I feel accused for my atheism."

"That's better than letting them regress to that medieval junk."

"I was wondering—I've read Zen haphazardly, not nearly so painstakingly as you have—would Zen offer a more comforting version of death than the one I gave?"

"Don't be ridiculous."

"I'm serious. It's important."

"Of course Zen doesn't offer anything more comforting."

She sighs. "I keep seeing those two stricken faces."

"Read them some funny stories tomorrow. Take their minds off the cat."

She shakes her head. "That's a cover-up. They'd see through it, hate it."

"Zen would teach them that all life is finite; that there's nothing beyond—Absolutely Nothing. They'd learn to accept The Great Void."

"It sounds stoical."

"It is. You take one day at a time. Enjoy it for what it offers."

"That's enough?"

"It has to be enough."

That tidbit on The Great Void which Melvin uttered a year ago glows like a garnet among the cinder-phrases he has muttered in eleven years of marriage. The aging kewpie who brings to the dinner table each evening his headache and colitis and no more vocabulary than "those dopes at the office"... "those clods at the Pentagon" is more like a creature who has crouched eight hours in a mine-shaft than a middle-aged scholar who has spent the day in a government office.

His peevishness seeps into Willo with his semen, and hours after he has drifted into that wined sleep, she consoles herself with memories of her other lovers. After sex, they had always talked. Nothing profound; just tender morsels fetched up from childhood. These tales had been essential to Willo, more essential by far, than the act of sex. —*Maybe it's a poet's form of prostitution,* she muses. *I used my body to suck out those precious monologues.*

Ben used to tell her about his boyhood in The Bronx: *"I was earnest and ambitious. I wanted to learn, learn, learn; embellish my mind, catch the attention of someone important. I begrudged the time wasted commuting to and from school. So I decided I'd use that interim for memorizing poetry. Can't you just see this pimply-faced Jewish kid hanging onto the strap in the subway, sweating, swaying back and forth in the crowd, and saying to himself: 'She walks in Beauty like the Night...'?"*

Clay, who had grown up on a farm in Nebraska, used to talk about fighting with his younger brother: *"My mother would wring her hands and say, 'Don't! Don't!' and I would go on punching my brother. Then my father would come home, glower at me, and say: 'Hey, Clay! Did you push*

196

Warren into the weir well again?' He'd roll up his sleeves and hit me whomp! whomp! whomp! Poor, ignorant people: They didn't know how to cope with sibling rivalry. . . . Then my sister Margaret came along, and as soon as she could toddle, Warren and I ganged up on her. She kept following us around. We hated that. We said: 'If you want to play with us, you'll have to stick your finger into this socket.' And she would do it. And she'd get a shock. Poor little tyke. She'd do anything to play with us, and we were just a couple of bullies."

"My father was a cantor in the synagogue," she could hear Sam saying. *"He was also hyper-conscientious. I identified with him; I still do. Every time a Jewish holiday approaches, I get a sore throat or diarrhea or pimples on my ass."*

—Ben? Clay? Sam? Are you good fathers to your imperfect children?

Even Ned had talked, not much after, but a great deal during those "warm-up walks" before sex. Just as Naomi was struggling against that Catholic background, so Ned was struggling against his Baptist boyhood in New Orleans. In that wheedling Southern voice that sounded much like Truman Capote's voice (and also something like Melvin's voice when she first met him), this debonair intern would mimic the squawkings and the hootings of the revival meetings. At the university, nearly everyone she knew was kicking over his religious background; some with rage; some with humor. Ned was the only one of her acquaintances who retained a shred. *"I believe in hants,"* he confessed to her. *"Hants?"* she asked. *"H-a-u-n-t-s. 'Ghosts' you northerners call them."* *"Not really?"* *"Yes, really! I've heard them. I've all but seen them."* Her mind at that time, thanks to Clay, was wrapped in a fresh foil of atheism-humanism that instantly deflected any ray of religion. Still, to humor her poor 'pupil,' she said: *"Do me a favor: If you should die before I do, pay me a call."* *"I will!"* *"That's a promise?"* *"That's a promise."* *"Don't scare me."* *"I can't promise not to scare you."*

197

"Well, tell me how you'll communicate. Then I'll be prepared." "No fair. I'll think of something appropriate when the time comes." Laughing, they had hugged and kissed like a couple of kids plotting a prank. . . . Again and again, Ned had returned to the subject: a strange one for an intern, yet not a strange one, perhaps, for a man who had been reared in a Southern household by a bevy of widowed ladies. Perhaps all this charming old-lady talk gave the clue to his failure to play a virile role in the sex-act.

In that voice rich and smooth as applebutter, Pete used to ladle out the story of her bizarre grandmother: *". . . a sort of gypsy-person. She went through five marriages in five countries. . . abandoned her children (one daughter for each marriage) early in life, usually by leaving them in expensive boarding schools. For a long while, no one heard from her. They assumed she must have died. Then one day my mother got a letter from her half-sister in Chicago. Sure enough, my grandmother, Louisa, had appeared at the door, broken in health, penniless, her clothes in tatters, and her daughter had to take her in. Then one night, at about midnight, our doorbell rang, and there she stood: a peculiar creature, like no one I've ever seen, like something out of the movies, and of course we took her in. She turned out to be a regular troubadour. In return for room and board and medical care, she doled out a pack of stories about her adventures, probably lies, but my God! They were entertaining!"*

—Pete? Do you have a woman? Or do you still prowl the beaches?

The vignettes are like a set of phonograph records which Willo takes out and plays one by one these lonely nights.

Melvin is her only lover who has never talked after sex. If she starts to talk, he grows annoyed. Twice, early in their affair, she had started to tell him about Pete, and he had cut her off with: *"Are you trying to make me sick?"* Another time, seeking a neutral subject, she had drifted into a discourse on kindergarten; how baffling the American culture had been to her at first, and then, with paints and crayons

198

and praises from the teacher, how exciting. *"If there's anything I hate,"* he had snarled, *"it's recollections from someone's childhood."* Always, without fail, after sex, Melvin would reach out and flip on the radio or the phonograph. Sometimes she would wait ten minutes, fifteen, thirty, for the noise to abate, like a pedestrian waiting on the curb for the green light, and the most then she could ever elicit from Melvin was a statement about a restaurant in Rome or a bookstore in London or an art shop in Tokyo—nothing revealing, just the name of the place and *"It was great. You should have been there."* About as inspiring as a price tag hung on a piece of furniture. "Inarticulate" you'd call it in an ordinary person, but in a man who had traveled on three continents and had put in a decade at leading universities, how would you classify this lack?

When the radio or the phonograph had failed to quench her need for intimate conversation, Melvin would interrupt her with: *"Let's go to a movie."* And they would get up and dress and for the next few hours the actors in a Swedish film or an Italian film would feed her curiosity. . . . If they had seen all the good movies, he would say, *"Let's go to a bookstore"* or to the art shop or to the record shop or the camera shop or the wine shop and again they would wander out into the campus town and for the next hour or two, Melvin would open his plump wallet and buy and buy and buy, and she would stand around fidgeting. If she would reach out to examine a book or a print, which she rarely did, Melvin would smile and whisper to her, as to a child, *"You don't want that junk, Honey."* He would select a book on foreign cooking for her. She'd thank him, try not to fidget, and after what would seem like half a day, they would return to his apartment laden with packages.

Over and over again, Melvin had flung her out onto this tangent. Over and over again, she had allowed herself to be flung. In those early days, she had generously placed his reticence on the plane of monastic Zen silence. What an illusion. Then for another phase she had cradled it in pathos:

199

a numbness, she told herself, from all those bereavements. Next, she had scolded herself for comparing him with the gifted Jewish talkers. Next, she had attributed it to his training in intelligence work, cryptography. It had not occurred to her until recently that it could have been *guilt, shame.* After all, when he met her, when he started sleeping with her, he was still very much a Catholic in his emotions; maybe she had been like a prostitute to him. —Or maybe she over-emphasized this facet of his personality. Maybe his family were simply non-talkers. They were acquisitive; they bought their entertainment: restaurants, plays, travels, wines, cars, cameras, phonographs, movies, books. *—Now I am custodian to their clutter.*

Here in suburbia, Willo has learned, Melvin's conversational crippling is far from unique. Nearly all the housewives speak the same stale, pompous doggerel. She had expected the middle class to speak more like university people. Wrong. Their language is but a slight improvement over the loutish working class language of her childhood. "YOU OUGHT TO—" She has come to cringe at that phrase. "YOU OUGHT TO—" That hook they keep flinging to her, as if to haul her out of her helplessness, out of her hauteur. *"YOU OUGHT TO come shopping with me for some plush carpeting and some nice nylon drapes." "YOU OUGHT TO get your family a backyard barbecue." "YOU OUGHT TO watch this television show." "YOU OUGHT TO come along with me next time and drop the kids off at this new place while we two go shopping."* And the place would turn out to be an area of chrome and plastic, where a series of coins in a series of slots dumped forth a series of gimmicks for temporary distraction. Worst of all was Beverly Cain, thrusting those Sunday School papers into her hand: *"YAWL OUGHT TO teach those boys about God! YAWL OUGHT TO teach them the meaning of Christmas! Why, my kids said Max and Tad don't even know about the crucifixion!"* And she, Willo, would smile politely and say "thank you."

There is a small category of more perceptive housewives

who talk of P.T.A. and community projects, but Willo, who is still aching with her own problems and with the problems of her children, has no energy left over for altruism. She is like a calipers: one Olympian-prong, one gutter-prong. At the moment of encounter, she measures each neighbor with a quick nip, then the relationship rolls away through her hollow middle. . . .

Across the street, next to the Cains, there is a new family, the Deans. Gertrude Dean, tall, blonde, aloof, appears to be Scandinavian. Her careful syntax and her precisely chosen vocabulary reveal a more reflective outlook than Willo has encountered for a long time; but she avoids Gertrude simply because Max despises her son Frank, who is in Max's grade at school.

Far, far into the night and even into the morning, while she walks around the house, with that slug's trail drying on her inner thigh, Willo takes more phonograph records out of her memory. Here is a record where she has described to her psychiatrist her suffering at those cocktail parties, where she was trying to adhere to Melvin's instructions for proper comments on the recent war, Truman, Eisenhower, The Marshall Plan. *"My instinct is to talk to conceal the fact that I cannot eat,"* she says. *"But even that fails: I find myself censoring all the spontaneous remarks, all the puns, all the imagery, until at last there emerges from my lips that little pastel pouf my husband wants."* The psychiatrist laughs: *"He sounds like the typical American male. He's intimidated by the bright woman. He feels safer with the doll."* She plays a second record: The psychiatrist is laughing and saying: *"I think in language you are a kind of tennis player. Your husband plays croquet."*

She had laughed with him. She cannot laugh now. Because the language-drought has reached Tad. It's closing in on him very fast. His words are withering. His gestures are withering. —*Is it a genetic flaw? What if words, spoken and written, are as agonizing for him as they are for my mother? He's a Leo, like her. . . . Or is he imitating his father?* She has watched Tad for evidence that intelligence has taken a non-verbal turn. Does he make things with his hands? Does he listen to music? Does he read? Is he sociable? Is he athletic? The answer is always NO. He is becoming a cipher.

She has tried to rescue him. With her own questions, she has invited him, coaxed him, to talk. She has listened to him. Listened and listened and praised him. It is as strenuous as diving for pearls, and far less rewarding. Now she has given up. It's a dormancy, she has told herself, a natural plateau ...or maybe the numbness is a retreat from her ambitions for him...a retreat from Max's bullying...a retreat from school...or maybe it is a flight towards an inner treasure.

But the more she observes Tad, the less talent she has for wishful thinking. Something tells her Tad has become the receptacle for Melvin's unshed grief...that unless someone helps Tad NOW, that trapped grief will back up into this frail boy, as it has backed up into his father, where it lodges as those headaches and those aching shoulders and that colitis and that crankiness.

—Oh, Love, help me with Tad!

Another record begins to play: *"—but you chose this remote man. It's as if you were saying you were not worthy of a communicative husband and father."*

—Yes. Unworthy. Wound for wound: His talking phobia to balance off my eating phobia. As if the center of me, the poet, needed this prison, sought this troll. I was born into a prison. I've always been guarded by a troll. First, my mother. Then Pete. Then Melvin. And within this cell, I perform my specialty: When the language grows hot in my mouth, Beverly Cain, and backs up into my throat, I handle it like a hank of hot taffy. I fold it   slap   slap   slap   back upon itself. I fold it and fold it and clack it and clack it and cool it and chop it into poems: "Crucifixion? I spell it c-r-u-c-i-F-I-C-T-I-O-N...."

One morning in November, Willo wakes, heavy with sadness. Stoically, she gives the family their breakfasts; and when they have gone to school and to the office, she takes her Sadness for a walk.

Up and down the streets, wherever she wanders, every lawn seems to be thrusting chrysanthemums to her   yellow ones   rust   white   pink   copper   bronze   lush ones, scrawny ones   everywhere, everywhere these flowers looking up into her downcast face. —*Daddy, oh my daddy, I see you walking down the railroad tracks with your black dinnerpail under your arm...your tired face...your little black coffin ....Daddy, I never said goodbye.*

Everywhere   everywhere on the green lawns these chrysanthemums. There, clumped like a white sleeping cat   there, crouched like a bronze tiger   large single ones fluffy and wistful as kittens. Every lawn has put them forth today like flags for The Fourth of July. —*Daddy, oh my daddy, I feel weak. That postponed goodbye is running out of my veins, undoing me, like yarn reeling from a dropped stitch....*

Everywhere, too, on the ground, whispering to her feet, fallen oak leaves —tan, rust, bronze...fingering her feet, like hands...—*Daddy, oh my daddy, through a mist, through a fragrance, I see you walking ahead of me   slow   thin   sedate   like a heron on a distant shore.   Years   years back before the school years, I think, you and Lester walked ahead...Maybelle and I behind   through sun-dappled woods   and Lester handed Maybelle a big oak leaf   and handed me a big oak leaf   and Maybelle laughed and said: "See, Mina! It's a hand!"   and we fluttered the leaves and giggled, "hands! hands!"   waved the leaves and giggled*

203

*"bye bye   bye bye" and you and Lester turned and laughed
and waved bye bye   bye bye   and you and Lester walked
ahead of us   not talking much   stopping now and then to
touch a tree trunk or some moss or a rock or to look up at the
clouds. . . . We came to a pond, and there was a rowboat   and
Lester lifted me into the boat   and you lifted Maybelle into
the boat   and Lester rowed slowly out into a carpet of
waterlilies   and we felt them pulling at the boat   heard them
whispering to the bottom of the boat   a whole family of
flowers tugging and whispering and murmuring   and Daddy,
you leaned over and pulled up—squeak!—a huge white
flower trailing a stem like a green snake and you gave it to me
and you leaned over again and pulled again—squeak!—we
laughed—another huge white flower trailing a green stem like
a snake and handed it to Maybelle   oh, huge white flowers
waxy as candles   serene as stars   glistening with drops of
water   and we drifted and drifted in silence   and Daddy, you
pointed to the shore where a tall gray bird was walking slowly,
carefully, and you whispered "Heron."   and we drifted and
drifted   the flowers in our small laps like wide waxy saucer-
candles   the yellow centers glowing like flames   the stems
dangling like snakes between our pale little legs   and we
laughed because we felt brave   and we drifted in the fragrance
of the flowers   swallowed the thick fragrance like honey   and
grew languid with the fullness   and we watched the heron
walking and listening and walking   and when he flew away,
Maybelle called, "Heron! Heron!"   and because Maybelle was
pretty and her voice was a warble I called with her, "Heron!"
and after a while you said, "He went home." And Lester
started rowing back slowly slowly and Maybelle and I looked
into the faces of the flowers in our laps   into the flowers that
were like dolls with faces   and Maybelle told her flower,
"He went home."   and I told my flower, "He went home."
With each stroke of the oars, we chanted, "He went home."
Like a lullaby. "He went home."   And then Mamma was
snatching me and snapping: "Yer hands are cold! Yer shoes
are muddy! You didn't have yer lunch!"   But I was full,*

Daddy, I was full of lily and perfume and peace. . . .
    *—Daddy, oh my daddy, now I remember: It's the eleventh
anniversary of your funeral.   Here, eleven years late comes
my grief   pulled up squeaking on a slippery green snake-stem
dripping perfume   my wet waxy white waterlily with its glad
golden eye   I'll hurry home and transplant it in a poem. . . .*

She has been writing the poem nearly an hour when Melvin
drives into the garage and hurries into the kitchen: "They've
shot Kennedy. . . . Turn on the radio. . . . In Dallas. . . ."

"My mind is filling up with poems," she tells Melvin.

"Waldorf salad? I was hoping for something exotic to go with the rest of that chablis."

Every single day since the assassination, he has come home for lunch "to get away from those long-faces in the cafeteria and all their sentimental talk."

"Given some solitude," she says, "I think I could write again."

He smiles blandly. "I thought I had rescued you from that bleeding-hearts phase of your college days. I hope there's some cheese pie left over from dinner."

—*Oh, little white attic. Apples. Peace.*

"Can you massage my neck, Honey? Right there. This is what the wives do in Japan...and my shoulders...."

"Every time my Muse drops a morsel into my begging bowl, Melvin snatches it..." she will write to her psychiatrist.

"It's just beginning to feel good." He reaches behind him, unbuttons her blouse. "Close the blinds, Honey...ah... lock the doors."

—*"Yet because he lost his brothers before the nation lost this Brother, I dare not deny him...."*

She tries to nudge him: "Don't you ever get engrossed in a project at work, Melvin? So many men—in fact, most of them—often work evenings in the office and on weekends."

"The rat race, you mean?" That bland smile. "Or hanky panky? No thanks."

Noontimes, she grows petulant over that stove. "I do need that chunk of solitude," she sighs.

"It's just a matter of organization. Is there some chocolate cake left? You keep frittering away your time on the boys. Make a schedule. Reserve a block of time for writing."

She tries: Mornings, after the three have left the house, she settles in a chair, blinds drawn, notebook in lap—
The phone rings. It is always Melvin: "Has the mail arrived?" "Did you send my suit to the cleaner's?" "I have a headache. I think I'll come home." "I'm catching a cold. I'll be home in an hour."

She tries not answering the phone: He rushes home in a panic.

"Poetry isn't some dinky hobby I can put down and pick up, like crocheting."

"I hate to see you getting so hooked. First it's the babies. Then it's those tranquilizers. Then it's that doctor. Now this. Just when I thought you were becoming a normal wife."

—*"You're a poet. You'll sublimate a lot."*

The poem shatters into shards, which she bundles into a letter to her psychiatrist: ...*I've been watching Melvin side-step the big painful emotions. "My two brothers died when I was nine," he told me long ago. "My father, when I was ten; my mother, when I was eighteen. I WENT ON AS IF NOTHING HAD HAPPENED." Of my relationship with Pete, he said: "As far as I'm concerned, IT NEVER HAPPENED." I'm forming a clear image of him at age nine, being enticed by that grief-numbed mother into an easy chair. At age ten, that easy chair had become a sort of womb into which she siphoned, steadily, steadily, books and music and gourmet foods. . .until at age eighteen, when she quit the scene, he was a kind of giant fetus.*

* *

She tries again: "Could you go alone to those parties? They're such a torment to me. As soon as we enter the room, my cerebellum shrieks that warning. Like an addict, I swallow the sherry. My high heels skewer me to the floor. Strands

207

of cigarette smoke spiral around me, and I become that caged bird cheeping pleasantries to those cowish Catholic wives. Surely, I'm no credit to you."

"You are. I ask so little; just put in an appearance for my sake."

And recently, contributing more than her share of smoke-strands to Willo's cage, is a new secretary, a plump young woman whose green eyes dart beneath stiff copper bangs, whose cheeks are clamped between two sharp wedges of copper hair suggestive of a burnished helmet, suggestive, too, of the spit-curls of the flapper era. Her mannerisms bounce jarringly between the belligerent and the silly: the flurry of grabs into her low-cut dress to discipline a black strap...the pluckings at the lace hem of the slip...the tugs at the thigh of the black mesh hose...all to the tune of phrases spurted from the corner of the tight slot-mouth: *"And I said to him: 'Get lost, Buddy.' "... "It's a lousy place, no kiddin."... "That jerk's barkin up the wrong tree."*

"I don't think I can endure another performance of that frigid floozie shuttling back and forth between Titillation and Ridicule," says Willo.

"Sally? She has a string of babies like a stepladder. She's married to a good-for-nothing cop. Poor Sally."

What Willo cannot say to him is that the worst part of those parties is to witness him, her short scholar, boozing himself into that pseudo-sociability. After a few drinks, his head starts bobbing like a cork on rough waters, as he nods agreement to the tall guys from the Pentagon.

"I see other husbands at those parties without their wives," she says.

"They're divorced, or predators."

"Not all of them."

"Those: Their wives are dumpy."

*   *

She sharpens her claws: "Could you take the boys somewhere? Maybe a trip to Williamsburg?"

"You know your babies wouldn't go anywhere without you." Mumbled without even looking up from his book.

"I think they'd like to go with you to the Smithsonian to see rocks and minerals, or to the children's performance at The Arena Stage, or even to the library."

He turns up the hi-fi.

She asks herself: —*If these were daughters, could I teach them to give a dinner party? to play bridge? to make a dress or drapes or slipcovers? The answer is NO.*

She sharpens her claws again: "If only I could have a rest from cooking meals now and then. Could you take the boys to a drive-in?"

"Drive-ins are so vulgar."

"To a Chinese restaurant, then?"

"Only if you come along."

"My phobia has returned in full force because I'm so tense these days. I'm afraid I'd transmit my affliction to the boys."

"Well, I won't take them to a restaurant without you. I'd look just like one of those divorced fathers....You know Sally, the secretary? She told me you're built just like a Barbie doll. Let's go buy you a slim dress."

It's like clawing a bowl of water.

Inspiration: Solitude: Max understands: "Sure, I've had it a few times. When everyone else in the house was asleep, and I'd been listening to a certain music—gosh!"

He cannot tell more, as a boy who has found a cave will not lead another person to it for a while.

Tad understands: "When I was getting well after chicken pox," he says shyly, "and again, after that strep throat—just lying there so quiet—gee."

—*Ah. The rendezvous with an inner call, after all?*

Melvin, of all people, should understand: he, who treats himself nearly every evening to hours of reading...hours of music.

"Please, it's no joke," she tells him. "Everything I give to others is subtracted from my poetry. I do need that tunnel of solitude. I do need your help in clearing away the domestic bric-a-brac."

"With Zen, you can create your own tunnel in the midst of Times Square."

"I've tried. I'm afraid I can't teach it to myself."

"I can. I've never had any trouble concentrating."

"You're lucky. Maybe it has something to do with that natural insulation: Fat."

"Maybe."

—*"Luxury makes the esthete,"* I read somewhere. *"Hardship makes the artist."* "Or maybe it's a lot easier to *take* from the printed page than to give to a *blank* one."

That bland smile: "Let's go buy you a gorgeous dress."

"Come back and guard my solitude," she had written to him in Japan. Now she will write to her psychiatrist: *"He stalks my solitude as another husband would stalk his wife's secret lover."*

During summer vacation, she teaches the boys to cook their own breakfasts.

"Look, Tad!" Max boasts. "I made scrambled eggs and toast."

"So what?" says Tad. "I made my bed."

When Max tells his father of their accomplishment at lunch, Melvin snarls, "Willo, you ought to be ashamed of yourself: teaching your sons to act like girls!"

She bristles. "It's so pathetic to be anxious about whether an activity is masculine or feminine."

"You speak straight from that Ivory Tower." That old whine has returned to his voice. "I've shielded you from the *real* world, where, believe me, boys do *not* cook and make beds."

—*You speak straight from that Catholic enclave. A New Age has dawned: My psychiatrist cooks every weekend. Censored.* She dares not diminish this already diminished man in

210

the presence of his sons.

Thus, the boys believe their father. From now on, they will be wary of this mother who nearly succeeded in tricking them.

Willo clacks this resentment, too, back into herself. —*Someday I will chop it into poems.*

"All right. So you want to write some poems," Melvin says one day. "If you can think of something sensible, I'll cooperate."

"Could you find a hobby of your own?"

"Sure."

He pursues her with that camera. The film, like a proboscis, plunges into her every gesture, licks up her every glance.

Her laundry room is confiscated for his darkroom.

Likewise, the kitchen sink: "Wash it very clean, Honey. I need it immaculate for processing film."

Likewise, the kitchen table: "Can you clear it all off, Sweets, and then spread some thick towels on it for blotting the pictures?"

Likewise, the bathroom: "Don't use it for an hour or two. I'm drying a strip of film on the shower rod."

Likewise the dining room table: "Can you place the meal somewhere else? I need the electric warmer for drying the blotted pictures."

Her Beauty, which bloomed afresh for Other Love, and only for Him, is turned by Melvin into a hundred pressed flowers. . .two hundred. . .three hundred. . .which he misers away into a locked filing cabinet.

"Could you try a hobby that doesn't involve me?" she asks.

He buys more stereo equipment, more records, new loudspeakers. Beethoven, Handel, Schoenberg, Bartok bay after her reverie as hounds after a fox, and again her shiny metaphors shatter into shards.

211

"Could I go away for a weekend—to a motel, maybe?"

Still not looking up from his book, still speaking in that bland tone: "A motel is more vulgar than a drive-in. Who would believe you were there to write poetry?"

"No one would know. I'd never leave the room. I'd live on apples and raisins and soybeans and water."

"The manager would know. He'd have a peep-hole."

"C.I.A. has made you paranoiac."

"That's not at all farfetched. The manager would have a peep-hole."

"All he would see would be a woman writing poems."

"I couldn't let you do such a thing."

"But why not?"

"Because I love you."

"If you loved me, I'd feel it. I'd be happy."

He scowls, like a surgeon who has botched a lobotomy, but expertly, that smile erases the scowl. "Come, let's go see that Swedish film."

The darkened cinema becomes, for Willo, that beloved London room. On the screen, a tall, tawny man looks out of the window into the mist. A small, pensive woman speaks, and Willo infuses her own soliloquy into the melancholy foreign tongue: *"It's a contest: Every time I open an issue, Melvin slams it shut. Is that the Libra-evasiveness? Is it the Puritan-squeamishness? Is it the C.I.A. cunning? Is it the bluffing which the short man brings home from the male world to his shorter wife? Is it the hinge from those massive bereavements? Or is it something in me that invites all this deprecation?"* The tall man ponders, sighs, and Willo endows him with: *"It's all that. Maybe the time has come to confront him."*

Those lunch hours at home stretch into two hours. "Work is slack. Morale is shattered," he tells her. "The others are out boozing in restaurants." He is always in that easy chair, reading, listening to music, snoozing.

She draws a chair up beside him. "For fifteen years," she says, "you've been reading those Zen books. Have you ever tried zazen?"

"I don't need zazen. I get my *satori* from reading."

"Somewhere I read about the truth behind myths: Man was driven from Eden after eating from The Tree of Knowledge. Maybe that means that incessant reading sets up a mental pattern which is contrary to the one zazen induces."

His hand darts out to turn up the button of the stereo.

She places her hand on his knee. "You're more *numb* than *serene,* Melvin: like a patient in an oxygen tent, inhaling music and printed words rather than the facts. Don't you think you need some help from a Zen master?"

"Nonsense. I've never felt better." He eases off his shoes and lays his feet in her lap. "Massage my feet."

Every day it grows more apparent to the neighbors that some kind of troll is holding the hungry waif captive in the Sanders house. With Christian zeal, they attempt to nourish her:

"Don't coop yourself up in that house all day," wheedles Beverly Cain. "Yawl come to Little League practice with us tomorrow."

"Come to the meeting of den mothers," croons Mrs. Do-It-Yourself Kit. "Both your boys need the scouts."

"Come on over. I'll teach yawl to play bridge."

Willo averts a finicky face from these gross goodies.

Only one neighbor is not hawking hospitality: "Excuse me for being unneighborly," says Gertrude Dean. She speaks slowly, out of a pale, melancholy face. "I'm Norwegian. Trying to adjust to this country, and having a problem-son are just too much for me. The only talking I do these days is to a psychiatrist."

"Good for you," Willo says.

She invites Tad for a walk along the canal.

"Only if Max does not come along," he bargains.

On the towpath, she points out huge wood chips under-foot; calls Tad's attention to the loud tapping overhead. "A pileated woodpecker, I think," she whispers; stops to listen to its assertive *chuck chuck chuck;* spots it at last high on a dead sycamore. "Huge as a prehistoric bird," she whispers. "—and red-crested and tailored in black and white like a character costumed for a ball or for the theatre."

Tad winces and turns his face from her. A delicate face,

startling in its girlish beauty.

Hopping from rock to rock, she leads him through the woods to an island where smooth gray beech trunks and rough tulip poplar trunks straddle the creek like a line of giants wearing ivory ankle bracelets.

"Beavers gnawed those," she says.

He does not answer. He recoils from her exactly as she recoils from her well-meaning neighbors.

At the Saturday night cocktail party, too, the hungry waif within the Barbie doll is apparent to everyone. The robust women in their bouffant Jackie Kennedy coiffures exude long spoons of cigarette smoke filled with their admonitions:

"If you're looking for a high-class school, don't be fooled by Montgomery County."

Their heads draw closer together, they lower their voices, and in short baby-spoons of cigarette-breath, they offer Willo these tidbits: "That's the egghead section. . . . My neighbor moved there. She's real bright, and she wanted a more brainy school for her kids. . . . Well, the very first month, this nice curly-headed boy with those big dark eyes kept asking her kid over to his house after school, and they thought: *oh, good, a friend right away!* . . . and guess what? They found out that 'nice boy' was hugging and kissing their boy."

"Doesn't that just make you *sick?*"

"Jews!—"

They withdraw from the huddle long enough to chug-a-lug more of those bloody Marys. Then they light up fresh cigarettes, draw together again, and in slow, sleepy voices, ladle out more motherly advice:

"I don't see how anyone can raise children without The Church."

The Barbie doll pipes up: "Some people like Zen."

"*Zen?* Our priest warned us about that one. He said he feels so sorry for these people who are led astray by those far-out religions."

Enter Sally, the copper-haired secretary, flushed from Sat-

215

urday overtime. She pats her lacquered coiffure, stuffs her brimming flesh into her decollete dress, scritches her cigarette lighter, and procedes to exude a series of smoky forks impaled with the morsels: "...He'd better not get any funny ideas....You think I'm kiddin?...He'll get his face slapped...."

Willo sips her sherry and allows a sphinx-smile to seep into her lips.—*Oh, Ladies, I envy you: Your Enemy is so specific. Mine is so diffuse.*

Willo retreats to the towpath, this time with Max. He is taller than his mother now, and his shoulders are growing broad and manly. They come upon a tree that holds in its high crotch a series of black loops, shiny as wet tar.

"Three snakes?" she guesses.

"Two?" His voice is deepening.

They watch the loops reel themselves, slowly, opulently, into a hole in the tree—one snake!

"Like a spine, crawling," she whispers.

"Like a bowel, moving," he laughs.

—*He's too charming. I must let him go. But how? To whom?*

Longing for someone, like Pete, who will release her again like a genie out of this suburban jug, she wanders to Gertrude, who is in her back yard, raking leaves. Frank is there, too, wandering about among the trees.

"I kept him home from school because he's running a slight fever," Gertrude explains.

Willo translates: *I kept him home because the kids at school keep picking on him.* The boy, who is very tall and very blond, moves about in a slow, shambling gait, his long limbs flopping slackly, like a rag doll's.

"Hi, Frank!" Willo calls.

He looks at her, as if dazed, out of pale bubble-eyes, and a shaft of pity shoots through Willo's ribs.

She talks a while with Gertrude about autumn, the schools,

and Gertrude says, "Living in this area is so hard for an inner person. My psychiatrist understands that very well. He suggests—just for a try—Boy Scouts for Frank."

As Willo leaves Gertrude's yard, a station wagon pulls up to the curb, and out of its front window emerges, like the face on a T.V. commercial, the handsome face of Beverly Cain. "Hey! Billy Graham will be in town Tuesday through Friday. How about yawl going with us to receive his message?"

She drives off, dragging behind her that cumbersome vehicle stuffed with those three convict-faced sons, two adolescent daughters in orthodontic braces and a black spaniel and a guitar and bags of groceries.

—Like a surinam toad with her family packed into pores all over her back.

Monday evening, shopping, as is her habit, at the least crowded time in the supermarket, while Melvin browses in the record shop next store, Willo faints.

After Melvin gets her home and onto the sofa, her words float in a monotone out of her white face: "My affliction is upon me again."

Melvin makes a squeamish scowl. "You don't know how I hate to hear that."

She continues in that stunned tone. "The other shoppers became surinam toads...hawks...predators of all sorts, and I was the little bird, the prey."

He sighs. "I don't want to hear about it."

But she persists. "Then my teeth turned to fangs. My fingernails turned to claws."

"You know I can't stand that silly talk."

"A psychiatrist wouldn't find it silly." *—Yes, hectoring mothers, conspiring sisters...and just as I was about to claw back and bite them, I fainted.*

"Haven't you ever tried will power?"

"Many times. It fails."

217

"How about throwing it all away, like you throw away my headaches?"

"I can't do it for myself. I need someone to do it for me."

He sighs. "You're so hot on having *me* do zazen. How about *you* doing it?"

"I'm too nervous to sit still."

"That's just the point. Zazen would train you to sit still. Maybe it would slow down that imagination of yours."

"I've read up on zazen in three of your books, and I'm going to try it," she tells Melvin the following Monday. "But for now, I cannot, I *will* not, go back into that grocery store."

"Don't be ridiculous."

"You don't understand, Melvin. I'm carrying a caged beast inside me. I can't take it back into that store."

Melvin wipes his wrinkled brow. "All right. You've conned me into your job. Hand me the grocery list."

As soon as he leaves the house, she goes into the bedroom, closes the door, and seats herself on the floor, like an isosceles triangle, and begins her zazen. She takes a deep breath... concentrates on the breath within her belly...a golden orb ...lets the breath out...concentrates on it going out...a golden spray...in out in out golden orb golden spray....

Willo rushes from Max's room, hugging a cream-colored sprawl that dangles opulently as a stole of ermine pelts. "The long underwear!" she gasps. "He didn't wear it!"

"That's nothing," says Melvin. He is at the dining room table, playing gin rummy with Tad.

Her tormented gaze tugs Melvin's gaze to the window of swirling snow.

"Don't fret," Melvin scolds. "Bake us a chocolate cake."

"Chocolate cupcakes with chocolate icing," pipes Tad.

Willo forces her way through the recipe. —*Do it for Tad. It's the first time in years that he's requested food.* She leans twice against the oven door, hoping Max's legs will soon be soothed by the heat of a campfire.

While the cupcakes are baking, she wanders back to Max's room, hugging the soft garment. Making the bed, she moves among objects suddenly raw with life: green chameleons relishing pearl mealworms in pink mouths...a dented trumpet...voluptuous auburn guitar...butchered golf ball... rocket...math book bearing a penned blasphemy along its soiled side...two toenail clippings like smiles on the brown tile floor.

She pats the underwear, nests it carefully into a drawer; thermal knit, double seat, reinforced knees; the best she could find; purchased for this Boy Scout overnight with Gertrude, who had bought two for her Frank, an enuretic. Poor Frank. What a contrast this room is to his room, which Gertrude showed her last week: an easel asquirm with an orange sunset, shelves full of doll-like figures of soldiers and Indians, a bed full of cloth animals dominated by a giant green velour dinosaur.

Here, on Max's nightstand, the class picture, in color: Max, center of the trio of tall boys in the back row, his generous roof of russet hair, his pink face, those navy blue Tartar eyes, that grin—glowing like a cathedral window. *"A leader,"* his teacher told Willo last month. *"A leader?"* his father had scoffed. *"A smart aleck,"* another teacher labeled him last year. From the neighbors: *"He knows too much about girls." "I'm glad my kids are average. I wouldn't know how to handle a whiz like that Max." "Smart? Sure he's smart. Let's hope he's smart enough to stay out of jail."* The yeas. The nays. The applause. The hisses. Always this turbulence around Max. Always this American uneasiness with that male vitality which the teachers in England had laughingly characterized as *"full of beans."* As for his participation in Boy Scouts, the approval was unanimous; here, at last, was the multi-vitamin capsule for every aspect of his personality that was out of control: *"Boy Scouts? Good! Now he'll learn something about God and his Country!"*

She sighs. He is her John F. Kennedy, her paradox, her brawny boy with the flimsy lining. She knows his inner pain, membrane by membrane, from faulty sinuses to gut-loneliness, as well as a diver knows an erratic coral reef....And there, in the school photo, at the end of the middle row, drooping, doltish, more like a puppet than a boy, nearly propped up by the teacher, is Frank Dean. —*Poor Frank,* Willo had mused, as she stood in his room last week. The awkward boy had brought her up hard against the narrow limits of her own compassion. She found it difficult to like him, just as she had found it difficult—no, impossible—to like Casey and Milo and Sikes and Agnes and her own mother and her slow-witted classmates and the damaged marines and the prosaic women of the neighborhood and at the C.I.A....even her own husband, at times. *"Snub him and you'll give birth someday to the worse-looking freak you ever saw."* Mamma's warning still grates like a pebble stuck in the gears of her earliest memories. Perhaps it is fortunate that she had been "barred" from the teaching profession;

perhaps she would have had nothing but scorn for all those children who could not fetch up a phrase like *"Sticks grow on trees."* or *"The raccoon is wearing huge sunglasses."* Perhaps her lifelong snobbishness was about to be "punished" through Tad. Poor, fading, receding Tad.... Washed by wave after wave of contrition last week, she had reminded Gertrude of her own stupidities: her inability to drive a car, her total lack of talent at entertaining guests, or at being a guest; surely these were awful blemishes in her intelligence. She had said to Gertrude: *"These Americans, who click along so swiftly in obedience to their technology, are not worthy to judge your Frank. Maybe he's unfolding, developing, according to a slow, Northern rhythm. Maybe he's another Hans Christian Anderson."*

The buzzer signals the completion of the cupcakes.

Melvin and Tad, savoring their indoor-status, assemble logs in the fireplace. Willo, spreading icing on the soft brown mounds, lets her gaze loop over to Dean's house, which dims and dims behind the thickening veil of snow.

The morning passes. The afternoon. The evening. The night.

In bed, beside the placidly-breathing Melvin, she envisions Max's purplish legs, like frozen turkey drumsticks, raw red throat, red whorls of cochlea conducting fever to the brain.

Into this dread, she coaxes the comfort of that London hearth, invokes the kindness of that London voice. But hearth and voice fail to bloom. Instead, she envisions Tad, two years hence, collapsing under the male-initiation rite.

Slowly, painstakingly, so as not to disturb Melvin, she arranges herself flat on her back, arms and legs straight and slightly spread, for a session of lazy zazen. Her belly, scarcely a meniscus in the shallow bowl of her hips, becomes a wallaby pouch. Into this pouch, she draws an orange glow... holds the glow until it swells to an oval...to an orb. Exhales a shower of sparks. Again: orange glow   oval orb. Her lungs her whole torso become a bellows   and she exhales a swish of

221

sparks. Orange hearth   bellows   swirl of flames.

"The Best is Enemy of the Good." It's not the London voice. It's Sam. Sam, warning her, in the words of Voltaire, that her dream-ideal shields her from flesh and blood humanity.

She inhales more orangeness, expands it with the bellows ...exhales it. She sees herself, as a tot, running from her mother's mediocrity...as a small schoolgirl running from her uncles' shame...as a pubescent girl running from her sister's dullness...from her father's fanaticism...running and running to that Golden Man...that teacher who would feed her from his strong green-veined hands....The thirty-three-year-old woman running to the calm Golden Man-Woman from whom she would be reborn....That Golden One who would nourish her from sweet orange-lungs...and guide her into Goldenness...running, always, always running towards The Golden One, who would lift her—Oh, Please!—out of the muddy mire of her own mediocrity....

"The Best is Enemy of the Good," Sam repeats, like a teacher holding up a flash card.

—*And my aversion to my family has stained Beverly Cain and Sally and even Melvin. "Refined" my mother used to call me, apologetically. She meant "proud." Pride is the first sin, say the Christians....I recoil, maybe not simply because I am proud, but because I can't bear for these people to contaminate my talent; my fragile talent which I've carried so many years, as a worried mother carries a very delicate baby. My first instinct has been—always—to protect it from the common people. It is so vulnerable. Truly, it cannot live unless it feeds on Tangerine-lungs.*

"The Best is Enemy of the Good." Flapping like a flash-card for the pupil who has not yet come up with the right answer.

—*Enemy? I faint. I'm an impotent enemy. My Rage is wrapped in Pity.*

In the morning, to the tune of sleet ticking on the window-pane, Melvin turns to her with a sleepy smile. "I dreamed Max was a basket-case. I guess I caught your anxiety."

* *

"Hey, Buddy," Melvin says to Tad after a big breakfast, "how about another game of gin rummy?"

Smiling with closed lips, Tad settles himself across the table from this jovial companion.

Melvin smacks the cards on the table in front of Tad. "Your turn to deal."

Tad glances up dubiously. Is this festive father the dragon who will soon vanish?

Washing the dishes, Willo glimpses behind the scene in the dining room. —*Do I see you now, Melvin, playing cards with your brother Nelson before Lee toddled onto the stage?*

At three o'clock, Frank Dean arrives home—popped from a station wagon like a cuckoo from a clock, and is grabbed by pale Gertrude.

At three-twenty, ditto for Max.

"Cupcakes!" he whoops.

Enthroned at the kitchen table, he says to his mother, "Cold? Me? No! The spaghetti was great, not quite cooked, sort of like kite string, but great. . . . Frank? O.K., I guess. Yesterday I saw his face all crooked across the campfire, and I said to myself: *'Now, why is that klutz wearing a beard?'* But it wasn't a beard. He was throwing up. Good cupcakes. May I have another? . . . For the third time, NO, I wasn't *cold.*"

Willo beholds, bulging beneath his jeans, like a drift of dingy snow, the thermal knit.

"Frank Dean's," he explains. "That Sis had two of everything. Yeah, *two.* After he threw up on our Bisquick, we all socked him and divided his junk among us."

Willo hurls a lasso-glance to Melvin, who slips out of it. "They're not *girl* scouts."

* *

223

Late that night, having made her rounds with aspirin, antihistimine, and ear drops, Willo launders, by hand, the long underwear, molding and re-molding with each squeeze of suds, an apology for Gertrude.

Willo writes to her psychiatrist:

> ...I'm running out of the strength you gave me six
> years ago. That flagellating Bible Belt has whipped Max
> right out of Scouts. His atheism became a major issue.
> The more the boys, and their parents, attacked it, the
> more he flaunted it.
>
> I tried to intercede, via a few mothers of Scouts, with
> Zen, but that flagellating belt whipped me, too. Did I
> once tell you Zen was a kind of fire extinguisher I'd take
> down off the wall for an emergency? In this emergency,
> it, or my lack of skill, turned it into a ten-cent store
> atomizer that squirted a pastel pouf.
>
> I've implored Melvin, with all his years of ardent
> reading, to teach the boys something about Zen. He
> says, "That's silly. The books are all on the shelf. The
> boys can read them for themselves."
>
> He seems less and less willing, or able, to give any-
> thing of himself to Max. He feels virtuous because he's
> played gin rummy a few times with Tad. Maybe this
> token is all the fatherliness my poor suckling-faced or-
> phan can give. My anger towards him is still sheathed in
> pity.
>
> Now Max is isolated again from his peers. I'm so
> afraid he'll try to break out of that isolation with drugs.
>
> So many fears. So many worries. Please, hold my
> hand....

Willo mails the letter. She waits the usual five days for the
letter to reach him, then allows herself the usual indulgence
in the fantasy of him opening her letter, savoring her words
...holding her hand...holding her in his arms. But the
fantasy does not flow.

She does zazen. The golden sphere is blue today, and the

spray is a blue mist. Still, no fantasy of her Love. Instead, this memory comes to her:

A tramp came to the back door. What a bustle! Mamma sent Cora and me to the cellar: "Get a can o beans and a can o peaches and a jar o that grape marmalade!"

She scurried to the bureau for my father's socks and shirts. "Now git!" She shooed us to the front porch.

The tramp reigned on the back stoop.

Mamma's voice drifted to us in tatters: "—I know what yer goin through. My own twin brother—"

His voice: "You said it! You said a mouthful!"

Her voice, jubilant: "Have some more; take some to yer chums. . . . My husband, he's a good pervider, I'll say that fer him, but he's got no feelins fer an outsider. Everthin is fer his daughters; upholds them somethin awful. I come last."

His voice: "It's a shame. It's a dirty shame!"

Her voice: "You think this is a nice house? Naw! It's my jail. That's what it is, my *jail!*"

Cora and I wandered to the back yard to see this father-confessor.

Mamma held her hooked index finger at her ribs in that gesture she considered more genteel than outright pointing: "The black-haired one, the pickaninny, she's my side-kick. A reglar little hustler. Whitey—haw!—she's her father's girl. Good marks in school. Don't lift a finger to help around the house. I feel sorry fer the guy that marries *her!*"

The florid-faced guest appraised us with bleary eyes.

When he'd had enough looking, Mamma said to us, "Where's yer manners? Don't stare at someone havin a bite ta eat!"

We retreated to the front porch. Again the tatters drifted to us: "Wisht I'd never got married. This ain't the life fer me. I'd like ta be somewheres runnin a kitchen fer fellas like you. Maybe an ole boxcar or a caboose with a coal stove an some ole dishes an some clean mattresses on the floor. . . . Nothin fancy, but clean n comfortable. Boy! I got a lotta good ideas."

"Bless yer heart. Oh, bless yer heart!"

After what seemed like time for a seven-course dinner, he walked up along the front porch railing, his coat fat with loot, his arms around two big brown paper bags. He sized us up with that bleary eye and said very solemnly: "You know somethin, young ladies? You got an angel fer a mother—an *angel!*"

We went into the house to have a look at this angel. Sure enough: She was glowing. She was floating. "Don't tell yer dad. He's narrowminded, tight. He don't like ta share."

Later that day I caught her looking in the mirror, patting her hair, smiling. "Somethin in my eye," she said when she saw me. There was nothing in her eye but pure pleasure. She had put on a clean dress. That lipless face grinned and grinned. Those lemur-eyes brimmed. "He'll write my name in a boxcar. All his pals will know me. Don't mention it to yer dad...."

Willo waits six days...seven. Still no fantasies of London Love. She does zazen again, and again, the memory of the tramp unfolds for her.

Lying awake one night two weeks after mailing the letter ...hours after a long session of zazen, the rain on the roof, the rain running down the rain spout...the rain puddling in the driveway...brings her his voice: "*—Are you still carrying her? I put her down on the other side of the puddle.*"

227

Standing barefoot on the sunny patio one day in May, brushing her hair and gazing into the face of an indigo iris, Willo's left big toe turns cold as ice. She looks down at the foot to see what has happened. She sees nothing, but feels the coldness sprial up around her hips, around her shoulders, and close over the top of her head, until she seems enclosed within a cold chrysalis.

"MAGIC." Spoken, yet not spoken; as if through telepathy. "FIVE SISTERS: GERTRUDE DEAN IN JUNE MARY SANDERS NAOMI MCALISTER LUCY SULLIVAN ELIZABETH CAMPBELL IN OCTOBER."

The chrysalis crackles, rises like a parasol, and Willo stands shivering, barefoot on the hot cement, still gazing into the face of the indigo iris. —*Pete? It's May fifteenth.*

In June, Gertrude Dean dies suddenly of a stroke.

In July, Melvin receives a letter from a distant relative: "*...Aunt Mary died July fifth....*"

In August, Willo receives two letters: one from the old university town: Ned has written: "*Naomi died of cancer the first of this month. She spoke of you often in her last days....*" The other letter, from Cora, contains a newspaper clipping: "Margaret Peterson, age forty-five, dies in car crash in Montana...." The clipping is dated May fifteenth.

—*Pete, my Love, what a gift.*

In August, Willo reads in the newspaper: "*Lucy Sullivan dies of leukemia....*"

231

In September, she reads in the paper: *"Elizabeth Campbell killed in auto crash...."*

—Two strangers. Yet now no longer strangers. All five joined in this journey...all sisters...all threads...all woven together with Pete into a mysterious fabric. Life merging into death and death into life. Maybelle, too....Daddy, too.... Melvin's brothers and his father and his mother   I, too, linked through you, Pete.   Love is the link.

Willo moves through the days, transformed. *—Oh, Pete, my Love, thank you for the wings!*

A school counselor has appended to Max's report card: "These grades are disgraceful. We've run out of ways to cope with this cynic."

Willo folds the note and places it in the pocket of her apron....The house is quaking with a Wagner opera. For five days, Melvin has been lying in the leather lounge chair. —*Libra; double? triple? Libra, sucking from that great breast MUSIC...sucking from that other great breast BOOKS.*

"Cynic." Willo takes the word off that high shelf of her mind and wipes off the dust of twenty years. *Cynic: sneering. Cynic: enemy of faith; enemy of hope; enemy of action.*

She reads Tad's report card: "Underachieving...bemused ...does not relate to peers."

Willo slips this card into her pocket with the other card. She walks out of the throbbing house, closes the door behind her, and sits on the patio in the April sunshine. Last quarter the report cards had carried the same warnings. She had hastened to the school for a conference. *"Max is precocious. He looks like Errol Flynn. He acts like him, too. He disrupts the class. He's often absent. He seems to be using drugs. Can you send this gifted boy to a private school?"* She conveyed the message to Melvin. *"Private school? That's just a fad, a prestige item,"* he snorted, and seeing the anguish on her face, *"I'll have a talk with the boy."* The outcome of the talk: *"Just a phase, Honey. I've been reading all about it in The New York Times. If Max doesn't change within a year, then we'll think about a private school."* She hurried to Tad's counselor: *"Tad needs vigorous involvement with an adult male."* She also hastened to Melvin with this information. Result: *"Just a phase, Honey. They outgrow these things."* A few more games of gin rummy.

Willo looks a long time at the daffodils: golden, cream, ivory faces. She closes her eyes, rests. After a while, she opens her eyes and smiles: —*I've eaten you, Pete. I'm strong.*

She rises and re-enters that room booming with Tristram. She hands Melvin the two cards.

He reads them, sneers, flips them over his shoulder. *"Wu wei!"*

She snaps off the Tristram. *"Wu wei?* Is this *wu wei* of yours anything more than *depression?"*

He drops his gaze to the novel in his lap.

"Melvin! We must salvage those boys!"

"Please. No soap operas."

"Listen: You used to say when they were tots that you'd be a stimulating father once they grew up a bit. They're fifteen and thirteen, and you're stimulating as a sponge."

He places his palm on his forehead. "Please. This is my vacation."

"You've had fifteen years of vacation, Lotus Eater."

He reaches out, turns the thunder back on. She snaps it off. She stands before him like a beacon. She flashes a glance to the three walls lined with books. "With books and music you've turned off the deaths of your two brothers." She flashes a glance to the fourth wall of stereo equipment. "With books and music, you've turned off the lives of your two sons."

He sits rapt as a cobra in a basket.

She sighs. "I share the guilt. Being a parent is the most heart-breaking job in the world. If I had it to do over again, I wouldn't."

He nods.

"I've checked with The Agency. They gave me a list of approved psychiatrists. I'm going to phone one called Michael Devlin, who lives a mile from us, for an appointment for Max and Tad."

"They won't like that."

"I've talked with both of them about psychiatrists. They seem interested."

"All right. Call your god."

"Not a god. Just a human being, I hope, who may act as a last-minute surrogate parent."

"All right." Still the cobra. "I've wondered for years when you'd come around to taking this step."

"Pity for you prevented me. Now the pity has shifted to our sons. Death is not the problem. Life is."

She goes to the phone and dials the psychiatrist.

"I always see the mother first, then the father, then the children," Dr. Devlin told Willo on the phone. Now Willo faces him in his office. He is a small roly-poly bald man who could be a twin to Melvin.

Willo tells him about her sons: "Tad, I think, is the more severely damaged of the two. I'm too involved to know why...."

The doctor sees a pretty face gone severe. Then he looks down and begins to catch the swiftly-told tale in his notebook.

"...Max is a sort of Heathcliff; stormy, dramatic, bright. Right now he hates school; he's using drugs. My husband has always rejected Max. I suspect Max is a vivid version of Melvin's gifted younger brother...."

The doctor listens to the voice: thin and flat.

"...These two boys are badly handicapped by my husband's apparent indifference to them, and by my coddling as an attempt to compensate for that indifference. They are both too fragile, emotionally, too vulnerable, to enter any kind of society outside the family. What I want of you—and this is a big order—is that you should help each boy build a bridge from his isolated home out into the community." She clears her throat, drifts into an evaluation of her husband and herself: "We are both poor parents. We are both misfits. I lack the social graces. I'm too angry, I guess, to learn them. Melvin lacks the skills of communication. He's too grieved, I suppose, to learn them.... He endures my addiction to our sons about as gracefully as I endure his addiction to me."

The doctor glances up, sees the thin, clenched hands.

"Melvin flaunts Zen. Yet I've never met a less Zen-like

236

person. Zen, as I understand it, is *playful,* to say the least. It makes maximum use of the unconscious mind. Melvin will scarcely acknowledge that he has an unconscious mind. I think when he latched onto Zen twenty years ago, he sensed that it had what he needed. I think while reading Zen literature and looking at the productions of Zen artists, he experiences an itch, a tickle of some dormancy that craves itching or tickling. But the process stops there. Nothing has been opened. Nothing has been released. It's just a flirtation. Let me give you an example: For fifteen years, I've been bringing him our simple family problems: 'Max is jealous of Tad. Could you play with Tad a few hours while I devote myself to Max?' Or 'The children have used me up today; I'd appreciate it if you could read them a story while I rest.' Or 'The children are bored. Would you take them to a museum?' For fifteen years, he's been smiling and answering, 'The children are fine. All you need to do is organize your day.' If I continue to insist that I really do need his help with them, he will turn to his trio of tranquilizers: whisky, recorded music, books. He will pour himself a drink, turn on soft music, or even thundering music, enthrone himself in that big easy-chair, and place that lovely Libra-smile upon his face. He's the image of the compassionate, listening husband. But it's just a pose. Quietly and slowly, as if he's going through a card-index catalog, he will proceed to cite a series of authors and articles and books to hush my idiot-cry...books, periodicals, and more books that will extend once more his sabbatical from parental involvement."

Her voice breaks. In a quick glance, the doctor sees the small, stern face that matches the voice.

"...I try to imagine what goes on in Melvin's office—what it is that drives him home for lunch every day...that drives him home each evening with a headache and a cramped bowel. I suppose it's just another facet of that role he plays at home. I imagine a co-worker presents him with a statement. The statement enters Melvin's consciousness like a fly or a gnat. His first impulse is to bat it away, squash it, get rid of it somehow. But he is not forthright. He's not a man of action. Probably he mumbles something which lets the colleague believe Melvin agrees with him. Yet Melvin seldom agrees. Almost every lunch hour he sputters to me about the stupidity, the grossness, of his co-workers. A few times I have said: *'Did you tell so-and-so that you disagree with him?'* Melvin growls to me, *'Of course not!* I'm not *rude.* I'm *not crude.'* It looks as though he is afraid to show his anger—even his mild disagreement—to another man. I think he does not know how to participate in a discussion. He is shockingly non-vocal. I used to wonder why. I could not believe it. Now at last I have come to believe that this flaw is the wound of the loner. Maybe it began when he was nine, when his brothers died. Maybe it began before that, when his younger brother was born; maybe even earlier. Maybe his parents never listened to him when he was a tot. I don't know. But whatever the reason, it seems he never learned to take a concept into himself, flavor it with his own experiences, and then pass the concept on to his fellow man. I think he spent his youth avoiding that simple social process. He must have spent most of his time reading, greedily reading, and listening to music; hoarding information and esthetic impressions like a miser. Now when another person asks him for a slice of that information, he feels threatened. He doesn't know how to let go of it, how to give it to the other person. When the other person proceeds to give Melvin his ideas, Melvin tightens with anger. 'Idiot!' he thinks of the associates; 'stupid ass.' You see, I think Melvin knows he has within him a huge treasure of knowledge; no doubt a much larger treasure than his vocal associate has, but Melvin is unable to utilize that treasure; cannot haul it up out of that pit and send it through the channel that would make it accessible to the associate. All he can do is sputter, 'You ought to go read the book.' He'll cite author, title, chapter, publisher, date, but he will rarely vocalize the *concept* he got from that source. It's maddening. It's pitiful. You know how a good teacher, a lecturer, an artist—oh, *any* civilized person—can present his ideas attractively, like a tray of food. Melvin can't. He serves, at most, the menu. And then he's angry because the recipient does not respond with a gusto of praise and thanks."

She sighs, places her fingertips on the vertical lines above her nose. "Imagine what it's like to be a boy approaching Melvin with a question about his homework, be it math or geography or politics. 'Don't ask me!' Melvin sputters. 'It's in the book over on that shelf. Go find it and read it for yourself.' " She massages the lines as if she's trying to erase them. "He's a bibliophile, not a scholar."

The doctor looks at the clock. "Our time is almost up."

Willo sighs. "I've talked an avalanche. This resentment has been accumulating ever since I broke off therapy in London nine years ago." Her feathery voice has turned hoarse. Her face is haggard.

The doctor chuckles. "It was most enlightening. Now in the few minutes that are left, I'll need your help on a few points. On Friday your husband will be sitting here with me. You seem to have a lot of concern for him. What, specifically, do you want me to do for him?"

"Open him. Let him know his sons are not his brothers."

The doctor smiles. "And Saturday at nine, Max will be here. At ten, Tad. You said at the beginning of the session that you wanted me to help each boy 'build a bridge from his isolated family into the community.' What, specifically, did you have in mind?"

"I'm hoping they'll learn to like you, to relate to you as—an uncle. A good uncle could help Max become more controlled, could help Tad become more assertive. The relationship would be a conduit into the friendships of other boys, of other groups."

The doctor nods. "And what about you? What do you want for yourself out of this long-awaited process of family-therapy?"

Willo looks bewildered. She laughs. Ten years vanish from her face. "I feel like the person in the fairy tale who is granted three wishes. Well, more than anything in the world,

I want to write poetry. For that, I need solitude and relative tranquility. If you help my sons, I'll gain some of that." Her face turns impish. Another ten years vanish. "Here's a more specific wish: Make Melvin stop coming home for lunch. Then, and only then, can my muse come to me." She rises swiftly. "Three wishes. That's a huge order."

Dr. Devlin chuckles. "I'm no magician, but I'll see what I can do."

The two men face one another like mirror images. Each smiles faintly at the recognition. The doctor speaks: "I always start off the first session by asking the parent to give a brief account of his own background: your father, mother, siblings, anything else that comes to mind."

"There were five in my family. We lived in St. Louis. My father was a very successful businessman: owned and operated a large department store. My mother was a librarian before her marriage. They were both very calm, quiet Catholic people. She was Irish. He was English." He folds his arms tightly across his chest and focuses his gaze on the doctor's shoe. "Then the summer when I was nine, my brothers both caught polio. Within the same week, they were—gone. My parents never got over it. My father died of a heart attack a year later."

Devlin says softly, "That was a terrible shock for you."

"A terrible shock. Nothing was ever the same after that."

"And your mother?"

Melvin wipes his fingertips over his frown. "She died when I was eighteen."

The doctor shakes his head. "You've had some awful losses."

"I guess so."

"Were you able to relate to others, to have friends after all those early losses?"

The arms tightly folded again: "Not at first." The voice chirping. "I read a lot. In college, I had fraternity brothers. In the army—the intelligence—I had buddies—if you can call those friends."

"Any girl friends in your youth?"

"None. I was too shy."

"I see...and you work at The Central Intelligence Agency. Do you enjoy that?"

"Oh, it's all right."

"Is there anything else you'd rather do?"

"I'd rather live off my investments. I've always been lazy, a sort of dilettante, I guess."

"Do you have friends at work?"

"They're very ambitious men, competetive, dedicated. I don't get in their way."

"Any hobbies?"

"Books, music, photography."

"Yes, your wife mentioned the books and the music. Now, what about the family—your wife and the sons?"

Melvin sighs. "There's nothing wrong with those boys. It's their mother. She's ultra-idealistic, ultra-permissive. When the older boy should be buckling down to his math, my wife is out walking along the canal with him. Or else she's in his room, letting him read her palm, or helping him cast a horoscope. The other day I saw a PLAYBOY magazine in his room. She knew all about it, just let him have it, anyway."

The doctor grins. "Horoscopes, palmistry, PLAYBOY. Those all sound like standard fare for today's teenager."

Melvin tightens his arms across his chest. "I don't go for all that hokum. The world is full of great literature to read. A lot of scientific breakthroughs are happening. I'd like my sons to be in on those."

"Of course. I agree. But I think these other things are *fun.* And the younger boy? How does your wife treat him?"

"She pampers him. She's in his room a lot. He's a slow reader. She reads his homework aloud to him."

"You express more concern for your wife than for your sons."

"Yes. She's the disturbed one. She worries and worries. She wants too much for them; compensating for her own dismal childhood, I guess." He shakes his head. "And that's some family of hers. We had been happily married a year,

242

and then I met them. That really shook me up.''

The doctor leans foreward. "Really? What were they like?''

"Exactly like characters out of a Steinbeck novel.''

"Poor people?''

"Losers. Skidrow calibre.''

The doctor shakes his head. "How did it happen that you married her without meeting the family?''

A faint smirk. "She seduced me. From then on, I didn't know what I was doing.''

The doctor echoes the smirk. "That was at the university?''

"Yes.'' He unlocks the arms and clasps his hands. "She pines for those days, I guess, when she was a Star. It's a shame the way those professors and psychology students did a snowjob on her; told her she was the greatest thing in poetry. Now she's forty-five, a nobody, and I know she blames me for taking her away from all that.''

"Does she have friends now?''

"None. She's an oddball, snobbish, shy. Can't get along with any of the neighbors. That doesn't do the boys any good.''

"You're right. . .and her hobbies?''

"The boys. Just those boys.''

The doctor nods pensively. "She seems to be under considerable tension. Was she like this when you met her?''

Melvin sighs. "No. She was a very good-natured girl. She was kind—very, very kind and very pretty. That's why I married her, actually.''

"She told me she wants very much to get back to writing poetry. What do you think of that?''

A delicate frown. "I'm not at all sure I go along with that.''

"No?''

"I don't like what writing does to her. It's an escape.''

"I'm wondering if she may need to escape from some of those household tasks. Maybe she needs to escape from those

243

boys."

"Of course. But I'd rather see her take up something like the A.A.U.W. or The League of Women Voters."

"Yes, a lot of women do find an outlet in those activities, but your wife's strongly bent in another direction, isn't she?"

"Yes, she is, but I don't think we should encourage that direction."

The doctor taps his pencil on his pad. "I've seen a lot of women like your wife—bright, ambitious, having raised the children, needing an outlet for all that maternal energy. You'd be surprised how much of that energy can be siphoned off in writing an hour or two each day."

"Well, I've some concern for my job. I can't use any of this exhibitionistic poetry."

The doctor nods his head. "Publication, you mean? I've known a lot of housewife-writers, and I've never known one of them to publish significantly." He smiles. "They're *women*. Writing for them is often the end in itself, not publishing."

Melvin nods. "Maybe. I don't mean to sound like a tyrant. But I associate her writing with those university days. She was vain. She still is. All we need is for her to display that confessional stuff to the wrong people, and they'll hoke her up with a lot of flattery and then exploit her. I've seen it happen."

The pencil continues to tap. "Well, let's leave that issue for another time. Let's get to those boys, Max and Tad. A picture is emerging for me now: I see the mother walking on the towpath with Max...then in his room, talking with him ...the mother in Tad's room, reading to him. I can't quite make out your role. Where are you in this picture?"

Melvin sighs. "In my chair, reading." He wraps his arms across his chest again. "I feel guilty. I've never done much for those boys."

"Why is that?"

He shrugs, frowns. "I don't know. At times I've wanted to play with those boys, but something always holds me back."

"What holds you back?"

"I don't know." He sighs, dabs at his forehead as if he's stunned. "I guess it's because their mother has nagged me so much to play with them that now it would be like taking orders from her to do so. It wouldn't be my own thing. I'd be acting on her orders, or on the orders of her London Adonis, or on the orders of those psychologists who hoked her all up with propaganda when she was a student."

Devlin nods, fervently. "There's a lot of truth in your analysis." He looks at his watch. "Our time is nearly up. In the few minutes that are left, can you tell me what you'd like me to accomplish—or try to accomplish—when I see Max and then Tad next week?"

"I don't think there's a lot you can do for that older boy. He's always been a wise guy. He doesn't want anyone's advice. The younger boy isn't so bad. Maybe you can perk him up a little—get his mother off his back." Melvin rises. "I do feel bad about neglecting that younger boy. I guess that's what I'm charged with—"

Devlin raises his hand. "Let's get this straight from the beginning: I'm not holding a thing against you. You've done well, considering your childhood." He shakes his head. "My heart goes out to any man who finds himself married to a latent lesbian."

Dr. Devlin finds Max every bit as dazzling as his mother claimed: also every bit as diabolical as his father said he was.

At the end of forty-five minutes, the doctor asks Max, "What do you want out of this therapy?"

Max chortles. "To be like other people. I want to get rid of books and classical music and all that egghead stuff of my parents. I want a motorcycle or a car, or both, and a colored television set and friends visiting me in my house. Most of all, I want those friends in my house."

The doctor sees that Tad, too, is as his mother described him; or worse. The boy is almost catatonic. He has barely talked during the sessions; he has answered questions with a shrug or one word or two spoken through closed lips.

"What do you want, Tad?" the doctor keeps asking him.

"I don't know."

"Do you want to continue living with your parents?"

"I don't know."

"Do you want to take a year off school to rest?"

"I don't know."

"Come on, Tad! You must want something enough to ask for it. Don't you?"

"I don't know."

The old pattern, the doctor concludes. That seductive mother has trapped him. Let's give the father a chance to set him free.

After three weeks in therapy, Max says to the doctor, "This is pure shit. I'm not coming back for more."

*　*

"I know an excellent boarding school for Max," the doctor tells Willo.

"No boarding school for a son of mine," Melvin protests.
"Please!" Willo pleads.
"No. A boarding school is just a place where wealthy people dump their sons when they can't cope with them."
"But we are somewhat wealthy, and let's admit it: we can't cope with Max."
"Investments have slumped. Do you want to take Tad out of treatment and use the money for boarding school for Max?"
She shakes her head.
"Can you earn the money by selling your poems?"
"You know I can't."
"Can you get a job teaching English?"
"You know I can't. Could we sell this big house and live in a smaller one, or in an apartment?"
"Don't be absurd."

In the middle of his junior year, Max drops out of high school. Willo pleads with Melvin, pleads with the doctor. Melvin shrugs. The doctor says, "Max is just experimenting with a new life-style. It's not the end of the world."

Willo becomes short-order cook for Max and his pals. Their rock music shakes the house like a cement mixer.
She flees to the attic, like someone clinging in the crow's nest on a stormy sea. —*"Luxury makes the esthete,"* she reminds herself. *"Hardship makes the artist." —Here I shall await the Muse.*

*　*

Tad will not look at his mother or speak to her. When she addresses him, he recoils, spastically, as if her voice is gravel poured into his eustachian tubes. When she awaits his answer, he grimaces and twitches as if the words are stuck in his

247

muscles.

From behind his newspaper, the smiling Melvin watches their struggle. Bravely, she addresses Tad again, very slowly: "Do you want me to order the plaid jacket from the catalog?"

The curly head jerks down between the hunched shoulders; the bony hand flutters up to the chin; the fingers scribble a long time in front of the wry mouth, as if to pull out the faint "yuk."

She reaches out to hand him a clean shirt.

He recoils in a spasm.

She tries to hand him a book. He twitches like an insect caught in the web of a spider.

He locks himself in his room.

When she knocks on his door, he growls, "Go away, Witch!"

Behind the newspaper, Melvin smiles and smiles.

Tad will not accept meals from his mother, but after she has gone to bed, he slogs down the stairs and into the kitchen, where he feeds himself large bowls-full of granola and honey and milk and can after can of tuna.

Each evening Melvin knocks on Tad's door, and is admitted, like a tutor, for assistance with homework and for an hour of chess.

They are awakened one morning at four by the ringing of the phone, and through the murk of her waking, Willo hears Melvin saying, "Yes, this is Melvin Sanders. Yes, I have a son Max. But you must have the wrong Sanders. My son is here, in bed." Sounds of Melvin's slippers shuffling down the steps to Max's room. "Max? Max?" tap tap Sounds of the door opening. Then Melvin is hurrying up the steps and saying on the phone, "All right. I'll be right down there."

Willo's heart pumps a bubble to her brain. Shakily, she scrambles out of bed.

"The police station," Melvin is saying, thrashing into his trousers. "Max stole a car. No, you stay here."

She waits. More bubbles to the brain. Tad is moving in his room. She taps on his door. "Max is in the police station. He stole a car."

Silence.

"Did you hear me, Tad?"

"Yes." Spoken as though through smiling lips.

"Won't you come out here and wait with me?"

Silence again. Then: "No."

Her heart pumps the bubbles into her throat, into her ears. —*It's Max's cry for help. Now his father will listen. Now he'll consent to the private school.*

She chants the thought over and over to herself, like a refrain, until the car is purring into the garage...and tall, bearded Max in mussed T-shirt walks into the kitchen, followed by his short, bald father. The room is full of a sharp odor. The room is reeling in the acrid odor of fear.

In the living room, Max seats himself on the sofa. His

hands are limp in his lap. His Tartar eyes in his pale face glitter like the eyes of a trapped animal. The T-shirt is gray with sweat; damp and exuding that wild odor of alarm.

Melvin sinks to the chair across from his son.

"How did it happen?" Willo hears herself asking.

Max says flatly, "I stole a yellow Pontiac down the street. The key was on the seat, and I just got in and took off."

—*Lonely. It sounds so Lonely.* "Have you done it before?"

"Sure."

Melvin says, "We have to be in court at nine in the morning."

"We must get some rest," Willo says. "Do you need aspirin, Max? Or coffee? Or some juice?"

Max shakes his head. He looks exhausted.

"Can you imagine what it's like to find your son in handcuffs?" Melvin asks her in a scolding tone.

She shakes her head. "We must get some rest. We'll help you, Max. We'll do anything to help." And to herself she says: —*Clean shirt, a light breakfast.*

Tad is standing at the top of the stairs. Tad with something like a smile on his face. The two brothers exchange a glance that excludes their parents. The two estranged brothers bonded in this glance.

"The trial will be in Baltimore, in the juvenile court," Melvin is saying. "Don't be surprised if your son gets reform school."

They drift through the day. Two days. Three days. Max on his bed, staring at the ceiling, accepting from his mother a small glass of juice...a glass of milk...tea. Looking out of animal eyes. Exuding that reek.

And beside her in bed, Melvin exuding that same reek. That odor sharp as thorns. And Willo thinking: —*He's suffering for his son. He's suffering WITH his son. At last....* And she visualizes a long period in which they visit Max week-ends in reform school. A humbled Max, calmed by much counseling. A warmed Melvin, wakened by the sessions of counseling. A mended relationship. The blessing in disguise.

Four days. Five days. They move about hushed, dazed, in their fetid suburban lair, waiting.

Then Melvin is saying: "Good news. The trial is off."
And dumbfounded Willo is saying: "What?"
Max grips his father's hand and laughs shakily. "Thanks, Dad. Thanks ever so much."
"It cost me five hundred dollars," Melvin says. "May cost another five hundred before we're clear. Max, you'd better get back into school." To his wife's blank face, he says, "I paid a lawyer to lose the paperwork on the case."
Max is chuckling. Max is telling Tad: "Stealing that car was *nothing*. I did that on a snort of whiskey. You ought to hear what I've done on speed. Wow!"
"What did you do on speed?" Willo asks flatly.
"I don't want to hear about it," says Melvin, and he goes out the door to work.
"Tell me," Willo persists.
His white smile flashing through his dark beard, Max says, "Vandalism. Colossal vandalism. You'd drop dead if you knew the truth." He runs up to Tad's room, and they close the door. They murmur and chortle.

Willo drifts through the days, putting the shirts—Max's shirts and Melvin's shirts, and the sheets, into the washing machine. . .taking them out. Folding them. She's still caught like an insect in that reeking web of danger.
At dinner, she twitches the grim silence: "I expected some *openness*. A confrontation, then confession, forgiveness, and HEALING."
Melvin sneers. "You and your fairytale mentality."
Max chuckles. "Mom, do you really think guys get rehabilitated in reform school? How naive can you get?"
Tad smirks. He's eating with an improved appetite. The

three males are united in this bourgeois feint.

Dr. Devlin says, "Your husband made the right move. Boys who go to trial—boys who are sentenced—tend, overwhelmingly—ninety-eight percent of them—to repeat their offenses. Boys who get off—" He shrugs. "They rarely repeat."

She gazes at the clean plump hands folded on the shimmering blue satin tie. —*Clean fingernails, Mamma.* She shakes her head and sighs. "This marshmallow-machismo leaves me uneasy. Think what would have happened if Max had been a black boy living seven miles from this spot, over the district line."

"I think of it often, Mrs. Sanders." He sighs. "We live in strange times."

—*Strange times.* Walking home down the tree-shaded streets, she hears an echo from her college days: —*"You're ingenuous. You've told all the wrong people."*

Days afterwards, weeks afterwards, washing those shirts and sheets, taking them from the dryer, folding them, placing them into drawers, Willo still inhales that odor of danger ...seems to see it, touch it, taste it. *Out, out, damned spot....* And with it she sees and smells the black boy, multiplied by ten, by a hundred, by a thousand...the black boy in sweaty T-shirt, in handcuffs...the black boy in court without a father; or if with a father, that father without money, without education, without "connections."...She sees that black mother washing her boy's shirt, that black mother lying awake in the night, knowing the GOOD in her son will soon be broken and scattered and soured into BAD...into meanness, anger...and the Anger multiplied exponentially and stalking through the labyrinths of this sick society.... Awake in her own bed, she smells again the putrid odor of Milo's clothes...hears her mother's washing machine chugging...hears her mother crying. And her mother's face merges with the face of the black mother. . .and Milo's face with the face of the black boy.

The Star of therapy is Melvin. He does, indeed, stop coming home for lunch: "We had an office picnic today. You remember Sally? Her two-year-old daughter sat in my lap the whole time. Gosh, she's a little *doll!*"

"Six of us went to a Chinese restaurant this noon. One of the secretaries brought a PLAYBOY magazine, and she read the letters to the editor aloud. Sally improvised the funniest answers I've ever heard in my life. That gal has the sharpest mind! And she's so frank. It's amazing."

"Four of us went to a topless restaurant today. That Sally was cracking a joke every minute. She kept us in stitches."
—Rip Van Winkle, wakened from that twenty-year sleep—. It will make an amusing poem.

"We're having a picnic on your old stomping grounds, down by the canal. It's Friday, and Sally wants you to be sure to come."
—Now that Max has been de-throned. . . . Did this trigger your cockiness?
"We can pick you up at noon Friday. You can relax with lots of wine."
"Thanks, but I want to work on my poetry." *—Brash girl is tonic for Bashful man. . . . It will make a hilarious poem.*

One evening, in the parking lot of the cinema, right after they have gotten into their car, Melvin leans over and says to Willo in a sly tone: "Watch this: I'm going to show you something." And he whams his door into the car parked next to theirs.
"Melvin!"

"Didn't you see that knick in our paint?" He flourishes the key in the slot of the dashboard. "I'll teach that nut a lesson."

"For God's sake, Mel—"

He beams. "You wanted me to be *aggressive,* didn't you?" He careens out of the parking lot.

Willo sighs. "I meant *openly* aggressive. *Open* aggression would mean explaining your grievance, face to face, to the owner of that car."

The car lurches to a stop at the red light. "You and that ivory tower."

"What's this new flamboyant driving?"

He purses his lips prissily. "You ought to take a lesson from a *real* liberated woman, a real spitfire. That Sally doesn't let anyone hassle her and get away with it."

All the way home, he smirks like a bespectacled dumpling third-grader whose Big Mamma has directed him to place a thumbtack on the seat of the class bully.

"Another picnic at the canal Friday. Lots of wine. Sally is going to bring two of her little girls. You come, too, Willo."

"No thanks."

"Other wives are coming."

"I have to work on my poems."

"Those *poems,*" he sighs. "You're such a *serious* person."

She glances up sharply and sees, across a widening rift, his narrow eyes appraising her. "You always looked as if you were about to cry. *That's* why I married you."

—Here come your regrets, Melvin; I'm not a ha ha secretary. She picks up her notebook and turns to leave the room.

"—Especially when you smiled . . . you looked as if you were about to cry."

She pauses in the doorway, feeling those narrowed eyes measuring her: *—so frail? so insubstantial compared with Sally?*

"—The saddest smile I've ever seen," Melvin muses. "It

255

nearly broke my heart.''

"You married your bereaved mother,'' she replies crisply. ''Also the grieving part of yourself.''

"You and your instant Freud.'' He shrinks from her and snaps on the radio.

She hurries to her room and closes the door behind her. She settles herself in the rocking chair and opens the notebook. —*I should have waited for him to uncover that insight for himself. Now he will only reject it, and his own inner growth will be delayed.* She sighs. When will she learn that she must give these thoughts to her notebook, and only to her notebook?...Her poignant face. Many had commented on it. Her silent cry for help. Many had responded. Father Vincent. Ben. Sam. Professors. London Love. Melvin. Neighbors. Some had helped her. Most had not. Had Melvin ever helped her? comforted her? healed her? He had given her a house, a series of houses, in fact, and food and clothing and books and movies and plays: the bourgeois package. Also: *"Rub my head. Massage my neck. Now my shoulders. Don't stop now...my back. My feet!"* —*It will take your mind off your own troubles,* Mamma would say.

Well, she had misinterpreted Melvin's needs, too; or had misinterpreted her ability to meet those needs. Swiftly, she scrawls in the notebook:

PITY

Pity, more passionate than Love,
drew me to you, Melvin.
Pity, I told myself, would make a nest
in which you would deposit your griefs.
Patience, I hoped, would hatch those griefs,
And one by one, they'd fly away.

Oh, I was ready for you!
All my life I had been preparing.
Long before you came along,
I was being pocketed with pity.
Pity accumulating, Pity misered
from Milo and Casey and Sikes and

256

Agnes and Mamma and—
Pity withheld, Pity denied, Pity
concealed from all those ghouls and freaks.
As a cliff grows pocketed with holes
of the cliff swallows,
I was pre-wounded with nests for you.

So what went wrong?
My patience turned to depression.
My dread conspired with your reticence
to create a chilly cave
where those griefs rotted.

Pity without Love hatched spooks.

She sighs. It is not a poem. It is a beginning. A tiny wad of life is here, like an embryo, throbbing within a nebulous shroud. It will need more warmth, much more energy to bring it to full life.

She turns the page to try again. The morning sunlight strikes the page, and in a golden oval, she sees Frank Dean, all six feet four of the gangling youth folded in a lotus position; he looks serene.

She turns another page, and in another flurry, she scribbles:

CHILDREN ARE NOT POEMS

"Children are poems," I said when I was twenty.
Innocence of youth! Arrogance of youth!

Children are children.
Poems are poems.
Both are *playful,*
but here the similarity stops.

A poem is mine.
I control it.

A child is not mine—not really.
I control, at most, its infancy.
It is silly; it is selfish,
to try to control more.

A child is not mine.
It belongs to the great continuum.

She turns the page to try a second draft. Again the sunlight strikes the paper. Again, she sees within the golden orb Frank Dean in the lotus position. There are others with him, all meditating, all serene. They seem to be in an ashram.

Max has been missing for three days.

"Don't call the police," Melvin has warned Willo.

Now it is early Sunday morning. Melvin is still sleeping. Willo enters Max's room and looks a long time at the sheet of paper he left on his desk. It's a song he was writing. Done hastily in red crayon, it looks more like a sketch of red roses on a trellis than musical notes on a staff. "THE TREES ARE CLAPPING THEIR HANDS" he has called it. *"Stop your crying. . .flowers are flying. . . . The pavement is hot. . . the forest is not. . . . Come in! The trees are clapping their hands!. . . Hate made a hole, and Love poured in. . . . "*

Willo showed it to Melvin yesterday: *"Look: your musical influence; my lyrical influence, "* she said.

Melvin was not impressed.

Willo folds the paper, places it in her pocket.

She goes to the kitchen, where she packs a hamper with freshly baked whole wheat bread and cheeses and apples; honey and figs and a thermos of lemonade. She laces up her hiking boots. Then she slings the hamper over her arm and heads for the canal.

A police patrol car cruises along beside her for a while. Beads of perspiration form on her upper lip. Then the car turns down the beltway.

The early morning sun has illuminated the giant boulders along the Potomac. They look ash-gray, silvery. Along the edge of the river, lush locusts and sumacs look geometric as trees painted by Henri Rousseau. Like an umbrella crested with tufts of pink fluff, the mimosa is embroidered on the Rousseau tapestry. The water is turbulent over the rocks.

She crosses the bridge to the towpath.

*   *

Sooner than she expected, Willo finds her bearded son. He is sitting on his sleeping bag. Beside him is a madonna-faced girl. She's wearing blue jeans and Max's gray sweatshirt.

Max turns to his mother. His eyes are bloodshot. "We saw you coming half a mile off."

The girl turns her pale face away and combs her opulent dark hair.

Max scowls at his mother. "You looked so *little.*"

—*That sneering look of appraisal exactly like Melvin's.* Smiling sardonically, Willo grasps the fabric of her baggy slacks, kicks out her heavy hiking boot: "Charlie Chaplin."

"We're not hungry," Max says.

"Did you hurt your eye?"

"No. I did not hurt my eye," he says very slowly as if talking to an idiot.

An awkward silence. The girl combing and combing her hair.

—*fills out that sweatshirt like Sophia Loren.*

"You can bring that breakfast home to Dad and Tad," Max says.

Willo fidgets. "Naturally, we've been worried."

"Natch. Mom, this is Nart."

The girl peers out of the drape of dark hair. "Hi."

—*such a white face. And Max's eyes so inflamed. Are they on drugs?*

Max reads her thoughts. "We're on heroin," he laughs.

"Not really," Nart says.

—*a genteel voice. A sleek beauty who has obviously not spent many nights in a sleeping bag on the rocks.*

"I wish you had some aspirin in that basket," Nart sighs.

"I can run home and get some."

"No, don't."

Willo says to Max, "Remember how we used to throw a headache or a stomach ache into the weeds?"

Max scowls. Her worried face looks old to him: Beneath the abnormally large eyes, the meagre cheeks have begun to sag, like tear drops. "Always throwing off bad vibes, Mom, polluting the world with petty, personal problems. You ought to throw off *joy.*"

Across the river, strong as a presence striding on the water, comes the peal of the bells of the convent.

Nart's face turns to the melody.

"Another thing you and Dad did poorly," scowls Max. "Atheism." He glances in the direction of the convent. "Not that God is in *there;* He's out here, for certain."

Willo dares not sit down. "The atheism was a terrible mistake."

Both faces turn to her in surprise.

—*Don't tell them. No fair snaring him now. It's too late.*

"I'm shocked that you would admit it," says Max.

—*Tell them. Pay the debt your generation owes to their generation.* She sets the hamper on a rock and seats herself beside it. Shyly, she looks away from the pair of appraising faces. "It was May thirty-first, nineteen sixty-eight, my birthday. For several days I had been trying to write a eulogy for John Kennedy, whose birthday was May twenty-ninth." Her gaze comes to rest on a clump of chicory. "In fact, for two years, mostly in May, I had been trying to write that eulogy. I kept seeing in my mind's eye a pair of gray eyes in a sun-tanned face. At first I thought I was recalling Kennedy's eyes, but no—his eyes were violet; these were gray. I couldn't figure it out. It was as if I were trying to remember someone, as if this gray-eyed image were trying to call my attention to some specific person. All afternoon, the gaze stuck in my mind. By evening, I could think of nothing else. I sat down by myself and tried to figure it out: Had a roofer or a repairman or some kind of outdoor man given me a message I had forgotten to give Dad? Had your former scout leader come to the door with a message I had forgotten to give you? Had the newsreels of Robert Kennedy's campaign impressed me deeply with his eyes? But no, these were not exactly his eyes, either." Her voice continues, small and monotonous, like a cricket's. "About nine o'clock in the evening, while I was in my bath, the face became clear. I all but 'saw' it on the tile wall: gray eyes, suntanned face, framed in foamy white hair and a foamy white beard. It was Walt Whitman. "When Lilacs Last in the Dooryard Bloomed" was the poem that came to mind as soon as I recognized the face. I went to bed. I couldn't sleep. I kept seeing the face, kept smelling lilacs, kept recalling fragments of that poem. I deduced that my concentration on my own Kennedy poem had pulled the Lincoln poem up out of my unconscious mind. Still, I couldn't sleep. Whitman's gaze was urgent. It felt as if he were asking me to read his poem. Since I couldn't sleep, anyway, I got up, found an anthology, and read the poem. It was beautiful. Still, Whitman's eyes seemed urgent. He seemed to be asking me to read something else. My eyes were drawn to the short biography. In the very first sentence, I read that Whitman was born *May thirty-first,* eighteen nineteen. It surprised me; pleased me; I was in great company— with Whitman, so close to Kennedy. I wondered if I had read that paragraph twenty-five years ago in college, had stored the information, then forgotten it....At any rate, Whitman's gaze faded away, and I went to sleep....The next day, though, and for a few days, I couldn't get the face of Whitman and the phrases of his poem out of my mind. Every time I sat down to work on my own poem, the face and the scent of lilacs intruded. Then, June fifth, Robert Kennedy was assassinated. As I heard the news on the radio, I saw Whitman's face again, vividly. I couldn't but feel that this was the tragedy he had been trying to warn me about."

She takes a breath, turns to look at Max and Nart. The two faces are waiting for more.

She looks back at the chicory. "Then, on May thirty-first last year, when I was *still* working on the Kennedy eulogy, the Whitman face came vividly into my mind again. He said—*It* said—well, not audibly, but as if through telepathy: 'ONE YEAR AND TWENTY-THREE DAYS   NIXON

RESIGNS   FIVE DAYS   THEN L. KING WILL BE
PRESIDENT.' *'King?'* I asked. *'Who is King?'* and that
'voice' said again: 'L. KING.' "

Shyly, like a child addressing adults who are not likely to
believe, the tiny woman steals another glance at Nart and
Max. Both their faces are wide open as flowers. "Then, on
May thirty-first this year, as Dad and I were driving to Arena
Stage, a force like a magnet drew my attention to The Water-
gate Apartments. Again, in my mind's eye, I *saw* Walt Whit-
man. He had that urgent look again. He seemed to be saying
something, not in real words, but through telepathy. Then
Dad's voice interrupted: *'A guy at the office calls that build-
ing "Ship of Fools."'* His statement blotted out whatever it was
Whitman was saying. All I could catch was 'Dean.' Then
Whitman glanced sharply across the street to the motel."
Still the cricket-chant drifting out of the tiny huge-eyed face.
"Was it Gertrude Dean, I wondered, who had died a few
years ago, speaking through Whitman? Or Whitman speaking through Gertrude Dean? And what was the message—the
warning—about that motel? Then we were at The Arena
Stage. The play was engrossing. I forgot about Whitman and
Dean. On the way home, as we approached The Watergate,
the same force pulled my attention: Whitman's face was on
Watergate. His glance arced across the street as if a match
had been struck against the sumptuous building and lifted
across the street to illuminate the motel. Then the words
'DEAN NIXON RESIGN TWENTY-THREE DAYS.' I
thought Whitman and Dean together were trying to warn me
that in twenty-three days someone would shoot from the
window of the motel to assassinate a prominent person on
the balcony of a Watergate apartment, just as Martin
Luther King was assassinated. I couldn't figure out 'resign'
unless it meant this prominent person—Nixon?—would be
wounded so badly that he would have to resign his office. . . .
Then last month, I did read in *The Washington Post* that
some burglars who had stayed in the motel across the street
had been caught bugging the Democrat headquarters in The

Watergate. I wonder if that's what Whitman and Gertrude Dean meant. June twenty-third has come and gone, and no one has tried to assassinate Nixon. Does it mean it will happen next year on June twenty-third? or the next? or what?"

The two young faces peel their gaze from Willo's face, slowly, like skins being peeled from an orange. They turn to one another.

"I'm flipped out," Nart says.

Max turns back to his mother. "Why didn't you tell me before?"

"It was too strange. I didn't dare speak of it."

"Have you told Dad or Tad?"

"No. I recoil every time I think of it. Tad will have nothing to do with me lately. Dad would interpret it as a symptom of emotional illness. Or maybe he would start 'testing' me, would turn me into a kind of ouija board of political information. I couldn't stand that."

Max grins at Nart. "Are you hungry?"

"Starved."

Willo places the hamper between them. Then she wanders down to a rock, where she sits watching the river.

"Good," says Nart. She smiles, showing small teeth curved slightly inward, like a child's. "That cured my headache." Her cheeks are pink.

"Nart left the convent last night," Max says. "We're going to hitch up to Vermont to a commune where we can learn to make dulcimers. Nart sings. I can write the songs."

Willo takes the folded paper from her pocket and hands it to him. He opens it, shrugs, hands it to Nart.

She studies the page. "Hey. You've got it all together." She looks worshipfully at Max. "It's right in my corner." She turns to Willo. "I call Max 'Gemin-Eye' (E-Y-E) because when he looks this way, he looks like Castro; when he looks that way, he looks like Christ."

Max makes a little disdainful motion with his hand. "Ego,

264

ego." He takes the sheet of paper from Nart, crushes it, springs to his feet, and flings it into the river. It bobs a moment like a waterlily, then in a rock-a-bye motion, it is carried down river.

—*Rogue, showing off for Nart.*

"I don't cast away pains, Mom," he says. "I cast away joys." He gathers the left-overs and stuffs them into his backpack: "Lunch."

Willo takes a wallet from her pocket. She removes the bills and hands them to Max. "Not much; all that I have."

"Thanks." He stuffs them into his wallet.

He and Nart wander down towards the river. Willo seats herself on a rock and watches them. —*How Nart fills out those jeans. Sophia Loren, yes.*

They begin to pick flowers. Chicory   pink mallows   white mallows   cardinal flowers   a bamboo-like grass. They climb to a ledge, where Max plucks a ragged lavender pompom.

"Bergamont," says Nart. "I love it." She plucks two of them.

They scramble down the rocks—Sophia Loren and Errol Flynn—and heap the flowers in the hamper.

Willo picks up the hamper. "Thank you." She turns to Nart. "Max says you left the convent."

"Right."

"With permission?"

"With*out* permission."

Willo sighs. "I'm an accomplice."

Max chuckles. "Yes, you're an accomplice." He takes Nart's hand in his.

*   *

Willo hurries up the towpath. The thick fuzzy pistils of the white mallows bounce like mute clappers within the satin corollas.   The pink mallows twitch like skirted hollyhock dolls.   The bergamont flutters.   The blue-eyed chicory watches her.   The spikes of the cardinal flower are splashed blood.

265

Half a mile up river, she turns to cross the little wooden bridge. Down river, where the giant gray boulders loom luminous as a cathedral, Max and Nart are waving to her. She walks to the center of the bridge, leans over the rail, tilts the basket, and spills the flowers into the river. They lay quietly on the water   blue   red   white   pink   lavender   like jewels. Slowly, reverently, the current arranges them   red blue   lavender   in an oval   pink   blue   red   an oval necklace. The necklace quivers beneath her for a long moment before the current slides it away and spins it towards some rocks. With a growl that sounds like HALLELUJAH! the river gobbles the offering.

As she walks off the other side of the bridge, Willo inhales a minty fragrance. A single blossom of bergamont is stuck in the reeds of the hamper. With each step, she inhales the aroma. . .letting the gray rocks. . .the last of the sumac   the locust   the mimosa   then the trees of suburbia   the houses the hedges   the police patrol car   the lawns   the minty aroma   wipe the AMEN from her face.

One afternoon at three o'clock, while Willo is slicing carrots for a casserole, Melvin walks into the kitchen with Sally. In an aura of sake, he calls, "Hi, Willo! We've had lunch at the Mikado, and we got into a big discussion on Taoism and Zen. I want to find some books for Sally."

Willo leans against the sink for support.

While he is searching the study for the books, Sally arranges her bulk in a chair at the kitchen table. The helmet-coiffure of yesteryear has been teased into a tousled mop. She taps a cigarette on the back of her hand. "Boy, that Mel's a terrific egghead," she announces. Tap   tap. The stack of spheres jiggles within the rubbery green dress.

Willo's fingers tighten on the paring knife.

The cigarette lighter clanks like a chunk of costume jewelry. "I told him he missed his calling." Scritch. "He oughta be a guru. No kidding." The spurted scolding manner somewhat subdued by the sake. The smoke framing her face in a blowsy lace. Today she is something out of Toulouse-Lautrec.

Self-consciously, Willo turns the blade of the paring knife away from this intruder.

When Melvin returns with two books, Sally's hand makes the quick dive for the bra strap. The green glance darts to Willo: "He's a guru. You better believe it."

Minutes after they have departed "for the office," Willo resumes the carrot-slashing with fresh ferocity.

At dinner that evening, Melvin says, somewhat sheepishly, "I'm afraid Sally is trying to turn me into a sort of father-confessor. The poor gal has a lousy marriage."

"If she wants help, shouldn't she consult a priest?"

"You must be kidding. Priests are *passé.*"

"I understand the agency is staffed with all kinds of counselors and psychologists. If she really wants help, wouldn't she consult one of those?"

Melvin looks annoyed. "No! She's not *neurotic.* It's her husband who's the no-goodnik."

—She doesn't want help; she wants an audience plus a free lunch.

A week later, Melvin arrives home for dinner, redolent with sake, laden with packages: two shirts, one shocking pink, one violet, and a Christian Dior tie that glows like a sunrise. "No one wears business suits to those picnics," he explains. In the other package: phonograph records: The Beatles, Paul Simon. "We may as well keep in touch with our kids."

—God, if You exist, release me from this jealousy.

But God does not release her, nor does Mary, nor Buddha, nor Pete, nor Walt Whitman. In those Zen books, also in those on Taoism, Willo has read: *"Precognition. . .happens to many persons after a little zazen. Don't dwell on it, or it can become a nuisance. It's only the first of eight steps in the spiritual ascent. You have a long way to go."*

"We had another fabulous picnic this noon. Sally's two little daughters just hung on me all the time. Sally read my palm. I have a very thick mound of Venus."

—Sally is inevitable to his healing. Sally is his sturdy red-headed Irish Catholic mother. Sally is the girl he never dated in high school. Sally is the daughter I never gave him. Boil it into a poem.

"Don't tell anyone: Sally is having a tubal ligation next week. Gosh, that gal is liberated!"

—Cow's tail: It's no accident that you've stuck with those Catholics-in-Action all these years. Yes, an hilarious poem.

*   *

Arrayed in the pink shirt and the sunrise tie and reeking of curry: "We whooped it up at a fantastic Indian restaurant this noon. Sally did our horoscopes. I'm Libra with a moon in Virgo and Venus in Leo. I improve with age."

—Does a concept have to clatter down through all the strata of society, klunk bottom, and bounce out the mouth of a Catholic secretary before it becomes palatable to you? Chop it into a poem.

Now in the violet shirt: "There's nothing to do in the office this week, so after lunch four of us went to see LOVE STORY. The girls cried. I nearly cried, too. Sally said it was the most terrific movie she's ever seen."

At last the snake flashes out of Willo's mouth: "I'd rather you'd bring me clap from a whore than the clichés from that secretary."

Melvin grins and turns up The Beatles. He knows there are forms of communication other than words. So does Willo.

After that, Melvin does not mention Sally. But Willo receives nearly every night the tumult which the ruthless titillator has scritched in him all day. She grows more and more reluctant in his arms.

One night, he strokes her vulva, reflectively, like a violinist fingering a flute. "Tell me how you and Pete did it."

She stiffens. "I don't want to talk about it."

He kisses the warm, fruity flesh. "Tell me. Lesbianism is the In thing. It's a real turn-on."

"Twenty years ago, when my telling would have helped both of us, you would not listen. You said it made you sick."

"Nobody talked about it then."

"Some people did. You called them Beatniks."

"You seem so tense," he says to Willo. "You've become a recluse."

"I need the solitude for writing."

269

"It doesn't seem to be making you happy."

"Everything I write is rejected."

He kisses the top of her head. "Try to be objective. Don't let yourself become ego-involved."

—*You're gloating, Melvin.*

His love-making grows ever more ardent, ever more artistic.

One night in his arms, she turns brittle. "These past years have wrung all the beauty off my bones."

"Your bones are beautiful."

"I can't help feeling it's—some young girl at the office you're handling—not me."

"Nonsense. I've fallen in love with you all over again."

"Don't tell me such lies."

"It's the truth. You were right: I was numb all those years. I want to start all over again."

"It's guilt you feel towards me, not love."

"It's love."

"It's pity."

"It's love. I swear it's love."

He takes up Chinese cooking: Chicken with walnuts. Sweet and sour pork. Scrambled eggs with fermented beancurd. Eggplant in ginger sauce.

"It's delicious, Melvin. I never would have believed it."

"It's just the beginning. What do you want me to do next?"

"Have Tad help you cook."

"Only one year until retirement," he tells her. "Then we'll share cooking and cleaning."

She sighs. "I'm worried about Max. He hasn't written for two months."

"I'm worried about him, too. We can't go back. We have to go ahead and try to do better. . . . People at the office are asking about you. Our picnics are so relaxed. Everyone's becoming so *liberated.* Won't you please come next week?''

She shakes her head.

"Please try. This Indian summer won't hold out much longer."

—*I'd vomit and vomit like a volcano.* "Tell your colleagues I'm menopausing."

"Sorry. I won't push you." He puts his arms around her. "Now you're the numb one. Would you like to try another psychiatrist?"

"No. I'm ashamed that I respond with so little gratitude to the new you. I think the turn-about has come too late for me."

He rocks her in his arms. "Better late than never, Honey."

Her anger will not budge.

One day while she is sitting with the notebook in her lap, her gaze strays to the newspaper beside her. She reads the small feature about some Carmelite nuns cloistered in the mountains of California. *"They pray for everyone who asks...."*

Swiftly, she writes: *"I'm exhausted from being your enemy. I'm not ready to be your friend. Pray for me."*

She slips it, unsigned, into an envelope, addresses it to those nuns; then tucks it into her notebook, for re-thinking.

Most of this December Sunday, Willo has been in the kitchen, making beef stew and granola bread. Through the door, she glimpses now and then Melvin and Tad playing chess at the dining room table. She notices, with surprise and also with some relief, that Tad has ceased to look like her. Within these few months, the curly golden hair has turned crisp and brown, the fragile face has broadened, the spindly neck has thickened, and his features have become cushioned in flesh. The lips have assumed a pouting expression, like his father's; the shy eyes are now half hidden, like his father's, behind a pair of horn rimmed glasses. *"Why, he's beginning to look just like you!"* she said to Melvin last week, and again, to her surprise, Melvin replied, quite merrily, *"I know it: If ever we get back to that family safe in St. Louis, I'll find my high school pictures and show you what a dude I was, with that big pile of curly hair on top of my head."* Melvin, she notices, looks younger these days; he scowls less; he talks more. Right now, sitting placidly over the chess board, he looks like Charlie Brown.... He and Tad are inseparable lately, either over that chess board or else sitting side by side in easy chairs watching the news broadcasts or the football games on television. In fact, most of this afternoon, up to an hour ago, they were calling to her from the television room: *"Bring our trays, please!"* *"How about another sandwich?"* *"Another glass of milk!"* *"What's for dessert?"* And with old-fashioned submissiveness, she had served this armchair virility, wondering all the while about the whereabouts of her wandering boy.

"Any homework I can assist you with during this vacation?" Melvin asks.

"I have to write a paper on Thoreau," Tad replies in his new deeper voice.

"Thoreau!" Willo calls. Her face brightens. "He was a marvelous man—so quiet, so skillful with his hands, so in tune with nature, so Zen-like—"

Without looking up from the chess board, Melvin says, "If there's any research to do, we men can handle it."

"But Thoreau is one of my favorite—"

Tad wags his hand in front of his face in that bizarre gesture of protest.

"Now, let's not have the limp-wrist act," Melvin says, patiently, and to Willo he says, with equal patience, "Zen-like? That's the label the hippies have laid on Thoreau. I'm sure Tad and I can produce something more original, if only you'll leave it to us."

Willo turns quickly back to the stove.

Smiling a little, Melvin addresses her back: "You've slaved all day in that kitchen, Willo," he says in a sugary tone, like a person coaxing the cat to go outside for the night. "Why don't you go to your room and write a poem?"

She places the two round loaves on the cookie sheet in the oven, sets the dial, places the large pot of stew on "simmer," removes her apron, and hurries upstairs.

In her room, she settles herself in the rocking chair and opens her notebook. No real poems yet. Just embryos within that film.

On the blank page, she "sees" what she has been "seeing" for a month: Max rattling along in an old truck driven by an old woman. She is chattering, and Max is laughing. The woman looks something like Mamma, except it is inconceivable that Mamma would drive any vehicle or that she would utter anything to arouse laughter in anyone. . . . Sometimes lately Willo receives another vision of Max arriving at the door, and with it she gets the date: December nineteenth. This is December nineteenth, dusk, and she has been on edge all day. . . . She takes up her pen, and in a jagged script, she scrawls on the blank page:

EYE

"I am willy nilly," I said to Father Vincent;
"I'm a thread that has come loose from the needle.
What I want   what I *need*   is to be thrust
back through the eye of that needle
and pulled right into FAITH."

Father Vincent laughed:
"Ho! Hasn't anyone ever told you
about the communion of saints?"
He told me. I listened. I believed.
Fickle girl that I was,
I dismissed the thought   or forgot.

Now, a quarter century later,
two gray EYES of Walt Whitman
(Are you a saint, Walt?)
have pulled me—sure enough!—into FAITH!

Saints? Angels? Poets? Whoever—
are you *punning* me?

I wish you would keep me *in stitches.*

She turns the page to try a second draft. A card slips out of
the notebook, and she reads it, or re-reads it: *Mr. and Mrs.
Melvin Sanders: You are invited to a Twelfth Night Party—
January six, eight p.m.—RSVP regrets only.*" It's written in
purple ink, in Sally's neat secretarial script. Willo places it on
top of another envelope—the one addressed to The Carmelite
Nuns, and on the fresh page, she writes EYE.

A stamping on the front porch. The doorbell ringing.
"Merry Christmas!" booms Max.

She plummets down the stairs like a waterfall.

"Merry Christmas!" he shouts. Shaggy beard. Face gaunt
and weathered. A pack on his back.

In an aura of kerosene-and-smoke scent, she is embracing
him, and for the first time since he was a little boy, she is

kissing his cheek.

"I smell beef stew! Oh, Mom! And granola bread!" he laughs.

—*I knew you were coming,* her sly smile says.

Beaming, Willo bustles about the table in tune to this fresh vitality.

* *

"I haven't eaten since yesterday." Max seats himself at the table and helps himself to a huge bowl of stew and a chunk of brown bread.

Across the table from him, the two gentlemen look down into their plates.

Questions ripple from Willo's lips: "Have you written any new songs?"

"Songs? No. Saturn has moved into Gemini."

"And Nart?"

Max takes a big bite of bread and chews contentedly. "Nart? Fart! We split up long ago."

Melvin sips his burgundy, then looks up and says, with painstaking civility, "I hope the wandering is finished. I hope you have plans for college."

A gust of laughter. "College? No way! Maybe when my hair falls out and my teeth rot and I have arthritis, then maybe I'll sit on my ass and listen to a professor spiel, and read books—"

Melvin takes another sip of wine. "We're grooming your brother for an elite New England college."

Max plinks his wine glass with his spoon. "Bully for you. One ivy leaguer in the family is enough. You need a bum for balance." He reaches into his shirt pocket and draws out a packet of snapshots and some scraps of paper, which he spreads out on the table, like a deck of cards. "Runaways," he explains. "Hitching, I keep meeting up with parents, who give me these pictures of their kids; also messages, addresses, phone numbers. I'm a regular missing persons bureau! Here, Tad, take your pick: Who do you want: Darlene? Sherry?

She's rich—from a snazzy New England school. Nadine? Cheryl? No, Cheryl's mine.... And I meet up with kids who give me a number and say, 'Phone my mom.'...''

Willo's face responds to the melody of this minstrel, "More bread, Max? Some honey?"

Melvin and Tad touch forks, fastidiously, to their stew.

"Still a finicky eater, Tad? You should have been with me. I eat anything. The rule of the road is: *If it makes a turd, eat it.*" He balances the slice of bread on the thumb-side of his fist and pours the honey on it, luxuriously. "I've been in Nova Scotia, on a farm." He takes a big bite of the bread and honey and chews a while. "I was hitchhiking, and I was nearly frozen—on the verge of pneumonia, I guess—and this old pickup truck comes rattling down the road, and this old woman picks me up. She was eighty-three. She kept taking out her false teeth, and at first I could hardly understand her." He takes another big bite and chews a while. "She took me to her farm. Old Lily Dade was her name. She made me hot tea and then some hot broth, and I stayed in bed nearly a week. It turned out her husband had died in the spring, and she was lonely. She wanted me to live with her. Gave me her husband's long underwear. Sure! We'd go out to the grave-yard, and she'd put her hand on his tombstone and say, 'Earl? I've got a nice boy here. I'm going to give him yer long underwear. All right, Earl?' Honest to God, she did! And we trudged back to the house, and she opened the trunk all reeking with moth balls, and she gave me three suits of thick gray underwear. Then after a few days, we'd treck out to the graveyard again, and she'd put her hand on the tombstone and say, 'Earl, this boy needs your brown jacket.' She ended up giving me all his clothes." He helps himself to another slice of bread and another ooze of honey. "We'd sit around at night with a kerosene lamp, and she'd tell me about Earl and the farm and how they came there when they were young, and she'd bake me a pie, and she'd tell me about their two sons who were killed in World War Two, and we played the phonograph. 'Thanks for the Memories.' You know that

276

song? Jesus, this long underwear is pricking me. I'm not used to a warm house—"

Tad and Melvin retreat to Tad's room to work on the Thoreau report.

In the kitchen, Max helps his mother wash the dishes. He holds the cookie sheet across his chest, like an accordian, and galumphs it, and light flashes from the metal along with the croaking sounds. "Thannnnnnnks for the underwearrrrrrr!" he croons. In a lowered voice, he says, "I'm still waiting for the June twenty-third crisis at the Watergate...waiting for Nixon to resign and for L. King to be president. I told Lily Dade, and she's waiting, too....Who in Hell is L. King?"

Willo shrugs. "I could be wrong."

"I'll bet you're right. I stayed at the Hare Krishna temple in New York for a couple of weeks. There were two monks there who had a lot of precognition. Lots of kids are clairvoyant at times. Old Lily Dade knows of people way out on farms who've had these 'messages'....What else have you foreseen?"

—I knew you were coming today, she nearly says, but she does not want to oppress him with her anxiety, which is always stalking him. "I was shown a vision of Frank Dean in an ashram, not once, but several times. Last week his father told Dad he had indeed gone to an ashram in Pennsylvania."

"Frank Dean? That figures. What's happening with the Cains?"

"William Cain comes over here sometimes to see Tad and to browse among our books."

"The erotic poetry, I'll bet, and the Zen."

"I suppose so. I don't snoop."

"And Tad visits the Cains?"

"He's dropped in at their house a few times after school."

"To fool around with their pistols and rifles?"

"I suppose so."

Max plinks three water glasses with a spoon. "I guess you know by now, Mom, that kids will go prowling for whatever their parents failed to give them. Better yet, for what their parents forbade them. The more taboo, the harder they prowl after it.''

''I know.''

''Do you know what's the most taboo thing in this family?''

''The conventional religions?''

''Guess again.''

''Neighbors?''

''Guess again.''

''Clichés?''

''Ha! It's funny that you mention those two practically in the same breath.''

''Drugs?''

He klinks the glasses, melodiously. ''Working class people.''

She nods. ''An unspoken taboo. Unspeakable, maybe.''

''We've never once been to Bronson, Michigan, Mom. I've never seen my own grandmother. Isn't that *disgraceful?*''

She sighs. ''I was protecting you from her, and from her brothers and her sister. Frustrations warped them long ago into caricatures.''

''They sound fascinating. I like the grotesque.''

''You like novelty.''

''There's more to it than novelty. Working class people are *cool.*''

''They're anything but cool. They're a regular vortex of needs.''

''So what? Who isn't?'' He picks up the cookie sheet and pumps more thunder and lightning from it. ''Thannnnnnnks for the unnnnnnnnnderwearrrrrrr!'' he croons. ''The fried potatoes, tooooooo.... Thank you, Earl Daaaaaaaade!''

In bed that night, Melvin groans, ''I have one of my old headaches. Could you massage the temples just a little?''

Willo strokes the throbbing forehead.

''What do you want to bet,'' Melvin whispers, ''that exhilaration of his comes from drugs?"

—*"Don't let Max be so bumptious."* "He's always been dynamic."

"The pain is just above the ears."

Patiently, as in the old days, she massages the aching areas.

"He feeds you a line. I'm amazed how you fall for it."

"He's my son. I'm overjoyed because he's home."

"Can you massage the neck now? Machismo is out of style. You ought not to encourage it."

She massages the tight, hot neck. —*Machismo? Bravado? I see now how it developed: in a vacuum; he's gone unchallenged by a male all his life.*

The next day, after Melvin has left for work, Willo tries to form a liason between Max and his father. "One of your father's big worries—and I guess he shares it with the parents of most teenagers—is drugs; especially when you hitchhike so much."

Max turns his palm to her in a gesture of disdain. "Drugs are everywhere; less on the road than in the colleges and universities."

"We can't help thinking, though, that in such a transient life, you'll become involved, whether you will it or not."

"A dealer? All right: I have turned drugs, mostly to academics. Professors are the big users of LSD, I guess you know."

"I wish you wouldn't, Max. You know now that those mind-expanding experiences are accessible without drugs."

He makes the disdainful gesture again. "Don't knock it, Mom; you're in no position to judge. You live in a little slowed-down world, like the poet said: 'out of the swing of the sea.' Most people are in a hurry."

During the next few days, Willo observes the growing clash of temperaments. Max keeps pitching his swift, hard balls of humor. Tad ducks all of them. Melvin ducks them, too, except for an occasional one which he catches, or attempts to catch, in that mesh glove: *how-about-going-to-college?*

Each night in bed Willo massages away Melvin's pain and listens to his comments: "What did I tell you? That high is over. Now he's down. He's in the sack all day."

"He's thin. He's been undernourished for months, and sick. He needs a lot of rest."

"He needs more dope. He'll be hitting the road any day now."

"He's depressed. No wonder. You and Tad keep withdrawing to Tad's room to work on that report and to play chess."

"We invited Max to play cards with us."

"Half-heartedly. Anyway, he's not a card player."

"He's self-centered, like you, but more so: he's just a performer."

"He likes to talk."

"Well, I've heard more than enough of his guff."

"I wish you could be friendlier."

"All right. It's all my fault."

She sighs. "It's mine, too. I've run out of conversation. I'm too isolated—as you say: too self-centered, to have much to offer."

"The ivory tower. I told you."

"I know."

He pats her flank. "You're cooking us some wonderful meals."

"But we eat them in silence, just as in the old days, and retreat to our separate rooms. It's like a boarding house."

"He ought to be thankful for a boarding house."

"He's full of talents—if you'd just give a little support."

"Support? A thousand dollars to that lawyer. Now I've offered to pay for college."

—a token   a rebuke—

"He walks in all brash and filthy and raunchy-looking. He eats like a tramp. Then he turns morose. He's an awful influence on Tad."

"He's warm. He's interesting. He's good for Tad."

"I hate to have him near Tad. I'm worried sick that any day now he'll be slipping that boy some dope."

*   *

On the last day of December, after Melvin has left for work, and after Tad has left for the suburban library, Max straps the pack on his back, accepts a bag lunch from his mother, and thirty dollars, and walks out into the cold, gray January morning.

As soon as he is out of sight, Willo puts on her coat and hurries to the corner mail box, where she deposits two notes: the "regrets" to Sally, and the message to those cloistered nuns in California.

"I'm exhausted from being your enemy. I'm not ready to be your friend. Pray for me." All that day, and the next, and the next, the message throbs like a mantra in her thoughts.

At a sidewalk café in Paris they sit, like a pair of mallards: Melvin in a bright green plaid cap and sun glasses and mustache and sideburns; Willo in tan slacks and a loose beige sweater. Between them, on the table, are two cups of tea and the morning mail.

Melvin shuffles through his: checks, travel folders, maps, more checks, and a postcard shiny with greenery. Then he glances up to watch Willo reading her letter. Something Cora wrote is tolling across her face. He sips his tea, reads the shiny green postcard a second time, and smiles; then he looks up to see Cora's message, still tolling across his wife's face.

Willo reads, *"—We were so tickled when Max dropped in on us. He only stayed four days, then headed for Ann Arbor but promised to come back soon. You sure must be worried to have him hitch hiking all over the country and Canada as well. Mamma says to tell you it was love at first sight. She sure is crazy about him and as her mind is slipping since Milo passed away she keeps calling Max Milo—"*

Melvin watches Willo fold the letter and lay it on the table. He hands her the shiny green card. "We've got a real scholar here," he beams.

Willo reads: *"All A's and A pluses the first quarter. It's a cinch. I like Vermont. Tad."* "Your tutoring has paid off," she says, and she hands Melvin Cora's letter.

He reads it, then sips his tea. "Nice of Cora to write," he says, and as if to cancel that Milo-Max merger, he repeats, "That Tad's a scholar."

She nods. "He's laconic."

Melvin shuffles Cora's letter into the maps and checks and travel folders. "Don't reproach me about Max." Behind the dark glasses, his gaze swivels to a scantily clad girl whose hair shimmies like a burlesque curtain over her breasts. "I'll make it up to the grandchildren."

Willo sips her tea. —*There, Rip Van Winkle, another halter jouncing its Bobsy twins for you. Dada. Dada.*

Melvin tries again to erase the remoteness from her face. "Investments are paying off like mad. I'll send Max a generous check tonight, and I'll write him a nice letter, too."

A mauve gaze drifts like incense out of her face. "I'll write to Cora and my mother." —*Dear Mamma, take my minstrel. Maybe he will sing you The Saga of Your Little Blue Dishes. . . .*

"I'll write to Tad, too, and send him a check."

The mauve gaze drifts beyond him and fastens to the spire of a cathedral. —*Last night, Melvin, when you were asleep, I had a strange—visit. For six years, I've been wondering how I could ever tell you. I could just say: 'I was informed in a vision that Max had gone to Mamma's.' I could tell you how it all started on the patio—with Pete. . .and moved to Walt Whitman, who told me L. King would be president. . . .*

"We can buy gifts for both boys if you like, and something for your mother, and something for Cora, too." His eyes stray to a languid lass in truncated jeans. Her naval returns his gaze like a sleepy papoose.

—*I told Max before he left home with Nart. He cheered. I told Tad before he left for college. He sneered.*

Melvin's glance returns to his wife's face, then retreats. Beneath her luminous gaze, the flesh has begun to sag slightly, like wax from a candle flame. "After we buy the gifts, what do you say to a spa? Then we'll buy you one of those dramatic caftans, and next week when we're in London, you can drop in on your old buddy."

—*At first I held it secret from you for fear you'd scoff—*

"How about it, Willo?"

"I have enough clothes, thanks." —*Lately I've withheld it for fear you'd try to turn me into your goose that lays the golden eggs—*

He glances at her drab slacks and sweater. "You ought to buy something smashing."

The incense-gaze continues to drift. —*I don't know how to approach you, Melvin. I've thought of saying: 'Those Catholics, so retarded about the flesh, turn out to be utterly wise about the spirit.'...I guess Sally would say: 'Hey, Mel! You threw out the Baby with the bathwater.'*

"Wouldn't you like to see your old London buddy again?"

She sips her tea. "I got what I was supposed to get from a good psychiatrist. There's no need to go back." —*Four days after I mailed that anonymous note to those nuns, Melvin, someone touched me on the shoulder. I was washing dishes, and without a doubt—*

Melvin leans across the table and takes her skimpy hand in his plump one. "Wake up, Willo. This is our long-awaited honeymoon. All this travel should put some fresh poems into your head."

Her hand, like a dowser in his, feels his eyes lapping up another pair of ripe breasts, then the matching derriere. —*I couldn't believe it. I thought it was my imagination. So I wrote again. Four days passed. Then when I was washing my hands* (*Why so often when I am touching water?*)—*someone tapped me again. . . .*

"How about it, Honey? Is that pretty head filling up with poems?"

Her gaze circles his full-moon face. —*I've tried it with other nuns in other convents, even with monks in monasteries. It's like dialing a telephone number. There's always a response, always something different, something astonishing. I keep trying to put it into poems, but words fail.*

"Why so pensive, Honey: Is a poem in process?"

Her gaze burns through his dark glasses. "For a long time, Melvin, I've been wanting to tell you something."

THE AUTHOR

Karen Snow's poems and prose fictions have appeared in a wide variety of publications. *Willo* is her first novel.

We at Street Fiction Press publish the fine arts of poetry, prose fiction, and offset design. Here are a number of other recent SFP Softcover Originals you may enjoy:

BABYBURGERS	by Andrew G. Carrigan and Warren Jay Hecht $3.95 ISBN:0-914908-25-1
CHICKEN BEACON	by Richard E. McMullen $2.95 ISBN:0-914908-26-X
ENGLISH STORIES	by Arturo Vivante $3.95 ISBN:0-914908-27-8
NO RELIEF	by Stephen Dixon $4.95 ISBN:0-914908-28-6

Street Fiction Press also produces The Periodical Lunch Collection, The Anon Anthologies, and Giraffe Imprints.